Darling Daughters

Darling Daughters

Elizabeth Troop

ST. MARTIN'S PRESS, NEW YORK

Copyright © 1981 by Elizabeth Troop
For information, write: St. Martin's Press,
175 Fifth Avenue, New York, N.Y. 10010
Manufactured in the United States of America

Library of Congress Cataloging in Publication Data

Troop, Elizabeth.
    Darling daughters.

    I. Title.
PR6070.R58D3   823′.914   80-52354
ISBN 0-312-18281-3

Darling daughters, listen to your mother,
I must go away and leave you to each other,
And one shall marry a rich man
And one shall go on an excursion to the Isle of Man
And one shall find her way home if she can.

Stevie Smith

1

I hate.

I have loved, in my time, people, objects, the smell of new books, the music of Mahler and Mozart, whisky and ice in a clean glass – but at the moment such things are alien to me. I tell myself it is a stage I am going through, that I am seeing the world in a distorting mirror, and that they are all still there, waiting for me to resume my interest. I hope they have not disappeared for ever. They are not dependent on my particular attention, I know that. They have other eyes, ears and noses to respond to their charms.

Meanwhile I carry on as if still human. I eat, wash, dress. I type my works, I visit the hospital.

The old women in the geriatric ward are laid out like waxworks. They have the white permed hair and the colourful nightwear of the new poor. Cajoled into a semblance of life by the cheerful nurses, they are propped into chairs at the end of their beds. One or two gaze at the bright consumer models in the weekly magazines; all vivacity and bared smiles. They scan articles on orgasm and troilism, or recipes for Osso Buco and Devilled Shrimp. Their mouths drool, their dentures slip. They cry out, like peremptory children, to be taken down the hall.

Eva, my mother, is among this brigade. The only dark head among the white flowers. With the stubbornness she has always shown towards nature and time, she has refused to go even grey.

A young doctor stops me on the way in.

'Eva is breathing a little better today. When did the attack start?'

7

I am tempted to say 'back in 1939 – before you were even thought of'. But I refrain. I like his use of 'Eva', it makes her seem a girl again. She looks a girl, in the over-large hospital gown, in the big bed.

I saw Eva last on Monday – she hadn't looked well, but I was busy, and ignored her. She had hoped I would go with her to the shops; I refused and she left, wheeling the plaid shopping cart that all women of her generation use, part crutch, part companion. They get under one's feet in buses, on the pavement, like the young mothers with push chairs. Thank God I have left one stage and not yet entered the other. I have opted out of the world of women with miniature wheels.

'She was fine on Monday.' I volunteer this with a slight air of defiance. He is stroking his moustache, which must be a new growth, with regularity and pride. I feel like slapping his hand.

'Really? On Monday she was fine?' He is used to the prevarications of middle-aged children. He gets them all the time. I have seen them, on previous occasions, standing staring at the still form of their nearest and dearest, not knowing what to say, knowing there is no time.

'She walked over to my house. We live near each other – she wasn't even breathless.' I sound like a child repeating a well-rehearsed lesson. A conditioned reflex, lying for or about Eva. She won't blame me for it – we are still comrades.

'This can't have come on in two days.' He frowns at me, trying to locate me behind the dark glasses. I wear them because they filter reality, and also ban the sun. I can't bear the sun to hit my eyes.

'No. She's had it all her life.' I feel that that is neat. I note it down on the *tabula rasa* of my mind. My mind is like a blank white quarto sheet rolled into the machine. The thoughts are the black letters, tap, tap, tap.

'It's a permanent condition then?' He looks serious, like a doctor in a television series. I wonder, suddenly, if they are all actors – the spruce doctors, the stern matron, the svelte black nurses – perhaps this is just another episode in a long-running cosmic soap opera? Does nature imitate television, or television imitate nature? I no longer know. I know he is too young to have seen much life, and too busy to have seen much television. How can he judge these old ones, all born before National Health took over the land? Their hearts and lungs and stomachs date from the First World War, or the Depression – they bear their lives within them, marked by their diseases like rings in a tree, or the tracings of fossils in a rock.

'She's always been in and out of hospital,' I say, partly to cheer him. After all, Eva and I know he won't be able to take in the condition of her much-tried body. The new ones were always surprised. 'How long do you think she'll be in this time?' I ask, naïvely.

'Give me a minute and I'll get out my crystal ball.' Touché. Are we exchanging a look of wary complicity? I should be ashamed. He is young enough to be my son. Well, almost.

Eva is sucking on a plastic tube which sticks out of a giant canister of oxygen. She looks like a child with a sherbert sucker. She becomes animated on seeing me, she mimes her joy with her eyes.

'Please don't,' I say. 'Go on with what you are doing.'

A nurse removes the canister and the tube.

'I'm going to do her blood pressure and her temperature. You can stay,' she says. 'Talk to her.'

I dry up at this.

'What a performance,' says Eva through her dry lips, crinkled as a dead leaf. Her painfully thin arm is exposed, and the black bag put round it. She is vivacious, enjoying the attention. A thermometer is put in her lips, for all the world like the Woodbines she used to hold there, all my childhood.

'Yes, what a thing to happen.' The black nurse removes the thermometer. She writes PEAK FLOW on the chart at the foot of the bed. I lean over to see. It means nothing to me.

'I was fine on Monday, wasn't I?' shouts Eva, for the whole ward. Good old Eva, she doesn't want anyone to think I neglect her. One doesn't forget the old routines.

From a side ward comes a cry, like that of a wounded animal. Pain. Everyone ignores it.

The nurse reappears.

'Drink your chocolate, Agnes,' she says to the gnarled figure at the end of the bed opposite Eva's. 'Come on, be a good girl.'

I recognize the tone; it is one I have used a million times, to my own children. Sometimes it works, sometimes not. Agnes stares into space. The nurse lifts the cup. Chocolate dribbles down the old chin. The cup is replaced on the trolley.

'Your mother will need the bed pan now,' the nurse announces, 'you can wait in the little lounge down the hall.' She draws the floral curtains round the bed. I go down the ward, past the waxworks, to the lounge. A dead television squats in the corner. Next to it is a hooded hair-drier, of the kind still used in suburban salons. The radio is playing softly. Al Jolson sings:

> Though April showers may come your way –
> They bring the flowers that bloom in May.
> So if it's raining, have no regrets –
> Because it isn't raining rain you know
> It's raining violets...

You could have fooled me. I have just walked over the common in the polluted London rain.

A woman in a wheelchair knits, counting 'eighteen, nineteen, twenty...' She drops a stitch, curses, and starts again, 'eighteen, nineteen...' Her head is full of plastic rollers.

'Would you like me to put you under the drier?' I ask. Unwise. Her feet drum against the step of the wheelchair. I am sorry, and say so. She ignores me, and I go over to the window. The rain is still slanting down but it is difficult to see it, because of the double glazing which also cuts off the sound.

A dog leaps and barks out there, with a solitary walker, but they are silent, as if in a dream.

There are a couple of dusty books on the window sill. I examine them. Both are copies of the New Testament. I open one at Corinthians 13, always good for a soul tonic. The words hit me, admiration and writer's envy in equal parts make me quiver. 'Though I speak with the tongues of men and of angels and have not charity, I am become as sounding brass, or a tinkling cymbal.' I close the book as the nurse comes in and puts the woman under the drier. She tells me I can go back to the ward.

Eva has been promoted to her chair. She pats the seat next to her. Her eyes are filmed from the drugs.

'You can bring me a decent nightdress, and some cold cream. My skin is so dry.' I hesitate. I can't possibly say that I am supposed now to be on my way to a church hall in Islington to attend a read-through for a television programme. Ironically, the programme is about my last book, which describes a fictional Eva and a fictional me.

'I won't be back until evening,' I say, and see the thin mouth tighten. I feel like a teenager asking to stay out late. I know what she is thinking, I always do.

Eva gives me a smile she has perfected over the years. It says: 'At least I suffer, am in the real world, unlike the fictional one you have chosen to inhabit. Watch me suffer.' Her mouth, however, says:

'I would also like my little mirror – it is on the mantelpiece; and buy me a hairnet, it must be a dark one, not grey. Write it down.'

I do, and go, monitoring my own footsteps down the ward. Some of the eyes follow me, like in Madame Tussaud's. That's how you know the real ones from the others. I turn and wave. Eva raises her thin arm and then lets it drop, like Gielgud playing Lear.

The doctor I spoke to is at the entrance. I am still holding the New Testament.

'Here,' I say, 'this is yours.' He catches it neatly. Smiles – it seems with recognition. He might have seen my picture on an old book jacket, or as a smudged photograph at the top of a review column. Or he could just be feeling friendly, going off duty.

'Ring any time, to see how she is,' he says. I pull my old Burberry raincoat tight around me, and put the *Guardian* over my head, against the rain.

'I'll be in and out a lot, I expect,' I say, my eyes scanning the forecourt. There are one or two cars and a stationary ambulance. Not a sign of a taxi; nor is there one skimming along the common road.

I dislike the common, having so often pretended to be contented here, with dogs and children and neighbours, playing hearty cricket, or coming to the public courts on Sunday mornings – producing in my relentless way two games haters and one junior champion. The common was always for me a place where I wished I might be somewhere else. Now it seems to be getting a touch nostalgic, my feeling for it. There is a couple in track suits playing in the rain. I spent a lot of time here, after all – it is the past, my past.

We asked the children once if they didn't feel their childhood had been idyllic, both of us hoping they would say yes. They said: not at all – they were bored by bland suburbia too. Yet we thought we were doing it for them.

The beautiful graveyard is being encroached upon by a parking lot; the headstones lurch like drunks, knocked by the bulldozers. An angel has been decapitated.

I chase a lumbering red bus, but the conductor rings the bell as I am stranded on the traffic island. It is typical, I think as I stand drenched to the bone, that I have not mastered the art every Western woman must learn – the ability to drive a car. She must transport bodies and artefacts from point A to point B. So I have written books – what use is that when you are out in the rain in the middle of nowhere?

The cars flash past. Time was when one might have stopped and offered a lift. No, I was never the type. One slows down, I look the other way. Thank you, but no. A bus arrives after fifteen minutes. I am the only one without an official pass of some kind. The bus is full of OAPs and students.

I'll ring Simon when I get in and say that it is impossible. This day is doomed. But as I alight at my stop I know I won't do any such thing – for if I do there will be no Kate Wainwright. It is, after all, what I do. What I exist for. Work.

The telephone is ringing as I enter the house. Simon, of course.

'Where on earth have you been? There are a lot of people waiting for you.'

'I've just got in. I'm drenched from walking across the common.' I don't mention Eva, or the hospital, I don't know

12

why. He rings off. He isn't pleased.

It takes the taxi nearly an hour in the rain to get to Islington. It could all be over by the time I arrive. But no, I see Simon's head looking out from the church-hall door, out and up, as if I might come riding in over the rooftops. It has stopped raining at last. He sees me and rushes over to pay the fare. He is polite, but grim.

2

The bunch of people waiting to flesh out my fantasy are sitting around as if they were in a permanent railway-station waiting-room, there are full ashtrays and spilled drinks and desultory conversations. Actors still seem to smoke, and they are temperamentally trained to take the waiting for granted, in green rooms everywhere. It is part of their life, on sets, in studios. I can't really see how any of this collection resembles anyone in my book; they are a motley crew, unlike the Northerners of wartime Britain who inhabit my pages. They must be hand-picked, Simon is good at that. If I have faith in anyone, it is in Simon (and now I suppose I include the young doctor at the hospital); both men seem to me to be an example of new professionalism; they are direct, democratic, and believe in the work-ethic which in the old days was always accompanied by the frills of professional behaviour. I like Simon's hard-nosed integrity – I wish I could belong to a group, a brotherhood, or sisterhood, like those I see in studios or in the hospital. They are far removed from the writer's onanistic and solitary act.

'Here's our author at last,' he says, putting an arm around my shoulder. 'I don't have to introduce her, you've all read the script, at least you *should* have read the script.' General laughter. I grimace, as I always do. I feel included, though, as much as I ever do. Part of the group, but a little outside. They are the spoken overt word, and I am the written, covert one.

'Let's get on, then.' There is more laughter, he doesn't know that it is one of his phrases, and he says it twenty times a day. Simon thrusts a chair at me; I sit at the long table littered with Coke tins and put my script down in a pool of unidentifiable liquid.

14

'We've had a good session, Kate, and it is going well. If you have any queries, please make yourself heard.'

We begin, and are absorbed for over an hour. Then he tells all but the three principals that they can go. They shuffle out, collecting coats and scripts, to buses or tubes. We won't all be together again until after the location trip to Blackpool.

'Goodbye, loves,' Simon shouts. 'Don't forget what we've done today, some of it was excellent.' He turns back to us. There is Rosamund who is to play Ellie, my mother, and Toby Armstrong, a rotund and talented actor. With his Falstaffian looks he is not what I imagined. My thin, ascetic, downbeat father will have to struggle out of him, like Cyril Connolly's thin man who is inside every fat man. There is a new girl I have not met before, who is, I suppose, to play Sarah – the young me.

Rosamund, fortyish, quick and lively and dark, has elements of early Eva, or Ellie as she is in the book. In spite of the Fiorucci boiler suit and the fox fur, she is, underneath, the same kind of female. We have worked together before. She grins at me now, offering a cigarette, and asks if I managed to pour myself into a taxi after that lunch we had. I say, yes, and did she? She winks at me.

The afro-haired girl with the WRP badge is the one unknown quantity. Abigail. My suspicion of her might be slight jealousy; I have a love-hate feeling about these new fringe girls, with their political ideals, broad smiles and disregard for clothes. I would have dearly loved to be like that, but was born into a more rigid time. I like their freshness, and their unisex attitude to the opposite sex. She holds out her hand for me to take, and shake.

'Abigail Jones – I'm to be you, it's funny, isn't it? I suppose you are Sarah? You must be. I loved the book.'

'Thanks. I am, sort of. You know—' She is charming and disarming. And confident, or seems so.

'You probably saw Abigail at the King's Head, in the new American play,' Simon says *sotte voce*, but loud enough for her to hear. Bastard, he knows I have been lazy about such things lately, the black dog on my back – depression.

'I didn't,' I say at her. 'But I am sure I have seen your work.'

I thought I knew the face, but could not place her – it could have been Riverside, or even a television soap commercial, the WRP badge did not always exclude such things. I used to be infallible with faces and names, but that is all going. 'I'm sure you'll be marvellous,' I say, as she and Simon look gloomy. I must watch myself, I don't anticipate being put in the maternal, approving role. That is one role I feel I can give up now.

They work their way into the parts. Rosamund, in spite of the clothes and the ringed, expressive hands, is becoming Eva/Ellie. Toby, if I discount the physical presence, is beginning to sound like my father. Abigail is having a good try at being a few years younger than her actual self, and she has got the voice right. The scene where Sarah and her father meet on the beach is growing before my gaze. I can't remember any more if it happened, or if it is one of my fictions. One of the sad processes of fiction: when exposed, it floats away like an errant balloon, the string is cut. Actors take it away, it is theirs, and not mine. I begin to relax. Let them have it. It is theirs as much as mine now.

Rosamund, when not reading, stares into space, and smokes. She is hidden in a grey cloud. I wonder what is going through her mind. She's a little younger than me – and is playing my mother. Odd. But then, I am no longer young Sarah, however I may feel. I saw Rosamund once, in the provinces as Cleopatra; but I think she would be the first to admit her career has not taken off in the way she had once hoped. Now she juggles her private agonies and public necessities deftly, as we all do. We should get together, I think, we should swop our sad and merry tales, two women of a kind. Soul sisters.

Simon stands and stretches, well-pleased with the way things are going. I realize that the day, which started so badly, has taken off and soared. Rosamund slings her coat over her shoulders.

'See you in Blackpool, then, love,' she says to me. 'Bring your bucket and spade.' And she is off. Toby kisses me on the cheek, murmurs to me that he is on a diet, and will be nearer the part when we meet again. So he knows my slight doubt. Abigail lingers, Simon walks her to the door. He gives her a hug, and a slap on the behind. She closes the large door, reluctant, I think, to lose the afternoon.

'You look upset. Or did.' He knows me well. 'You forgot to eat, didn't you? There's a humble caff somewhere around – let's go.'

He gets me tea and a stale bun at the counter, without asking me what I want. For years I was asked by Dominic, my ex-husband now, exactly what I wanted. All the time. The secret is, I never care. Simon knows I would rather not be asked.

'You know, Toby and I are aware you weren't too happy at his playing your Dad,' he says, biting into his own bun. 'He's losing weight, and he'll get the voice down.'

'Weren't there any small wiry Northerners?' I ask. 'Isn't he going to be, simply, too grand?'

'In a word, no. Trust me.'

I sip my tea. I do trust him on Toby, but maybe not about Abigail.

'Is Abigail right for the part?'

'Those RSC girls are very clever.' He has never said she was with the RSC; I should have known. My *accidie* has made me stupid. But he has pushed his granny glasses back over his nose, a nervous gesture he has when telling little white lies. He is unsure. I know him at least as well as he knows me.

'Apart from Abigail, what's worrying you?' He pursues me, always, like a little terrier.

'Eva. She's back in hospital. It seems bad this time. That's why I was late. I have to go back, she needs some things.' I was going to say, 'you know Eva', but, of course, he doesn't. He knows only that we are still entwined like the gnarled roots of a tree, in that indescribable way some mothers and daughters remain. Unlike the way I am with my own daughter, Jenni.

'Don't worry – it has happened before.'

'It was a crisis, she was rushed in as an emergency, and I didn't know.'

'You can't always be there.'

I am never there, that is the trouble.

'I've got to get back. I felt a bitch leaving her.'

'You are anything but that. You are one of the most generous people I know.'

I wince a little at that. He sounds like Dom, after years of living together. I don't want Simon to start those easy banalities with me. Of course, he might believe it.

'Did you see the old movie on Sunday afternoon?' I ask him. He shakes his head. He sees his two little daughters on Sundays. He takes them to the zoo, or a film.

'It was partly scripted by Scott Fitzgerald, and his bits stuck out like a sore thumb. *Three Comrades,* it was called. Get this: Franchot Tone says to Margaret Sullavan, "He's too good for you." She replies, quick as a flash, "We're all too good for each other." Great, eh?'

'How do you know that was a Scotty bit?' Simon asks.

'Because I do. And that's why you like me.' I risk a lot, saying that. But I don't say 'that's why you love me.' He puts his arm around me, and we leave the café, and go out into the rainy street.

I make my way to Eva's flat, to search for a clean nightdress, and cold cream. The place is a muddle, my heart sinks as I enter; the light flex is swinging bulbless from the middle of the ceiling; I had promised her I would get an electrician to fix it, and had forgotten. Cobwebs festoon the place, like Christmas streamers someone has forgotten to take down. She has stuck an Anglepoise lamp on the dressing table, it is the only light, and it illuminates the family pictures of all of us she keeps there, like a shrine. We lurk from every crevice, at various ages, Peter, Miles, Dom, Jenni – and of course myself. On holidays we had neglected to include her in, at functions we had not invited her to. I get out quickly, getting her one of my own nightdresses from home, and picking up cold cream from the late-night chemist near the hospital.

At the hospital they have eaten their evening meal, and are almost ready for bed. Like a lot of little girls they are sitting up, as if waiting for a goodnight kiss.

Eva is not pleased by the fact I did not find her own nightdress. She says the cold cream is the wrong brand. Tomorrow I must go back and find the nightdress in the third drawer down, and the cold cream behind the mirror on the mantelpiece. Where is the hair net, *and* the small mirror? I have brought Peter's old transistor for her, with an ear plug, and she puts it in and says she can't hear anything. The ward is too noisy. I sit there, deflated as a scolded infant. At the end of the visit I feel as exhausted as if I'd done twenty pages.

Back at home I switch on the television, a box of Kentucky Fried chicken on my knee. I eat like a starving woman, with my fingers. There is no one to mark my greed. Gone are the years when I staggered down from a day of typing to do the family meal at this hour. I always poured myself a stiff whisky before the two halves of the day separated themselves. Evenings I devoted to scattered arrivals, to arguments about homework versus television, or discussions of Dom's day. All gone.

When I let myself into the house these days there is the distinct aroma of junk food. I'm a junk-food junkie, I tell myself, cheerfully. I sneer at the row of fat cookbooks. It is a kind of triumph after so many years of snob eating.

I watch a programme on education, in which a bunch of councillors, MPs and parents argue the case for bringing back the grammar schools in their old glory. A lady in a floral dress gets very excited. I can't get into the debate – my children are old and gone. I switch to a repeat cop thriller on the other side.

The pussy flap bangs, and Macheath the tom bounds in. I've forgotten to get any cat food. He has to make do with the tiny bones of the Kentucky chicken. Peter christened him Macheath while in his Brecht phase years ago. It dates him. He rubs against my legs as I go around the house, switching on lights as if expecting someone. He is still hungry. I fry him an egg, which he refuses. He flounces out, leaving me to go around the ghost rooms, looking for imaginary burglars.

Peter's room looks as if he has just left, although he has been in Edinburgh for a year now. I smile; the room is so like him. There are the traces of his phases; the military stage, the astronaut boom. The earlier ones, the Babars and Tintins, and the Rev. Awdrey's little books on railway engines are stuffed in with his university textbooks. He is a hoarder. Miles hasn't kept a thing, his room is like a monk's cell. His blazer is the only thing that reminds me of him, it still has fluff and toffee papers in the pocket when I put in my hand. It feels as if he might bounce in and ask me if his cricket flannels are ready, but of course he won't. Jenni? Jenni says she never lived here, not 'lived' that is, in spite of the Laura Ashley wallpaper and clothes she demanded, and which still cover her room maddeningly, with tiny flowers.

Dom cleared all his stuff out when he left, but I only have to look in the bookshelf to be reminded of Dom.

The telephone disturbs my trip. I go down slowly, so that whoever it is won't think I am waiting for a call.

Simon. Who else? I long ago alienated friends and relations, with my unsociable writing habits.

'I'll be over later. If I may? I have to see Gilly and the girls. Some crisis or other – you know Gilly. Won't be late. Can you contain yourself until then?'

I hang up. What a strange phrase. Of course I can contain myself. I have been doing it for quite some time now.

I'll reread the book, it is time I did. A bit of self-abuse never hurt anybody.

3

I always do a double-take when Simon is at the door, for a split second I think it is Peter. It's a superficial resemblance, the glasses, the dark hair, the jeans, the fact they both have an air of the eternal student, Trofimov, in *The Cherry Orchard*.

'I solved the problem with Toby – *Daddy*, on the telephone. We worked out what was wrong,' he says.

'Don't call Eric "Daddy".' I snap it out before I think. I could bite my tongue. It isn't anything to do with him.

'Sorry.' He looks tired. I wonder exactly what I am doing. I would rather, in truth, go to bed with a good book – even my book. I shut this thought out of my mind. I know I am lucky to have him, as long as it lasts.

'Shall I cook you something? An omelette?' Funny, when I had to cook I resented it, but now I am always trying to feed Simon. Repeat three times: try not to be maternal.

'No thanks. Gilly made me something. She said it was an omelette as well.'

'How are they all?'

'Measles. She thinks they have measles. She isn't sure, being Gilly.'

'It isn't that easy to tell. It's not so stupid, not knowing,' I say. Girls of a feather flock together.

'I hope you've had it – them – the measles?'

'Oh yes.'

I remember the rooms darkened to prevent the light hitting the eyes, the fractious children. I'd had it with them. Family solidarity. Poor Gilly.

'I like Gilly,' I say, out of the blue.

'I like her too. Just can't live with her.' He slaps my behind, which annoys me, because I remember the Abigail slap, earlier.

21

Still, my behind is slimmer these days, and I am slightly pleased to find it slappable.

'You aren't taking anything away from them, you know. I've told you.' Big of him. I wasn't considering it. Much more mundanely, my thoughts were on the difficulty of amusing sick children.

'I was really wondering if they would like some jigsaws. We have a lot upstairs. Of course, there might be pieces missing.'

'Forget it. She can always buy a jigsaw.'

How was he to know she could get out to buy jigsaws? It wasn't easy to get out when children were sick.

'Jigsaws can be a godsend sometimes. You have no idea...'

I clear the table of its debris and make two mugs of instant coffee. It is fun working with Simon. We are doing an adaptation of a Conrad novel called *Chance*. I put the lamp on the table. The intensity of it reminds me of student days. Writing is a lonely business – this is a delight for me.

'Toby won't do a comic Yorkshire, will he?' I am still worried, obviously. I can't bring up Abigail again.

'I told you.'

'I know.'

'If I didn't know you so well, I'd say you had an Electra complex. You just don't want us to do your Dad. I mean *Eric*.'

'I just heard a talk saying the one person who didn't have an Oedipus complex was – Oedipus.'

'I don't think Freud ever suggested he had.'

I laugh. I like the speed of the reply, like a good return in tennis. Our minds play good tennis; our bodies too. Wham, bam, thank you sir. Good doubles. Now, why did I think *doubles?* It must be because we are both tied up emotionally with our previous partners. Me, nostalgically with Dom, he, actually with Gilly and the girls. The silken cord.

'Let's get on, shall we?' He doesn't recognize the remark. I ruffle his hair. He removes my hand.

We stop in a while for lager. He has brought a six-pack of Stella Artois. It amuses me that I can last an evening on lager. Dom and I belonged to the drinking generation – we would have needed a bottle of malt whisky for an evening at home.

Dom would be amused at the new naïve me. Simon does not

drink much, he smokes the odd joint, but not conventional cigarettes. The difference in generations.

'You do think Abigail is right for me, then?' He looks shocked. I realize he thinks I fancy her. Perhaps I do, and don't know it. *'Sarah,'* I say.

'I thought we were on to Joseph Conrad. You'll be surprised at Abigail.'

'I bet.'

'You'll feel better when you get up there. Blackpool. Stir the old roots.'

'I just don't want her to make it too – modern, politicized. She's so *new*. She won't unzip your flies, will she?'

So now it was out.

'You are being a bit silly this evening. She isn't like that. She knows we are committed.'

'Are we?'

'Well, I am.' He yawns and says he feels like bed. He says I look tired. At the beginning of the relationship a remark like that would have made me fearful that I looked old. Now I know he means I look tired.

I go up first and look in the glass, automatically. I have cropped my hair and I am thinner than I was. I wear jeans all the time, and shirts from Jean Machine, left by the boys. If I put on the bedside table lamp and shut off the main light I look twenty. Well, thirty. I switch off the main light. I recall Eva's hanging flex. Simon falls over a cold cup of coffee on the floor as he leaps in with me.

'This house is more of a junk pile each time I see it. Why don't you clean it, or get someone in?' He picks up the cup and deposits it on the windowsill, the only clear place.

'My tidy days are over.' I like the grotty bedsitter feeling the house is acquiring. 'I used to run a tight ship,' I say, snuggling against him. 'Dom liked it that way. He always said he didn't – but he went mad if socks were unwashed or shirts unironed. Or crumbs in the bed. He hated crumbs in the bed.'

'He wouldn't be happy now,' Simon grumbles. 'So, you are rebelling?'

'I just don't think about it.'

True. It isn't a conscious behaviour pattern, I just let things

23

be. It is part of my cure, from being a wife and mother. I was a compulsive *Hausfrau* – I can now let things ride. My work has never been better. The dog, recently deceased, has left stains from his last illness all over the carpets, I can leave them as a kind of tribute to his ragged charm. If others were here I would be at the stains with a carpet shampoo. The china is running out, all that eternal marriage china – I buy paper cups. I smash and throw odd saucers against the patio wall when I feel like it. If examined, my actions might seem vindictive, against Dom's defection, or even mad. In fact I am happier than I have been for years. I am discovering me. The Kate, or Sarah, who was buried. I want to get back to the point where young Sarah stepped off the coach, fresh from Blackpool. The dissolution of objects is part of that retracing. The old deep freeze lurks in the garden, pots of geraniums peer out of its apertures. A broken Habitat lantern swings from the Russian vine. The birds have made a house in it.

Simon and I make love, effortlessly, with no questions asked or answered. No half-refusals, no turning away, no sadness; it just happens.

After, as he sleeps against me, I think of the rows of beds in the geriatric ward. All those women have at some time loved, been loved. When night falls, Eva tells me, their cries rise through the dark. They mumble names of loved ones that are nothing to do with the passing nurses, and the others awake beside them. The words ascend in the silence. 'Though I speak with the tongues of men and angels –'

I sleep, finally. No cries come from my mouth, I think. No cry disturbs the peace of my sated, once-marital bed.

4

The next morning Simon is up, has made coffee and scrambled eggs, and has gone out for the *Guardian* and the *Daily Mail.* I cancelled the paper deliveries when Dom left. I never seem to read them, and they depress me. It is part of my new isolation, not catching up with events.

Simon reads Nigel Dempster's gossip column first, which amuses me, it is so unlike him. If he ever becomes a permanent fixture I shall have to tell him I can't possibly eat breakfast. But I munch, dutifully, when he is here.

I open the *Guardian,* and the first thing I see is Dom's cheerful yet earnest face staring at me from the financial pages.

'Dom is in here,' I say.

'Mm.' He is on to the sports pages. Reading about some transferred football hero. He is so different from Dominic, it is as sharply a temperamental as an age difference. Sometimes I think we were misguided, Dom and I, in feeling we had made some kind of progress, in our woolly-minded liberal way. Really, we just lazed along, supporting the *status quo.* What happened to the sixties? Nothing, Dom would say still, fixed in his middle-class middle-brow England – whereas I would say something was lazily lost, mislaid, some chance went. And Simon? He seems apolitical. He has the penchant for working-class culture that all his lot have – soccer and beer. 'I'm quite good at what I do' – that would be Simon's ethic. I have the feeling Dom would say the same. Where are the fanatics of yesteryear? I ask myself. Frequently.

Dom and I, in the early years, wanted the lot. Progress, ourselves and everyone were to be included in that. Watery socialism, of the Harold Wilson technological revolutionary kind. Commitment was the hot word then. Funny how Simon used it to describe what he felt for me. Dom had seen nothing wrong with the old puritan work-ethic. Neither had I, as a good Northern girl from the wrong side of the tracks.

I notice I have inadvertently put a buttery fingerprint on the face of my ex-spouse. Sorry, Dom.

'You are very quiet,' says Simon.

'Thought you were reading. I don't like having the papers now I've given them up. I listen to the birds in the garden, dream. Now I've seen Dom, and read about inflation.'

'Sorry. Can I have a bath? Is there any hot water?'

'Of course. It is still a functioning household in some respects. The machines clock on and off. Shall I run it for you?'

'No,' he says, 'I'll do it.'

Dom would have loved me to run his bath, but for that reason I never did it. Now I know, mustn't fuss, mustn't be too eager. Will I be allowed to dry bodies?

'I'll come up and dry you.' He doesn't object to that.

I clear the table. It is odd; first there were breakfasts *à deux,* Dom in a business suit, and everything very efficient. Then the infant messes, high-chairs and slop. Homework-evading sessions, with cereals and toast crammed in mouths as they left. Then the student times, hangovers and spare bodies on the spare couches, appearing tousle-haired and bog-eyed, for Alka Seltzer or tomato juice.

Now, it appears we are back to *à deux,* at least for odd days of the week. He isn't a permanent guest, not yet.

I take a towel from the airing cupboard and go in to the bathroom. I dry him like a child, rubbing the wiry black hair until he says that's enough, and I slap him on the rump with the damp towel. I am in love with male bodies, the harder and leaner the better.

'Thanks, mum,' he says, and chases me along the landing.

Downstairs, jeaned and sweatered again, he is serious. Trofimov again, ready for off, as they say in the North.

'Can I drop you anywhere?'

'What, like this?' I am still in Dom's old towelling robe.

'Well, you are the fastest dresser I know.'

26

'And undresser?'

'That too.'

I tell him I have to lunch with a publisher at one, and that I have to read the book. It is a white lie, he doesn't spot it. Dom would have known.

'So, see you late Friday.'

'What happened to Thursday?'

'I have to go to Belfast, for that conference. You remember.'

Now I do.

'Come to dinner on Friday?'

'As long as it isn't Kentucky.'

'It won't be. I'll do something grand.'

'You're on. See you Friday.' A peck on the cheek, impersonal really. He is gone. *Take care,* I say, but to myself really.

I go up and wash my face with some exclusive black soap I bought at Harrods once when panicky about old age and wrinkly skin. I usually forget about it. You are supposed to rinse three hundred times or so, I get tired after about three. I put on my jeans and a Southern Comfort T-shirt. Working uniform. I scrub out the bath. Was ever a man born who would scrub out a bath automatically, after using it? I'd like to meet him. It had been in my mind to scrub the house, after Simon's remark of the night before, but I reconsider. I like it this way.

Dom and I used to have a routine we fell into when we had dinner parties. 'You are looking very ugly today, my dear – are we expecting guests?' Alfred Jarry, *Père Ubu.* It always made us laugh. I miss Dom sometimes; would like to ring him, in his Suffolk cottage, but Lois would never understand.

It was something Dom said he would never do, start all over again. 'Imagine,' he would say, 'beginning *all* that again – how can they do it?' That was when our friends split up and remarried and had new families. 'Poor sod,' he would say, but only about the man. 'Poor sod.'

That's what I think sometimes. Poor sod.

In some ways we still have what we had – a youth spent together, learning about living with another human body. But it is an underground stream that runs between us.

27

I have never exposed it in my work. But when I get stuck for an idea I might. *Caritas* stops me. Charity.

I curl up on the bed with a book. Mine.

5

On Thursday night I wake from a frightening dream. The dream was a mixture, of Eva in the ward, with the common converted into a brown heaving sea. Waves dashed against the beds, with their cargoes of old bones.

There was young Ellie, just married (do I remember or did I invent?) and the young Sarah (not me) watching her.

Throughout, as in most dreams, was the suffocating sense of guilt. Betrayal of trust. I go down and make coffee and watch dawn come up over the patio wall. It is the worst time of day, the dark recriminations of dreams are bad enough, but I have the novel to haunt me too. Dawn is difficult alone. It is hard living without the proximity of other bodies. Minds are a worse lack. Not being able to spill out worries is a real lack. One can even do that with one's children, up to a point.

I *will* learn. Eva learned. Eva might seem a simpler being than me, but all complications are cancelled when it comes to stoicism. Eva and I were such comrades once, in the world without men. All through my marriage I saw Eva's mouth tighten at my defection into the family syndrome, saw her edged out. She didn't want to be part of it too much, she had disapproved of it for herself, and taught me to disapprove of it too, especially in the bourgeois style Dom and I affected. So I was ambivalent, though, if pressed, I would have admitted I embraced it thoroughly. Now I am where all women seem to end up – in Eva's camp. She soldiered on alone. Can I?

My desire for the normal has split us in a way we never were split by poverty. I produced other human beings and I felt I owed them a different view from that bleak one.

The price paid, if a price is paid, is removal from what Eva and I (or Ellie and Sarah) believed was life. But is Eva's Samuel

29

Beckett-like climate, which is not theatrical (she preceded him) the right one? For a writer, maybe. You can't fake it, for that reason. I know Eva thinks I have faked it, and she may be right. I couldn't ask as little of the world as she did.

So here I am, exposing our wounds. I go around, wringing my hands, like a suburban Lady Macbeth. Spilled psychic blood – and the past murdered willingly. But if I am Lady Macbeth, who is my lord? All this is dawn nonsense. Does Eva care? For all I know, she may be delighted.

The destructive, or maybe constructive part of the defence mechanism of a writer always rears its ugly head at some point. I defend myself in this dawn trial. You have to try and shape life – I thought this as a child, and will always think it. Passivity is not all, especially not for a woman, not now.

When I've said that, I've said nothing, as I well know. For Eva stumbled on the first rule of living, which is just to live. From day to day. Blind unseen plodding, as my grandmother did before her. I couldn't do it – I wanted progress. Why then does Eva's passive existence seem nobler to me at this point? It must be the vengeance of time, the dying of cells, the mad dance of hormones, the preparation to be a waxwork. Is this house – the mausoleum of the nuclear family – a memorial to those years? Or are the memorials those flesh-and-blood creations of mine, who are out there, somewhere in the night?

I wander over the museum of our life. There is a faded square for each picture Dom took – he had to be persuaded that I was no longer into possessions. One particularly amused me, a Léger print, which caused a row on our first visit to the South of France. I had snapped it up, before looking at the pictures. Dom accused me of being a consumer, of not enjoying the day, the real pictures on the walls. In truth, I just wanted to encapsulate it, and wrap it up and take it home. The children howled, the day was ruined. We had our Léger, and now I have the blank patch. I prefer it.

I am learning at last what Eva once told me, what Ellie tells Sarah in the book; that to 'have' things forever, you must lose them, give them up willingly. It has taken me a long time to know what she meant.

When the television programme is over I will move to some

large empty space, a warehouse perhaps, and again become a piece of human flotsam. I can't wait.

Until then I must avoid falling back into my old posture of waiting, wanting, hoping, demanding. What I learned from the years of marriage and children is that there is no secret to being capable, no secret to possessing or being possessed. All one has to do is hold out one's competent hands.

Letting the hands fall to one's side is a more difficult matter.

6

Simon rings from Belfast to say he is leaving from the airport and that he will be back at about four. He wants to have another read-through with the three principals. I hesitate; Eva is on a super drug, with side effects that are making her ill. I suggest they all come to my house – the key is under the flowerpot as usual. Simon hangs up. I have promised to ring them all and arrange it – I myself will have to go to the hospital. He doesn't seem to get the point that there are some times when fact is more important than fiction. I can't blame him – I have always been like that too.

I hire a car to take me to the hospital. I cringe at the thought of driving up, and try and convince the driver to drop me outside, on the common road. He, being obliging, insists on taking me into the forecourt, and getting out and opening the door.

I am ashamed of this, in front of the nurses. I have heard them complain about the bus route, and the fact they have to wait fifteen minutes or so, going on and off duty.

I pass the Greek woman in the side ward as I go in. She is the one who howls – the animal noise I heard on the first day. Raging against the dying of the light. She lies, naked as a babe, her legs drawn up over her protruberant old woman belly; her female relatives, who are always there, sit and knit, and watch the people who pass with their dark inscrutable eyes.

This is not the way Eva and I carry on, nor the others. We carry sagging brown bags of fruit, and bunches of flowers to show our solidarity. We would like to be Greek but are not. This is what we do.

The food trolleys are squeaking down the ward. Eva cannot eat; she has, earlier, been wrapped in wet cloths and had a cool

32

fan on her thin carcass to bring down the high temperature. She looks yellow and drawn.

She tells me she does not take the pills they give her; she says she hides them in the transistor. I don't believe this, but make a note to check with Sister.

Eva complains she now wants her blue dressing gown. Will I go and get it for her? Her thin fingers pluck the sheet. I write down 'Dressing Gown' on my cheque book as if it were a title of a new work. Eva says we have a long time, a nice long time together, as the doctor is not coming until four, to check on her. I look at the clock. It is 2.30.

I look at her tight, withdrawn face. She dozes. I am no use here. At three, when there is the interruption of tea, I tell her I must go. I know what she thinks – see the condemnation in her face. But I'll be back, I tell her, with the dressing gown. I feel my voice is already getting the note the nurses have in theirs, which I used to have in mine when I made excuses to children. She has a paroxysm of coughing to make her point. She makes her point.

I pass the Greek lady, silent now. Radio One blares from the little lounge. The woman in the wheelchair is still knitting, counting: 'Twenty, twenty-one, twenty-two.' I begin to run.

At home, they are sitting around the kitchen table. Simon, Abigail, Toby and Rosamund. My family. Simon looks up as I enter.

'Hello, love – how is she?' Their faces are all concern. He hands me a book, an Irish poet he knows I like, Seamus Heaney. 'I brought you a present to cheer you up.'

Much to everyone's surprise (and my own) I burst into tears.

7

A doll's house, standing in a row of doll's houses, red-brick, built in the 1920s by a speculative builder, contained Ellie Shand, peeling onions for a stew.

The houses were solidly built, with integrity; however, their similarity and the neatness of the rows denoted condescension. Their present occupants, in the depression of the 'thirties, nevertheless knew they were lucky.

Ellie did. Young, married, with a fat child in the garden, she did not really care if the tears running down her tanned cheeks were induced by physiology (the effect of onions on her tear ducts) or general misery (her marriage to Eric Shand). Whatever the reason for the waterworks, she would have gone on peeling.

She attacked the transparent globes with thin artistic fingers. Domestic chores did not appeal to her; not for her the delight of new recipes to tempt the homecoming husband. For one thing, Eric often did not come home – or when he did it was after closing time and the dinner was ruined.

If Ellie had been of a later generation – or even in her own one, educated – she might have analysed her situation. As it was, she accepted it. Women were not used to scrutinizing their minds, bodies or hearts, in the 1930s. It was assumed that whatever happened was one's 'lot'.

Ellie knew without being told, although she was told, often, that her lot was a happy one. She had a man, a house, a baby. What every woman desired.

21 Rathmines Avenue, then – semi-detached, with two bedrooms and a box room, two reception rooms (one the Northern parlour, used only on special occasions), a bare, gadgetless kitchen and an unheated bathroom. A large garden,

which Ellie had tended over four childless years.

The sea-girt clay soil was good for roses – roses bloomed in profusion. The whole place reeked of roses.

At the back of the house was a marshland, not to be developed until after the Second World War. As yet it was just a place of mystery and adventure for the local children who ignored nature's warnings of king cups and reeds, and the council's warning – a large sign saying 'DANGER'. Two children had drowned there since the houses were built, but then, children were as numerous as roses.

Neatness and respectability, those two English virtues, made for boredom. Ellie thought that was why murder of the domestic kind was the English hobby. The net curtains opened only to look for a wayward child, or to spy on what the neighbours were doing. Sometimes Ellie thought it would have been better to have landed on one of the sprawling pebble-dashed council estates; where noisy brawls were enacted on the child-scarred grass verges, and life was more open. But the estates were *common*. Ellie knew that though Rathmines Avenue was dull, it wasn't common.

Petit-bourgeois, the life there might have been called if sociologists had been invented. Shopkeepers, barbers, clerks, retired couples, and the odd person who had come down in the world a little, like Eric, inhabited the quiet streets. The men worked; the women, as a rule, did not. There was a black Ford outside Ellie's door – this was unusual. Not many had cars. Ellie didn't drive – few women did.

The chill wind of the depression had not really hit the town, although there were less visitors due to the lack of money in the industrial areas. An odd unemployed male lingered around, waiting for the pub to open, but it wasn't how Ellie had heard it was in the mill towns or the mining communities.

She peered out at her baby, a chubby girl. The child gurgled and cooed in the black perambulator, under the silver birch tree.

Sarah, the infant, bald as a coot, waved a celluloid rattle into the air, into the china blue sky, as if all were right with the world. Ellie was disturbed by the affability of babies; she had not expected that. Had expected wails and tears, not a positive human being joining her and willing her to enjoy life too. She found it annoying, just as she had disliked the way the baby hung on her breasts and pumped away, enthusiastic for the thin bluish milk that flooded out, against Ellie's will. Ellie soon put a stop to that, a nice sterilized bottle was much more under her control.

Sarah was what was known, locally, as 'a good baby'. She weighed more each week, she smiled at all. She was a complete enigma to Ellie.

Ellie saw the child's dimpled feet flashing under the tree. Slivers of light hit them. She had planted the tree, the young silver birch, five years ago, and it too had flourished, like Sarah. She had been a young bride then. Now, all she knew was that she would not still plant a tree.

She didn't blame anyone for her misplaced hopes – not Eric, not even herself. If she had been able to do that, she might have wept real, not onion-triggered, tears. As it was, they stopped as soon as she had enough onions for the casserole. She blew her retroussé nose vigorously; then she rushed upstairs for powder and lipstick to restore the damage. Her main virtue was stoicism – her vice, vanity.

If probed, which she was not, Ellie would have confessed that little interested her except the preservation of her slim, girlish body. She was, after all, only twenty-four.

Ellie didn't want to acquire the form of most of the young mothers around her – after one or two children they resembled floral cushions in their flowered pinnies – sagging, succouring, finished.

The doctor had said, after delivering Sarah: 'What a beautiful body.' He had not meant the child. The change wrought in Ellie was emotionally charged – she had never had flattery before. It winged around her anaesthetized head. It took away the aftermath of pain.

It made up for the fact that Eric had not bothered to come in and see his child for the first twenty-four hours, and had then said, 'Oh, a girl.' He had sat puffing his pipe smoke over the red bundle in the basket at the end of the bed until opening time.

He had not been told off by the nurses because of the air of authority that still clung to him, as ex-Labour candidate, ex-councillor, and local man-about-town.

The young doctor's remark became for Ellie her talisman, her inspiration, her hope. She had gone into the maternity home to bring out a baby and had brought out an ideal. Now she exercised daily, behind the net curtains of the matrimonial bedroom, window opened on to the deserted street. The voice of the BBC lady instructed her: 'AND one-two-three, knees bend – AND UP. Straighten that spine, ladies AND four-five-six, AND breathe deeply, seven-eight-nine. STRETCH those arms and AGAIN ... '

Ellie wanted to be a perfect physical specimen, like the German maidens she saw on the Movietone and Pathe Pictorial newsreels, making themselves fit for Hitler.

It seemed to her that if she had such inspiration it would give her life meaning. The dominant male, wasn't that needed? The hypnotic sway of those white-clad bodies in the mass inspired her. There was nothing like that in her life. It made her guts melt, in the way they had on her honeymoon, not for Eric, but for Wagner and Puccini at the Opera House. Her girlish heart beat faster now only for Tristan, on the wind-up gramophone in the front parlour.

Ellie had never bothered to penetrate the vulgar parts of the town, with the Tower erect over the Central Beach, or the delights of the Golden Mile. She avoided Kiss-Me-Quick hatted trippers, factory girls and lads on Wakes weeks holidays, carrying their pink candy-floss like bouquets of flowers.

Not for her the Fattest Woman on Earth, the man with a baby growing out of his stomach, the Rat Man, the Gypsy Fortune Teller, or Epstein's Adam, scandalous because he had displayed the first man's private parts. Ellie had always considered herself a cut above the average. She would not have danced the evenings away – much less the afternoons – to the Mighty Wurlitzer. She would not have tried to 'click' or 'get off' with the young men scattering the town, spending their year's savings on a wild week's spree. Ellie had watched them when she first came to the town; first the giggling girls, cotton skirts blowing in the wind on the Promenade, then the sad intense young men, Adam's apples bobbling with impatience and desire.

> When I grow too old to dream,
> I'll have you to remember—

Ellie shuddered. She hated songs like that. She had learned to prefer Wagner. It came from having an older husband who could tell you things. Eric had implied to her that she shouldn't feel superior in this way, yet he in his turn tried to elevate the workers, as if they were not good enough as they were. He was more of a snob than she was. He told her that the ballroom was the *Schönbrunn* of the masses, that the white Woolworth building was pure *Bauhaus*. She had no idea what he meant, but she knew he was trying to make a silk purse out of a sow's ear.

She didn't respond to his schoolmasterish side, although it had attracted her as a younger girl. He had tried to educate her, in the early days, had pushed books on to her thin lap; Ibsen, Wilde, Bertrand Russell, Bernard Shaw, all his favourites. She had accepted them gravely, been amused by Shaw and titillated by Wilde. She didn't know what it was that Oscar Wilde had done. She listened to classical music, liking only that which stimulated the orgasmic feeling she never had in bed.

Her mind, like her sensuality, remained inviolate. Which is why, in a sense, she fell for the threat of violence implied in Adolf. She thought a lot of men and women must feel the same, look at the enthusiasm he engendered, all over Europe. She could never confess this to Eric. He had given up on her passivity, he would have been shocked at the strain of submerged masochism lying just under the skin.

Restricting herself to the prim suburbia she was offered, Ellie wheeled her baby through the bowling green grounds, where wallflowers bloomed. There was even a flower clock, showing the pretty, empty hours. She joined Boots' Library and read, daringly, D.H. Lawrence, and Michael Arlen. She wished to be Iris Storm, in *The Green Hat*.

The summer silence, away from the tripper-filled sea was

broken only by the click of bowls, or the cries of young children on the swings. If there was the odd drunk hanging on to a lamp-post in the middle of the afternoon, or the scent of piss from the gents' urinal hidden in the bushes of the municipal gardens, Ellie ignored these.

It was tempting to think there was nothing wrong with this life; just as people assumed everything was all right between Eric and Ellie. It was easy here to see British life leading to British death – the cemetery was as proudly laid out as the park, and just as pleasant for an afternoon walk.

But there was the brown-webbed magic wireless, to bring other voices for company and delight. Dance music, too. There was the voice of the Führer, screaming out over Germany, and the cheers that met the hysteria. There was the threat of a scream in the silence, even Ellie knew that. Even Ellie knew that Eric was disintegrating, in front of her soft brown eyes.

Alone, except for Sarah of course, in the living room, she would dance around, to Henry Hall and his Radio Dance Orchestra.

> No more money in the bank,
> No cute baby we can spank.
> What's to do about it?
> Let's put out the lights and go to sleep.

It seemed to Ellie the whole world had done that. Put out the lights and gone to sleep. She mooned for the London she had known as a girl, a place of colour, vitality. The big city. Ellie had worn short skirts, bobbed her hair, worked in Bond Street; long ago, when she was young.

She had replaced all that with the smell of baby talc, the scent of pinks and roses in a suburban garden – and the sour, whisky-smelling breath of a man she now realized she hardly knew.

Ellie had in return what everyone thought important. Security. Only in the shrill voice of Hitler, insistent and wild, could she hear intimations that something could break through the non-living of this life.

Even so, he had really nothing to do with her.

8

'Hark the herald angels sing
Mrs Simpson's pinched our King.'

Two little lads, sheltering in a doorway from the rain, sang it as
Ellie passed down the wet road. Past the red-brick houses and
small shops, down to the chemist's, Ellie wheeled the push
chair, tottering on her unsuitable high heels.

The child's sick face loomed out from behind the mackin-
tosh pram apron. Red-eyed Sarah, flushed and whining (no
one to leave her with) was threatening another childhood
fever.

Ellie needed the reassurance of patent medicines, Fenning's
fever cure and Vick ointment, boracic acid crystals for the red
weepers. She caught an image of herself in the darkening
windows of the Co-op. The post office, which sold fresh-baked
bread, as well as stamps, and the wool shop, where Ellie
bought the pastel skeins she made up into the articles she now
sold to make extra money, were both closed.

She stopped at the paper shop for Woodbines. It smelled of
newsprint in the winter, and ice cream in the summer. The
man behind the counter told her she was smoking too much.

He stared after her, approving, she thought, her new Wallis
Simpson hair-do – centre parting, wings of dark hair drawn
down severely. She sucked in her cheeks, to make her high
cheekbones more prominent, running in the rain.

Sarah moaned softly, as if to remind her that duty came first.
Ellie didn't like it when the child was ill – it took her mind off
herself. She *had* to worry, no one else would. Sarah wasn't
often a trouble, she was a self-absorbed child, as Ellie would

have wished a child of hers to be.

Ellie raised her cockney-inflected voice (she was still a girl from the South, and it was there, in the vocal chords, no matter how long she was in the North) and asked Mr Tavey's advice.

Mr Tavey, who had been about to turn the OPEN sign to CLOSED turned it back quickly on seeing young Mrs Shand. He pushed his rimless glasses over his pate, which was as pink and hairless as a baby's bum, and his equally pink and white dentures clicked as he smiled at her. The strident call of Mrs Tavey, like some predatory bird, rang out from the rear of the shop. There she lay bedridden, in the back room; Mr Tavey had rigged up a mirror so she could see most of what went on.

'I thought you had locked up, Horace?'

'Well, there's an emergency prescription, you see, my dear,' he shouted. 'Wants her tea.' He winked at Ellie. 'Now, what is it, some more "Evening in Paris"? Another town-hall do?' He insisted on seeing Ellie as a socialite, wife of a successful man, not knowing, or pretending not to know that all that had gone.

'It's Sarah – she has a fever. I didn't know what to do.'

He put his glasses down over his lusting eyes.

'You didn't call in the doctor?' Ellie shook her head. There was no money for doctors these days.

Mr Tavey moved a little nearer to Ellie. There wasn't a man around who hadn't envied Eric Shand his London bride.

'I didn't want to bother the doctor, thought you would know what to advise.' Ellie fluttered her lashes at him, feeling ridiculous. It was pathetic, she knew, but who else was there? 'Should I have called him in?' Drops of rain from her raven black hair fell on Mr Tavey's suede shoes.

'You've taken her temperature?'

Ellie said she didn't know how.

'I'll show you. You must have a thermometer in the house, where there is a child.' He moved to the cabinet, shook out the glass tube and stuffed it in Sarah's mouth. 'Don't bite on this, Sarah, there's a good girl.'

He ignored the calls of 'Horace, Horace' from the back

room. Ellie thought they were like the calls of Brangaene, in the second act of *Tristan*, disturbing the love duet.

'You are watching?' he asked. Ellie jumped to attention. Men were always trying to teach her something. Her mind always wandered on such occasions. Sarah bit through the thermometer.

'Do something, she'll die. My baby—'

Swallowing the broken glass of his own annoyance, Mr Tavey wiped out the child's mouth with gauze. Sarah's pouting lip was cut, bled a little. She grinned at them. Mr Tavey fitted the broken bits together to prove to Ellie that the child had not swallowed any. Then they both chased the elusive pool of mercury around the floor. Eventually they gave up, Ellie tearful, Mr Tavey flushed. His glasses were steamed up with exertion and desire.

'Won't be long, Florrie,' he shouted, remembering he was a married man. 'A child with an injury, that's all.'

'You had better just give me a Fenning's powder and some crystals for her eyes,' said Ellie. She was not pleased.

'And a thermometer. You ought to have one.'

'If you insist.' Ellie sighed as she thought Wallis Simpson might, when made angry by incompetence.

'If you can't get her to take it by mouth, try her armpit, or rectum.' He put the thermometer and the patent medicines in a bag bearing his name and a pestle and mortar.

Ellie wasn't sure she knew what the rectum was. And was sure she would never manage it, looking at Sarah.

'I popped in a lipstick sample, just to cheer you up.' He moved near again. Ellie grabbed the push chair. 'On the bill, as usual? Not the lipstick, that's a little gift.'

'Thank you,' said Ellie. And ran.

He could hear her, pattering down the road. He listened to the high heels tapping, like the sound effects in a radio drama.

He turned the sign back to CLOSED and stood in the dispensing area, out of sight of Florrie, and brought himself to a climax, scattering his seed down the white sink. Then he went in to make tea.

★

42

It wasn't often she was out in the dark, Ellie realized. She had forgotten lights reflected in rain puddles, cars going somewhere, swishing along the wet roads.

In London there had been a constant threat of excitement, even when none occurred; there were restaurants, cinemas and dance halls, all offering their pleasures – here there was just the howling gale from the sea.

There was always the box, the wireless, which saved her sanity. They were the only voices she heard – her friends. They, and the grocery lad who called once a week, and the Prudential man on Fridays, were the only contacts she had. Insuring one's own death was a curious thing to do, but her mother had always done it – sixpence a week – and though Eric didn't believe in it, she continued the family tradition. Sometimes she felt death had already happened.

It was such a male society, here in the North. Eric had his men's clubs and his political meetings. He never brought his friends home any more. His political pals had been polite, after the initial shock at her youth. You had to pity them, they weren't used to girls like her. Their own wives were fat and comfortable as sofas – nice to sink into, no doubt, but hardly a challenge. She could see they thought of her as a challenge, but it was one they were not going to take up.

The wives worked hard for the Party, they soon weighed up Ellie – she would be no use knocking at doors, canvassing in this conservative town. Nor was she the type to provide home-made jellies and cakes for jumble sales. They left her alone.

Eric stopped giving her lectures about Karl Marx and William Morris; he began to stay out more and more, sometimes he snatched a meal at his sisters' house. Or had the odd snack in a pub.

Ellie always kept the pan of marrowfat peas bubbling on the stove for him, as she had been instructed to do in the early days. She got used to hearing him stumble in, long after she and Sarah had gone to bed, and remove the pan lid, drop it, clatter the soup plate and curse as he burned his mouth. He had been a confirmed bachelor, that was his trouble. He's had a mother's and sisters' attention, she thought, he hates the intimacy of a strange female. His stubbornness made him resent it. His own mother had been dominant enough to stop him taking up an Oxford scholarship. She had needed him to help support her large family. He had never forgiven her for that. Or forgiven women in general, it seemed.

After all, he was about Mr Tavey's age. She had seen him as Ronald Colman, or Gable. He'd had glamour for her, with his dark eyes and moustache, his long overcoat and felt hat. Now she saw he was not Gable or Colman, just an elderly man eating mushy peas.

When they had married she had not thought that in a few years he would be old, though many had told her. He had become old rapidly, after the defeat of the last election he had slowed down, acquired a beer gut, and gone rather bald. Yet she could see what had attracted her; he was a more worthy love object than any of the young men she had known in London. How could she have known that he had a fatal flaw? (And wasn't she, in some sense, that herself?)

Eric seemed to ignore young Sarah. One evening he had stared at the child while Ellie washed her in a bowl in front of the fire – the bathroom was too icy for her – and he had remarked how odd it was to have this small animal in the house. He found it difficult to show affection. Ellie was not the one to teach him.

Ellie was scared that the indifference might maim Sarah in some way. There was nothing she could do about it.

Lack of emotion seemed to shrink the tiny house still further. The furniture was oppressive, the food dull. There was no life, everything she touched seemed to shrivel, thought Ellie. Except the garden, which blossomed and bloomed in spite of their spare souls. Except the mass of bubbling green peas on the stove.

Now, after the visit to Mr Tavey, Ellie bathed Sarah and stuck her in the back of the armchair she sat in, behind her, for company. Ellie would knit, with the background of the broadcast opera, *Manon Lescaut,* on the wireless – exalting her emotions by proxy. The King was ill, there was scandal about Edward and Mrs Simpson. Was it only romantic for Royals? Ellie lit another Woodbine and stared into the fire.

Eventually she carried Sarah up the wooden hill to Bedfordshire. She murmured this in the pink ear as they went. The scent of Vick's vapour rub lingered in the air like an exotic perfume. The room, their room, had ice strips on the insides of the panes. They could see their breath.

Sarah's small bed was in the corner, she was warmer in there with them. Ellie opened the window the regulation three inches, as she had been taught by her own mother, even though the temperature was sub-zero outside. You could hear sometimes in the distance the hiss of a steam train. Beyond that there was the sea.

'Neck, mama, neck—' Sarah whined.

It was a ritual she had got into, and now she demanded it every night. Ellie would put her on their large double bed and lie beside her, covering them both with the black eiderdown. The child then manipulated the small tendon on Ellie's neck, rhythmically, pressing back and forth, with almost sexual urgency until she fell asleep. This was the only thing that would send her off. Ellie had to submit to it, until finally the small hand dropped. She hoped Sarah would grow out of this soon; she was worried about it, and had no one to tell. Her own mother would think it peculiar, Eric would not know what she was on about.

In some ways, too, she would miss it if it stopped. It was, oddly enough, the only physical affection either of them had.

She examined her reddened neck in the looking glass. She heard the back door open, and the lid of the mushy peas pan lifted. He was early, early for him. She descended the red Axminster like Wallis Simpson confronting Mr Baldwin. Her temples throbbed with anger, she was annoyed at the disruption of her neat habits, which were all she had. There was the evening paper, spread out, and the plate of green mush. What right had he to come home at 9.30?

He looked up and asked her if she would like a cup of tea. She saw there was no pot on the table, and assumed he wanted her to make it. She went out and filled the kettle. Might as well talk, she supposed.

'Sarah is off-colour.'

45

'Did you call in the doctor?'

'I took her to Tavey's. He told me what to do.' She refrained from saying they could hardly afford to eat, never mind pay doctors' bills.

'I told you to call the doctor. Your side of the family is riddled with TB.'

She banged the teapot down.

'It's just a cold – I told you.' Why was he bothering, suddenly? She hoped he wasn't going to get interested in Sarah, now.

There was a pound she was keeping for emergencies in the old biscuit barrel. She might offer it to him – he would surely go out again then. She could hear the broadcast of *Manon Lescaut* if he went.

'The garage isn't doing well,' he said, folding up the paper. 'I've put it up for sale.' He had bought the ailing garage and an almost defunct mineral water bottling company with a small inheritance, but it was a bad time for investing in small businesses. She didn't know, either, how he equated this ownership with his socialist principles, but knew that if she questioned it, he would say she was politically naïve. So she kept off the subject.

'Will you be going out again?' It was all she cared about now.

'I seem to have run out of small change.' He wiped his mouth on the napkin he insisted on, even with mushy peas. He left a trail of green on the pale linen.

'You can have a pound, if you like.'

'Trying to get rid of me, eh?' It was an attempt to be jocular. He was up, and had his raincoat on before she had closed the lid.

She and Sarah would miss the garage. They didn't go often, but it was a nice walk over there, to the long shed where the smell of the motor oil and petrol was comforting, and the rough talk of the men a solace on a lonely afternoon. She wondered what the men would do, when they were laid off; they were all quite old. The mineral water company she knew nothing about, except that he brought home lots of headed paper, which Sarah used to scribble on.

46

'Don't wait up for me,' he shouted at the back door.

'I gave up waiting for you years ago,' she said to herself, going over to the wireless and switching on.

9

After the wedding, soon after, Eric left Ellie in the care of his two sisters while he went off on Party business. They looked her up and down, eyeing her cheapish London clothes. She had sobbed, up in the guest bedroom, while they decided what to do about her. Their Yorkshire voices rose up to her where she lay.

The sisters had been asked by Eric to use some of his inheritance to buy a small house, which they did; Rathmines Avenue, near them, was their choice. They furnished it too, with moquette suites and reproduction Sheraton, not bothering to confer with indecisive Ellie.

As a tribute to her modern ways, they chose two ugly silhouettes; a green and red parrot, and a lady smoking a cigarette in a long holder. She took the last as a criticism of her habit. She hung them in the front parlour, they didn't use it much.

Ellie had to admit that the house had a certain style – she could never have done it all herself. She knew she had no 'taste'.

The sisters took her to Manchester, to buy *good* clothes – tweed suits, silk dresses with coats to match, all designed to make her look good on the political platform, at his side. They chose also a fox-fur stole, expensive shoes and underwear that surprised her. It was exotic, sexy, and, she thought, would make Eric run a mile. She felt embarrassed, as they chatted with the sales girl, admiring Ellie's figure. They were really more masculine than Eric.

Sarah was the eldest (all eldest girls in the family were called Sarah) and she was slender, grey-haired, and had a marvellous peaches-and-cream complexion. She wore tweed suits and mannish jumpers, and strode with her Airedale along the sands. Frances was different. She looked more male, but in fact spent all her time dressmaking and cooking. She had dark hair, like Eric's, and an incipient moustache.

It was evident they resented the secrecy of their brother's marriage. They wondered, obviously, what had led him to do such a strange thing. He had shown scant interest in women before (except for Ellie's sister, Lena, and they did not know about that; knowing nothing of his London life) and the shock to them was intense.

The elopement had been as big a surprise to Ellie as it was to them. The excitement of it (so like Hollywood) had been negated by the clumsy deflowering that followed it. There was nothing of Hollywood in that.

Her own destroyed expectation was that of a twenties girl, nurtured on films and dance tunes, who hoped her sexuality, of which she knew little, would sweep her into marriage with some unsuspecting male. She had been willing it to happen since she left school at sixteen, and worked in a milliner's shop in Bond Street. Some day he would come along, and her history would be recorded, as every other girl's was, into the formalized rituals of marriage, birth, anniversaries, all noted by appropriate cards and gifts. Her own parents had not had a marriage like that – but everyone did now. This was the modern age.

Eric was a better prospect than the callow boys who hung around the church hall or the palais. A friend of Eric's had told her to beware, that the reason he liked her was because of her boyish figure and cropped head; she had not known what he meant, and had taken his hand off her knee, where it had rested during the conversation. Rested electrifyingly, so that she felt its imprint long after the hand was removed. This had never happened with Eric, but Eric was, she thought, too much of a gentleman to put his hand on her knee.

Eric rarely touched her, except to take off her coat in restaurants, or hand her out of a car.

Did she disgust him? It was hard to tell. She had no experience. The local lads had been timid with her. One used to sing: 'The moon has raised her lamp above – to light the way

49

to thee, my love – To theeee – my love.' That was not electrifying either.

Eric with his dark pin-stripe suits and his carnation in the buttonhole *seemed* worldly. His political speeches, wild and exciting, were contrasted with his fatherly concern for her. Therefore his bedroom fumblings were a complete surprise. She had wanted his instruction, but not just in literature and politics. She was, in every way, a very passive girl.

He neither looked at her nor talked to her before the act that joined their reluctant flesh. She knew little of men, had never seen her father more naked than in his long nightshirt. She could not recall seeing her mother naked, even. When she saw Eric's private parts, so red and different from the rest of his pale blue-veined body, she had wanted to laugh, hide her face. When they swelled, showing his interest in her, she was shocked.

She surveyed other married couples with interest after this. Did they all commit that unspeakable act? No wonder his sisters had never married. No wonder they thought her slightly cheap.

Her mother's zipped-up, prim mouth had never spoken of sex. Affection was rarely shown in the family. Perhaps romance was only for the films, for Greta Garbo and Fredric March. That was why films were so popular.

Her sister Lena told her it wasn't so. But who could trust Lena – her mother said Lena was an animal. Had shouted it one night when Ellie had woken to find the bedroom they shared a mass of moans and whispers; the sheets blood-stained, the chamber pot full of blood. That night's activity was never mentioned and the next day Lena was pale and sick, but still able to go to work, and their mother's mouth was shut more tightly than ever.

This secret female rite had caught Ellie's curiosity – neither of them mentioned it; she knew only that it was something to do with Lena's fatal attraction to boys. If blood and tears were the result of 'it', then Ellie wanted none of 'it'.

It was about this time that Ellie learned to flirt, dissemble, dress up, make eyes, and generally distract men from herself by this mimicry. It covered up the fear she felt for the male sex.

The simple-minded youths fell for this, thinking it sexuality, she was considered a hot number. She was capable of charming them out of any overtures they might make. They never tried with her the vulgar pawing they did with other girls.

With these devices Ellie avoided the thought of what she would do when finally faced with one male, alone in a bedroom. The tricks might not work then.

They hadn't worked. Eric, fascinated by Lena's more direct attractions, had begun by treating Ellie as the little sister. He had led her to a mirror and wiped off the lipstick she smothered herself in; he had told her to pull down her skirts, given her books to read, offered to send her away to school.

'School?' she laughed at him. 'Never. I've had enough of that, thank you.'

When Lena married and went to live in Yorkshire, Eric too disappeared up North. He had become a Labour Party agent in a border constituency. He came back to London frequently and, perhaps as an act of kindness, began to take her out, to plays, restaurants, concerts. He showed her the House of Commons, saying he hoped to sit there one day. She liked the novelty of it; it was not what she was used to. He made her feel secure, older, more of a person.

Once married, the tricks were out. Instead of melting, fusing, like at the end of a film, there was only a terrible falling-away from each other. Lying under the black eiderdown in Rathmines Avenue, staring at the cracks in the ceiling (settlement cracks they were called) Ellie submitted to the sexual embrace as she might have done to a dentist probing a painful tooth. Was life to be a long series of dreaded dental appointments?

She desired a child, to make a change, but none came. Even the four-month miscarriage, hopefully named 'Peter', did not bring them closer. That was when Eric started to stay out more. To give him credit, he had mourned this lost child, had sat at the bedside for hours, had put out his pipe. He lost the temptation to leave her alone. But when she got back to the silent house, he left her again. They tried once more, and the result was Sarah.

'She looks like you,' he had said, on seeing the girl child.

51

The final condemnation, Ellie supposed. But by then she had the doctor's remark to fire her into self-interest at last. Her beautiful body would sustain her.

The sisters came, bearing baby clothes and gifts, and informing her that all eldest girls were called 'Sarah'. And so it was. Ellie, who had fancied 'Penelope' or even Iris (Storm), acquiesced. Sarah it was.

They said also that the baby was pure Shand, which was true. After the first initial resemblance to Ellie she turned out to have their dark-eyed tenacity, their broad Yorkshire forehead. Ellie, who had hoped for a twin soul, could only despair. She had carried an interloper in her womb. The only solace was that, now she had done it, whatever the result, she would not need to go through the experience again.

The sisters soon seemed to indicate they knew enough about being a mother to know that Ellie was not a good one. They hired a nurse, but after a few weeks the nurse, from the best agency in London, dropped poor Sarah, and Ellie, in an unusual fit of courage, dismissed her. Sarah, weaned, was an easy child, all chuckles and responses. For three years Ellie devoted herself to this new game. Then Sarah began, without warning, to oppose her.

The child ate with a pusher and spoon quite skilfully, finding her rosebud mouth with ease – but then she began to act up; pouring the food in her Beatrix Potter plate right over her curly head. Ellie could only construe this as criticism.

The child seemed to have inherited the dogged nature of the Shands. From the time of the upturned plate, she had no desire to eat. Ellie spent hours enticing her; making soldiers of the sausages and castles of the mashed potatoes – playing games designed to conceal the fact that the food should go into the firmly shut mouth. Eventually the concoction known as muesli, which Ellie had culled from a medical journal article about the Bircher-Benner institute in Switzerland, did the trick. All day Ellie cut up nuts, grated apples, and made the dish known as 'Snow-fruit' for her wilful daughter. The sisters said this was ridiculous, and that all the little besom needed was a few sharp slaps. But Ellie was more than a bit afraid of Sarah, and went on cutting up nuts.

When Ellie mulled over what had happened to her, she saw she had been fooled by the cinematic hopes she had sustained; the elopement, the older man, the rise in status. Now she knew that had been a fantasy – the fact was that Eric had decided he needed a wife; the Party had implied it might be better to present an image of charmed domestic life to the electorate. Anything else was suspicious. Eric procured a family for them to publicize.

As it happened, thought Ellie, the joke was on him. The misery of it had made his not inconsiderable gifts decline. He was getting too old for some members of the Party to have faith in his ability. And then, there was Ellie's passion, Adolf Hitler, waiting in the wings.

10

Ellie and Sarah, in the Princess cinema matinée performance, watched the swoop and glide of Ginger Rogers and Fred Astaire. Ginger's dress swirled as Fred dipped and moved her across the marble floor. Ellie sighed. Mother and daughter eyes devoured the scene; Ellie wished to be dipped and swerved by Fred Astaire, Sarah wanted to *be* Ginger Rogers.

They came out, blinking, into the grey sea light. Ellie always bought fruit and vegetables in the arcaded market. There was the odour of rotting cabbage leaves and oranges which littered the entrance. Outside, tuning his fiddle, was Sarah's friend, the First World War veteran, who was always there, propped up by his wooden leg. He began to play.

'Can you play "Oh no, they can't take that away from me"?' asked Sarah, as she swung, upside down like a monkey, on the chain that went across the loading bay. She swung while Ellie shopped.

'Never heard of it,' he said, sending a yellow-green gob of spit out among the leaves.

'What are you playing, then?' She reversed herself down, in case he could see up her knickers.

'The Beethoven violin concerto.' He spat again.

She went in to find Ellie, hidden in the throng of Friday afternoon shoppers. Sarah loved the market, particularly the toffee-spinning machine, where long pulls of honey and sugar were stretched out on metal arms, just as Ellie had her stretch out her arms for the skeins of wool to be wound. There was a smell so delicious she nearly died from it.

Next to the toffee stall was the most beautiful place on earth. The stall of celluloid dolls, with feathered head dresses and sequin-spangled dresses always hypnotized Sarah. She could stay there for hours, trying to decide which was the most beauteous; pink, purple, yellow or blue. She could never make up her mind. Of course, she had never been offered one, if she had it would have been the most difficult decision of her life to choose one colour over the others. Round-eyed, each week she changed her mind.

'Come on, dolly daydream,' Ellie said, laden with apples, sprouts and bananas. She was good-tempered, because when she had been to the cinema she was under the sway of the film for hours. Sarah was different, she hated leaving the dark illusion – it didn't suit her, coming out into reality.

'Can we go to the art gallery, please?' Sarah never wanted to go back to Rathmines Avenue. The gallery was the next best place to the cinema, she sometimes thought she liked it better – but Ellie never spent as long in there, as they had been so often. It was just like a house really, and in the hall were little glass-covered cases with coins in them. All up the stairs were pictures, including one Sarah found very ugly: *The Shrimp Girl*, by Hogarth. This girl's red grinning face haunted her, because she was used to thinking that prettiness was all, like the dolls, like the ladies on the screen. Yet the face on the stairs had something which made it memorable. She didn't know what it was. The picture she liked best was a group of gentlemen in brocade waistcoats and knee breeches, standing in a long drawing room. That, in its way, was as pretty as the dolls. On the tram, on the way home, she would try and decide which was best – seeing the dolls or the pictures. She needed them all, in a way. Men were searching for shrimps on the beach, trousers rolled up, backs bent; their baskets beside them. That seemed to say to her, with a small inner voice, that she was to be reminded of the shrimp girl, anyway, because the real was best. But mostly she wished life was like the cinema, because when Ellie put the key in the door of 21 Rathmines Avenue, the excitement was over for another week.

So Ellie would let her dress up in her old Manchester opera clothes, evening dresses and velvet cloaks, and she would swirl around, mirrors in place on the floor – being Ginger Rogers, until tea time.

The wireless was their joy. Sarah would peer into the

webbed box, hoping to see the little musicians creep out of the back, when the band finished, but she always missed them.

Another game was to slant the mirrors and look into the looking-glass world, like in the Alice story Ellie read her. The floor slanted, and the other Sarah seemed more real, and so she was frightened, not knowing which was the real Sarah. Finally she learned to pick out the words in the Beatrix Potter books; Pigling Bland and Jemima Puddleduck were not just pictures, they did something, and the words told you what they did. Pictures showed them – words explained them. It was more important, to explain.

She started school. Fearing the other children, because they had brothers and sisters, and knew what to do, she was timid in class. She was put at the back because she could read. She watched the others having the big cards held up at them, capitals first, then the small letters. Finally they sent her around the other classes, to show them how she could read, and for this she was isolated in the playground, the boys jeered and the girls stood in groups and giggled.

'Do you like school?' Ellie asked, as Sarah sat listening to *Children's Hour,* eating her boiled egg.

'It's all right.'

'Have you made any little friends?'

'No.'

'What do you do at school?'

'Tear patterns, sing. It's boring.' The time Sarah liked best was when it was 3.15 and they put the small chairs on the desks and sang, 'Now the day is over, night is drawing nigh...' The song always seemed frightening, but then there were the mothers waiting at the gates. It was over for another day.

Ellie knew life couldn't go on this way. The garage had gone, so had the mineral water company, and she was reduced to collecting a pound a week from the sisters. Eric just sat in a chair all day, head in hands. He got up only to get a plate of mushy peas. Often he would forget to do that, and only looked up to ask Ellie what time it was. It became scary, the way he asked, every few minutes, a hundred times a day.

He was just the shell of a man, you could see that. She didn't know what to do about it. He looked right through her, and

Sarah, as if they didn't exist. They no longer listened to their programmes, because he was always there. Sarah used the box-room to play in, after school.

Eventually Ellie called in Dr Glebe. He said it was a nervous breakdown, and that Eric should rest, take it easy.

'No problem there,' said Ellie. 'He does nothing else.' Dr Glebe said she shouldn't worry him – but how could she, she hardly spoke to him? She didn't tell Dr Glebe that.

She wondered what had done this to him – his mother, the Party, or Ellie herself? The sisters assumed it was the marriage. They could be right.

She imported her mother. There was nothing else to do; she had to get a job.

Gran, in her tightly laced Portland brogues, bunions bulging, arrived to take over. She was glad to be needed, anxious for control. Sarah, to whom Gran was the tightly-bunned lady in the garden snaps, was apprehensive. Now life would be different. From the moment Gran removed the long pin from her battered felt hat, had hung her grey overcoat in the cupboard, the house was, in some way, hers.

In the kitchen, she took the peas off the stove and tipped them away.

'That will be the end of that nonsense. He needs some good beef broth to build him up.' She had taken off her shoes, to release her corns, and put on her slippers. Otherwise Gran was formal in her dress – it depended on the time of day. Mornings, she had a pinny over a cotton frock, in the afternoon, a *front* made of lace was tucked into the neckline of a more suitable dress, for modesty's sake. Respectability was her armour, cleanliness her god.

Eric, who had been a permanent fixture before, now got out of the house as soon as possible, to public library or pub. It was her way of curing his nervous breakdown. He didn't have to see Dr Glebe again. Gran never spoke to him; she talked about him, if there was an occasion when he was there, in the third person. She sniffed when he came in, as if a stray dog had entered and lifted its leg.

Sarah marvelled at the power of her personality. She had them all organized in no time at all.

'Why do you dress up, Gran? There's no one but us here.'

'Either you are fully alive, or you are dead. There's no in between. *He* is trying to make up his mind which he is.'

'He's writing a book,' Sarah offered, in defence of Eric.

'*Book* my foot. Nervous breakdown my foot,' was the answer to that, as Gran beat a carpet over the back line. She hit it as if she had Eric slung up there, for her delight.

Sarah would see Eric, on her way back from school; he would be sitting by the bowling green, or in a promenade shelter. She worried about him, because he seemed so alone, more even than her. Ellie was looking for a job, and was remote too. Only Gran chattered incessantly, like a large parrot.

Gran, one evening, handed Sarah one of the beloved celluloid dolls. It was the purple one. Sarah, sensing a bribe, and not knowing how to deal with the situation, cried. It seemed that the doll had been bought because Ellie had found a job, and would not be around so much – she was making the transition to being a working wife. Sarah howled more loudly than ever.

'Why are you crying? Don't you like the doll?'

'I didn't want the purple one.' How to explain that Gran had chosen for her? That the decision should have been hers?

'You're an ungrateful girl. And your poor mother has to go out and support you. I've a good mind to take the doll back.' Gran would never have understood about the rejection of all the other dolls, by choosing the purple one.

Ellie was to work in Woolworth's, selling buckets and spades and beach balls to visitors. It was the only thing she could find to do.

Sarah had lost, as well as Ellie, the voices from the wireless. All her friends had gone, Larry the Lamb, and Mr Mayor, and Romany.

'You can talk to me, instead of listening to rubbish,' said Gran. But Gran would never let Sarah say anything, really.

Without its companions on the stall, the purple doll was ugly. It was garish, like a lady in evening dress still out on the street in the morning. Her feathers and spangles seemed repulsive now, to Sarah; she took the kitchen scissors and cut the flimsy dress into ribbons, then she stuck the shears into the doll's hard flesh, where the heart should have been. There was nothing inside when she had prised the celluloid open. The doll's beady black eyes stared at Sarah. She got out her Little Nurse's set and bandaged the gaping wound. Then she stuck on her an old dress from Nana, the rag doll. She threw Miss Purple on top of the wardrobe. 'There you go. I hate you,' she said.

Sarah didn't like Gran's sayings. *'We're poor but we're honest'* was one.

Were they poor? It seemed to her they lived as they had always done. Gran had her widow's pension, Ellie had her money from Woolworth's. Eric was the only one without cash. It was rumoured by Gran that the sisters gave him pocket money. He often ate there, too; when the climate at Rathmines was too ciy for him to brave coming home.

Gran was always aware when he stumbled in.

'Don't know why he bothers to come back at all,' she would sniff. She seemed annoyed that Ellie and Eric still slept under the same black eiderdown, together. Sarah wondered if she wasn't jealous of Eric.

Whether they were poor or not, Sarah knew herself to be dishonest. She used her school milk money to buy ice cream from the 'Stop Me and Buy One' ice-cream cart. She stole gobstoppers from the paper shop, when the man was looking the other way. She touched her private parts. She stole a single red poppy from the garden next door, even though it was the only flower blooming there. She was discovered in that sin, for she put it in an alabaster egg cup, admiring the brilliant red against the translucent white. She was made to go and apologize to the ancient couple next door – and worse, she was invited to tea with them, the following Sunday, and every other Sunday. Gran's zeal had let her in for untold misery.

The Dodsworths were decaying in the next house which was a replica of their own, but the other way round, as if she were at last in the mirror world of Alice. Now, not only was she a thief, she was a liar too, having to pretend to enjoy the thin tea in bone china, the wafer-sliced bread with margarine on it, and the bleatings about religion.

The Dodsworths were fanatical – they thought Ellie wrong

to work on Sunday, showing no sympathy when Sarah said: why was Woolworth's open, then, if it was immoral? They thought people should stop existing on Sunday. Out of boredom she had made the mistake of rolling on their tiger rug, in front of their cold hearth; now she had to do it every time she went. 'Mr Dodsworth shot that tiger,' Mrs Dodsworth said, wiping his dribbling mouth with a napkin.

Mrs Dodsworth was worried that Sarah didn't know much about Jesus. She brought in little cards showing Middle Eastern scenes, camels and palms, all in garish pastels. Sarah, who, if she thought about it at all, had not considered Jesus's sartorial aspects, decided they were in bad taste and threw them in the rubbish. Worst of all in the Dodsworth house was *Miss* Dodsworth, who brought in the tea and swept the hearth, and jumped if you spoke to her. She wore a mob cap, like the female animals in the Beatrix Potter books. The house smelled of death. It was something to do with the herbal cigarettes that Mr Dodsworth had drooping from his dried lips. Sarah felt they were hanging on to her visits as the only activity they had. Instead of making her sad, this made her angry, and she slashed at the flowers in their own garden (there were none in the Dodsworths since the poppy) until the petals fell.

Gran too was obsessed by death. She had done laying-out in the Yorkshire village where she had lived. Washing corpses, and tying up their jaws with rags, so that the relations wouldn't get a fright. She rearranged their limbs, so as not to cause a shock for the living. Sarah thought that Gran probably preferred the dead; they couldn't answer back. Gran had her own laying-out clothes in her tin trunk – a peach silk nightdress and silk stockings to match. No shoes. Did you need shoes for Heaven? They probably had neat lawns up there, and it would be sunny – that's what Sarah thought. St Peter at the golden gate would be surprised when Gran got there, in this peach affair. Gran seemed on good terms with God – He had her approval. She spoke to Him sternly, as if He were a more important, older version of Eric. It was rather like the way she spoke to Ellie, when she was discussing her life, or telling her not to use so much make-up.

Ellie's authority, never in excess, was declining. Sarah felt she was taken over by Gran. Sarah slept with Gran in the second bedroom. Plump and fleshy, Gran was lovely to rest with, soft as the feather bed which covered them. The feather bed, giant-sized, was enough for them both. It had covered Gran and Grandad all their married life, and now it was she, Sarah, who accompanied Gran into sleep. From this warm nest, in the early morning, Sarah watched Gran prepare herself for her day. There was ritual cleansing; a bowl of water carried from the bathroom and put on the old wash-stand, this to avoid the possibility of meeting Eric, who was never up anyway, and the scouring of neck, arms, shoulders, armpits and what she called nether regions, began.

Then the Anglican religious rites; the mumbled prayers, instructions for God, for the day. She had knelt on her old knees, having put on again the voluminous nightdress over the new-washed body, so as not to offend God. Then she made the final strip-off, pouring her purified flesh into one of two iron corsets – one tea rose, one white (they were alternated daily) – and she laced herself into these like armour. She captured the elusive mounds of flesh and imprisoned them ruthlessly. Standing, a sagging mass, her breasts hanging to her waist like empty shopping bags, her ample belly sticking out – like Sarah's young belly did, also – she persevered. She couldn't see her privates, as she called them, under this mountain of belly. Gran liked her food, and it showed.

Her legs were like two pillars, encrusted with vines, the vines were varicose veins, wrapping around, trailing purple clusters. The lisle stockings were pulled on, with groans, and attached to the corset by bumpy suspenders. She did this deftly, in spite of arthritic hands. A vest followed, and a slip, and rayon drawers with elastic round the legs, and finally her frightening shoes. It was over; she had garbed herself for the battle of the day.

Sarah realized that if life was a battle, then Gran was a general. Ellie and Sarah were in the ranks. Eric, poor Eric, had been court-martialled, discharged with dishonour.

In her nightdress, in bed, Gran might resemble a cloud, a cloud of feathers. With her armour on no one could get near to her, or defy her. Yet, even dressed like this, she was incomplete without the two rows of teeth, that had floated overnight, like two giant goldfish, in the glass by the bed. Before she left the room, arrayed, she had to brave the bathroom to scrub them. Her mouth, before she left, was soft and Ellie-like – when she returned the teeth gave her even more authority to beam out her instructions.

Last came the hair, which all night had hung down her back in a wispy Chinaman's pigtail. In the day it was wound severely into a bun, secured by iron hairpins, which fell out at intervals and traced her route, like the bread dropped by Hansel and Gretel in the fairy tale.

The bits of hair that came out in the process, were wound into a ball, and placed into a crocheted hair-tidy that had been made by Lena when she was seven. Sarah wondered why Gran didn't just put the hair in an ashtray, or a waste-bin, but she did see that would have destroyed the function of the hair-tidy, which had no other reason for existence.

Next to the hair-tidy, which hung on a mirror edge, was Gran's Indian carved box of jewels, full of glass beads, paste brooches and dress rings. Sarah was not allowed to play with these, although she secretly fingered them when Gran was out, which was not often. Gran treated them as if they were the Crown Jewels.

Gran's new campaign was to let a room to summer visitors. It seemed no accident to Sarah that the room chosen was that used by Ellie and Eric. Ellie was to move to the box room, and Eric asked, ever so politely, to move out to his sisters' house for as long as the guests stayed.

For a while no visitors came – it was too far from the sea; then, at the height of the season, they managed to snare a family from Surrey, two little boys, twins, and their parents.

Eric moved out, with his pyjamas in a carrier bag. Sarah was beside herself with excitement, although Gran told her it was nothing to do with her.

The twins were a revelation to Sarah. One was called Peter, the other Paul, just like the game adults played with bits of paper stuck to their thumbs – 'Fly away Peter, fly away Paul, come back Peter, come back Paul'. Gran said they wouldn't come back, they didn't like the room, and they were too far from the beach.

They ignored Sarah because she was a girl and inferior. Gran told her that. Little boys always treated girls like that. Sarah didn't mind, because she was not put off by that fact; she was trying to decide which twin she preferred. It was easy to tell which was which if you remembered that Paul had lost a tooth.

She liked to watch them in the bathroom, peeing. They didn't do it like her, squatting, but stood up, and used their little hose attachments. She asked Gran when hers would grow, and Gran said *never*. She asked Ellie, and Ellie told her not to be silly.

So Sarah tried to pee like them, standing up, and was smacked for it. The Martins took her to the beach one day in their black Ford that was just like the one outside, which Eric and Ellie never used – it now had a wheel missing. Sarah wore trunks just like Peter and Paul; they asked her where her tits were and she said here, pointing to her chest, which was just like theirs, with minute nipples. They threw sand at her but she thought that was part of their getting to like her.

She told the Martins she rarely went to the beach because she was a sand grown 'un, which meant she was born in Blackpool. They really did not go because Ellie thought the beach was common, especially when there were trippers there. They didn't mind a walk along the cliffs, out of season when the old people sat like clothed statues, staring out to sea.

The twins and Sarah built a sandcastle, and brought water for a moat. Or, Sarah was allowed to bring the water; the tide was out for quite a stretch. When she poured the water in, it soaked right into the sand, and she had to go back for more.

The parents, who seemed to Sarah to be very young, played with a beach ball, and then lay, covered in suntan oil, on towels. She tried to think of Eric and Ellie doing such a thing, but could not. It wasn't likely they would ever do that.

When the castle was finished Paul and Peter put on little paper flags, and then they jumped on it and destroyed it. She cried. She would have liked to ask them if they had bought the flags and buckets and spades from Ellie, but though the words came to her mouth, the time never seemed right to let them out.

The tide was coming, fast as ever, but they seemed to ignore it. The parents still lay there, turning bright red.

Under the pier it was dark and eerie, like the ghost train at the Pleasure Beach. The twins pushed her into one of the pools which surrounded the balustrades of the pier. She spluttered and choked, until Mr Martin ran up and got her out, and carried her over to where their things were. They tipped her up and got the sea water out of her lungs, and then they gave her a ride on a donkey. She promised not to tell her mother, so as not to worry her. She promised because they had given her the ride and might pay for another one, but they never did. She still retained the memory of the excitement, and the sandy feel of the saddle between her legs.

On the last day of their holiday they bought her a celluloid windmill, with transparent pink arms that blew around, making a noise.

They waved from the back of the black car, shouting that they would be back next year.

'We'll never see *them* again,' said Gran.

11

They didn't get any more guests. Eric moved back from his sisters' house, Ellie moved back to the big bedroom, and Gran sulked.

'I shall have to think of some other plan,' she said, settled like a nesting bird on the bed, with Sarah, for an afternoon nap. Sarah was reading *Chick's Own*.

Sarah missed having Ellie around now that it was the school holidays. Gran was no good for fun. Sarah missed the pictures and the times they had cooked fairy cakes together and mowed the lawn. It seemed that everything changed all the time. There was talk of war.

'We'll all be in the next one, women included,' Gran said. 'Of course, I was in the last one, packing shells in Woolwich Arsenal.' Sarah admired that. She admired Ellie too, for going out and bringing money home. She was a bit afraid of Ellie's old interest in Adolf Hitler. Gran said Ellie would be shot for that, or interned, if war came.

'Will I be in the army, Gran?'

'If it lasts long enough you will.' Gran said *he* wouldn't be, he was too old.

He seemed more cheerful, having got over his nervous breakdown without anyone knowing how. Sarah thought it might be because he liked staying with the aunts. He winked at her, and said they made good puddings there. Ellie and Gran were not good at puddings. He started bringing Sarah sweets again, as he did before he was ill, but Gran confiscated them. Gran said she thought he was having a bit on the side from the lady at the wool shop, but Sarah thought why would he want any wool?

Eric had started his book again. He got out all his notes and spread them over the table. Gran told him to move into the front parlour as they couldn't cope. He went in there, unlocked his roll-top desk and got out the typewriter. He played Wagner on the gramophone. Gran asked him what the book was called.

'None of your business,' he told her.

'That's a good title,' she said. It was hard to get the better of Gran. It was called 'The Beginnings of the Labour Movement.'

'Stuff and nonsense,' Gran said to that.

'How that man can stay in there, with her out at work, I'll never know,' she grumbled.

Sometimes they heard the yells of Brunhilde accompanied by the clatter of the typewriter, but not often. This angered Gran; she had taken to opening the door suddenly, so Eric put a chair against it.

When Gran got angry she was inclined to have what she called one of her heart attacks. Ellie said they were bilious attacks, from eating too much cheese at night. Whatever their cause, they were frightening, with lights on, doctor called, Gran giving a performance looking blue, and having a few days in bed. Eric always got his mushy peas again while Gran was indisposed.

Gran had home remedies for all ills. Arnica for bruises, alum for mouth ulcers, senna pods for constipation (but for Sarah, California syrup of figs), iron tonic and Parkinson's Little Liver Pills, or Beecham's pills for good general health, sal volatile for fainting fits, and brandy for shock. All these she carried with her. A good strong cup of tea was also good for what ailed you.

She would appear again to find Eric had made inroads on to her territory. He would be back in his old chair, reading the paper, his book suspended.

'Lift up your feet, I want to sweep just there,' Gran would say, brandishing the Bissell carpet sweeper, neatly nipping his ankles. He would get the point, and rise and go to his desk; *Das Rheingold* would flood the house.

'Some people have the life of Riley,' Gran would say.

'Who *is* Riley, Gran?'

'Never mind.'

66

She said also that some people knew on which side their bread was buttered. Sarah thought everybody must know that.

She read a lot, it was a way of escaping from Gran's world to a better one. She met Eric in the library. He winked at her, said he was doing research for his book.

'Has she driven you out as well?' he asked her.

'I'm trying to change these. They won't let you change books on the same day you got them out.' She had read them all that morning, with Ellie working and Gran rampant.

'Try some of the books in the shelf by my desk. You are a good little reader from what I hear.'

It was the first time he had taken her seriously.

'I met father in the library,' she told Gran. Then could have bitten her tongue.

'Like father, like daughter. Always got your head in a book. As for him, he should get a job there. He'll get his reward soon, he will, for women won't support him for ever.'

Why should he get an award? Or had she said 'reward'? Gran was very mysterious sometimes.

'What do you mean, Gran?'

'I just mean things might not always stay as they are. That's what I mean.'

Sarah guessed she meant the war. Or did she mean the war between her and Eric?

'Why don't you like him – father?'

Gran wrung out the floor cloth as if it were Eric's neck.

'Like him? *Like* him?' There was such disgust in her voice that Sarah ran out, into the parlour, straight to his books. She looked them over, picked one out. It was called *The Doll's House*, by Henrik Ibsen. It looked like a children's book.

12

From behind the scrubby bushes in the recreation ground where Mad Jack lurked, the man emerged, his raincoat stained with vomit.

He retrieved his trilby and stuck it back on his head. He ignored the bunch of children aping his drunken walk.

'Been sleeping it off, then?'

'Ssh. That's Sarah Shand's dad.'

'It isn't – it's Mad Jack.'

'Get off, I tell you – it *is.*' They giggled. Sarah was considered stuck-up.

'Mad Jack's in jail. Have you ever had a Milky Way from him?'

'What do you think I am?'

Eric went down the road. He was careful to avoid his sisters' house, with its neat windows, from where they kept an eye on the passing scene. He noticed the children were playing a game with him – it used to be called 'Grandmother's footsteps' – when he stopped, they stopped, when he resumed walking, so did they.

'Get away with you,' he roared at them. They scattered.

He was blessed regarding obstacles, like all drunks. Traffic, sparse at this time of day, avoided him. Lamp posts parted as he walked the pavements. People kept at a safe distance. He seemed to be making for home, until he remembered the she-dragon was there and not soft Ellie. He longed for a plate of mushy peas.

He should be more belligerent, he knew, with the old battle-axe, especially when in his cups. It was becoming like a music-hall joke – the mother-in-law, the wife. He despised himself for restricting his world to such mean dimensions. The conspiracy of the females made him wince. The three of them, for he had to include Sarah in this coven of female disapproval, diminished him – he had no answer to their contempt. No one knew or cared what he had lost.

He had put up with the humiliation of Ellie's job, though it was really against the northern principles of his generation. He had suffered also the indignity of not being asked about it. Nor had he been consulted about her mother's coming in and taking over.

Eric wondered why Sarah was not out playing with the other children. They isolated her, those two, and spoiled her as if they were making up for some deprivation. The old she-dragon had Sarah chained. She was wrecking whatever remained between him and Sarah. He felt the child's scorn; his own self-disgust was complete when he saw her eyes, so like his own, on him. Her condemnation was worse than theirs – she was half his, after all. In her he sensed the moral outrage he also felt, a judging of his behaviour. He hated this, but the cage he had pulled down over himself was complete. He was imprisoned inside it. His decline, so fast since the marriage, had decidedly finished – the Left of the Party no longer considered him, while the Right had always hated him. The sapping away of his political power, though seeming to coincide with marriage, could not really be blamed on Ellie. That naïve and passive yet powerful girl had succeeded, though, where even his own mother had failed. Castration was the name of the game.

Lena, her sister Lena, had at least been a life force, while Ellie – who could say what Ellie's force was? The dark force, all the negativity of the female – Lilith, Kali. Before he married he had known nothing of it, now he felt himself an expert, and hoped his little daughter would accrue none of it from those two witches.

Strong, positive women were the only ones he could understand. There were many in the Party. His sisters, too, could be relied on. There was little malice in them. His mother had never given him confidence, true, and had denied him Oxford; but that was out of a real necessity, and not a foolish feminine whim, of the sort he suffered now.

His mother could have been right on that. He had not been

69

ready for Oxford, as it was then.

It could be that she, kindly and perceptive as she was, had saved him from self-knowledge at an age when it might have destroyed him.

Was it his mother who had taught him to avoid intimacy? He couldn't remember, it was too long ago. Before Ellie he had not had to face up to intimacy, he had always refracted emotion away, reserved it as a future ideal. For a man of fifty, used to the world, it should have been feasible to narrow down the intensity to one object, a wife. He had started out wanting to right the whole world and ended not being able to convince one other person. He felt he had nothing to say now, to the public mass or the private soul.

Except, always excepting, Sarah. He would like to have influenced her; but how could he, after she saw him emptying his guts under the silver birch tree?

When she had first gone to primary school he had been entrusted with escorting her, after Ellie began work. But in the afternoons, he had strayed into the Working Men's Institute, right by the primary school, on the way back. Sarah would wait on the step. They would creep into school late, into the cloakroom where the red pegs had names she knew and he did not. Her world. The faces in the class would turn to her, as she slipped in and he closed the door. Poor Sarah, she would never forgive him. Eventually, she always howled when he offered to take her to school, and Gran took over.

He still bought sweets for her, which she accepted solemnly – he never knew if she ate them. There were some now in his pocket. He threw them in the bushes, the neat privets of Rathmines Avenue.

He struggled to put his key in the lock. It was amazing how one's talents became refined down into such small victories.

She, the she-dragon, was peeling cooking apples in the kitchen. Their acid aroma cut through him. The sour smell made him retch.

Sarah was sitting on the floor, engaged in making paper dolls. She was drawing a complete wardrobe, it seemed, with little tabs on the shoulders of the clothes, and fitting them over the cut-out dolls. She was absorbed, her tongue moved with the scissors' movement. He recalled the sensation of being so absorbed – he hadn't had that for years.

'To what do we owe this honour?' asked the bitter one, plopping the cut apples into a pan.

He drew his breath to give her a piece of his mind, but Sarah looked up.

'I came back to do some work. The *Manchester Guardian* is interested in a couple of articles.'

She sniffed. He went into the dank front room. It smelled of lavender furniture polish. The roll-top desk had been closed, and his papers put inside in a jumble, as if they were of no importance.

He put them in piles, and rolled a sheet of blank paper into the typewriter. Then he sat, wondering how to begin.

Gran pummelled a mound of pastry in a bowl. Sarah put her fingers into the pan of apples and pulled out a piece. She nibbled at it; it was very sharp, and she winced.

'I don't know who he thinks he is kidding,' said Gran.

13

'How goes it, Eric?' The publican, like all publicans in the area, was an old friend.

'Not bad, I'll have the usual.' He sat in the corner, with his paper. The civil war in Spain was over, no thanks to his assistance, either way. He felt a sense of utter futility – all these past few years he had watched events unroll – the stupid Abdication crisis, the Coronation, now this, at least real; and he had done nothing but dwindle in his own life, down to what he now was. 'If I had been younger, I'd have been there,' he said, pointing at the headlines.

'You'd have been wasting your time. They weren't sure what they were on about. They do say no one knew what side was shooting at you. It was all a big muddle.' He held up a glass against the light, and polished it.

'I'd at least have known what I was fighting for,' Eric said, going up for a refill.

'Of course you would. We all know that.'

Eric sat down again. The International Socialist of the Public Bar.

'The Germans and Italians were just using it for a rehearsal, anyway,' said Eric.

'It's the Russians you want to keep your eye on. We'll be fighting them in the end,' said an old man, slumped in the corner.

Eric went out. They were all the same in this town, petit-bourgeois rubbish. No wonder he had never made any headway. Small-minded business people, all out to make a quick pound or two, and to hell with the rest of the world. Petty individualism. All you could do was destroy yourself.

By the time he reached the next pub he was angry. Crazy

72

Jane was in there, dressed in her old rags. He bought her a whisky. He sounded off about Spain.

'Watch your language, Eric,' she cackled at him, as she drained it down.

'Careful, Eric,' said the publican as he stumbled out. 'There goes a man who might have done more with himself.'

'Blasted commie,' said Crazy Jane.

'He weren't a commie – just a straight socialist. In this town that is a commie,' said a young man. 'He had a head on his shoulders, my dad said. Not that it matters now. After 1931 it didn't matter. There'll be another coalition, if war comes.'

'Get out – there isn't going to be a war.' Crazy Jane got up. 'And if you want to see your hero, he's out there on the promenade, sounding off to the seagulls.'

'Drink up,' said the publican. 'I'll stand you one. Let's drink to old Eric – there's nowt sadder, to my mind, than seeing a man destroy himself.' He poured a drink for the young man.

'You shouldn't sell him the means to do it with, then,' shouted Crazy Jane, as she left, wheeling her old perambulator filled with her worldly possessions.

'My God, it takes all sorts, doesn't it, eh?' said the publican.

'It does,' said the young man.

They clinked glasses.

14

'Sarah is more the modern-dance type,' said Miss Jeanne, of the famous Langley-Forster Dance Academy.

'You mean she is clumsy?' slurred Eric. He was a stand-in escort for Sarah, as Ellie was working and Gran had had one of her fateful cheese-induced heart attacks.

'No. Oh no.' Miss Jeanne pursed her mouth and raised her pencilled-in brows. 'You misunderstand me. I just meant Sarah is a bit wobbly on her points. Not enough bar exercises I dare say.'

Eric looked at her to see if the bar reference was a cheap crack. He was so used to female acidity that he heard sarcasm in every innocent remark. But this woman was too stupid to see he was half-cut.

Eric had never really seen Sarah dance, on or off points. He knew from his visits to constituents' homes that no Northern piano was complete without a hand-tinted photograph of a little girl in tutu, in the fifth position. They all wanted, for some inexplicable reason, to become ballerinas. He had never associated Sarah with that kind of thing, she seemed such a studious child. What happened to all those budding ballet dancers, with their scraggy arms and legs? They gave up, he supposed.

Miss Jeanne was right about Sarah, she was acting her head off as Little Boy Blue, a regular Sarah Bernhardt. Eric had seen *her* once, on tour, a formidable old duck. He hoped Sarah was not headed in that direction. He would rather see her as Ellen Wilkinson.

Eric could see that, unlike all the others, Sarah was believing in it too much.

'Sarah Shand, don't overdo it. You see the sheep, I know,

74

and you must make us see them, the audience must believe in those sheep.'

Eric took a swig from his hip flask, hoping not to see sheep.

'Now, come along, snowflakes. Not so *heavy*, dears.'

They appeared, surrounding Little Boy Blue and Little Bo-Peep.

Sarah had been a snowflake once, on points, but now she had been promoted, or demoted, depending on how you looked at it. She blew her silent horn with panache, and took Little Bo-Peep by the hand, and led her into the Magic Meadow.

Eric yawned. There was a pause for a scene change. Miss Jeanne's son carried on some cut-out trees.

'Bees, come on bees, please. Let's have the flowers in position. *Buzz*, Deirdre – be fierce.'

The old lady playing 'Flight of the Bumblebee' on the tinny piano stopped to rub her hands. Eric rushed over and offered her a nip from the flask. He could see Miss Jeanne, disapproving, from the stage. The other mothers (he was the only male) applauded.

Sarah, on the way home, clutched his hand in her wool-mittened one. He could not remember this ever happening before.

'Why are you playing a boy – did you want to?' he asked her.

'Nobody else wanted to. There aren't any boys in the class, they think it cissy,' she said. 'I could have been Little Bo-Peep, but she is stupid.'

'You are very good,' he assured her.

She looked pleased.

'I like it when we are doing a show,' she said.

'You are a real little performer,' Eric answered. 'You probably get it from me. I always liked being in the public eye.'

Sarah was too shy to tell him she wanted to be Ginger Rogers, eventually. She couldn't tell him about the way Ginger and Fred Astaire transformed the world on a dull afternoon.

'The shows are fun,' she said, in what Gran called her bossy tone. 'But Miss Jeanne gets very worked-up. Ladies are often bad-tempered – have you noticed?'

'I have,' he said.

Ellie was asked to go along to the school to find out why

75

Sarah was so violent in class; she had hit a boy sitting in front of her over the head with a book, and he had needed four stitches in the wound. When asked why she had done it, Sarah had laughed and said she was bored. There was also something worse; the young teacher blushed as she told Ellie about it. Sarah touched herself *there* a lot, and told the other little girls that it was nice to do it; they told their mothers, and the mothers complained.

Ellie, who hated facing any kind of authority, even a young female teacher, blushed, and wilted and apologized, and said she didn't know why Sarah was like that.

The teacher said was there any problem in the family, was Sarah a nervous child? And Ellie said no. Ellie said she would discuss it with her husband. Of course she would.

Ellie, back in the privacy of Rathmines Avenue, sobbed. She couldn't mention it to Eric, they hadn't spoken about things like that, ever. It seemed to her quite likely they had produced a monster. If she told Gran, or the aunts, they would suggest a good beating; they were a different generation. There was only professional advice – Ellie contacted the child clinic.

They sat, mother and daughter, in the bright environs of the specialist's office. Ellie stared at the bright posters and cheery curtains, wondering where she had gone wrong. It all smacked of a normal, stable world.

The specialist was hearty. He spoke to Sarah as if she were deaf or stupid, or both. Sarah twitched and stared at him as if he were mad. Ellie could see she was not making a good impression. He whispered awful possibilities in Ellie's ear, St Vitus's Dance (chorea), a heart murmur. Ellie paled. They ran tests, shook their heads. They could find nothing wrong.

Sarah was put to bed for six months; she was to be built up with nerve tonics and beef extracts and pills to calm her nervous excitability. Sarah sulked. It was going to be more boring even than normal life. She was fed milk dishes and had perfect rest and quiet. Jigsaw puzzles, crayoning books, wireless, all were forbidden for the first few weeks. She stared at the cracks in the ceiling. She was allowed to read. It was an entire universe up there, in her box room. She rocked herself to sleep, touching herself, there.

Mrs Dodsworth, of the dread Sunday visits, came to see her.
'Would you like to go to Heaven, and help God paint the flowers and butterflies?' she asked Sarah.

'I don't believe he does that. I don't believe he exists,' shouted Sarah. Mrs Dodsworth told Gran that Sarah was very ill indeed. She brought in religious books. Sarah screamed whenever she saw her.

'She thinks I am going to die! I'm not going to die, am I?'
Ellie banned Mrs Dodsworth. Gran was annoyed, and said to Sarah she might die, if she didn't mend her ways.

'Will I ever go back to dancing class? To school?'
Ellie said she would, when she was better. She had a bad heart. It was true, thought Sarah. That was why no one liked her; she had a bad heart. That's why she had hit Maurice Hays over the head with a book – that is why she knew the secret of the body the others didn't seem to know.

Now she wouldn't become the world's greatest ballerina, or Sarah Bernhardt. No one had ever got famous by staying in bed. She decided to become the world's greatest woman artist, like Leonardo. They did let her draw. She copied all the pictures from the *Children's Encyclopaedia.*

Just as suddenly as the world had decided she was sick it decided she was better. She had grown a lot, lying in bed, and lost a tooth, just like Paul, the twin, had. The other children welcomed her back. She had become, by being different, one of them. It was very odd. Back at school they were trying on gas masks, nodding like sea horses snorting at each other. She hated the feeling of being inside the gas mask, but it didn't do to show it. If you showed feelings they would put you to bed, imprison you for it. So she snorted with the rest.

She forgot once, and told the whole class she was in love with Billy Carson – swore it on the Bible. She saw the reaction – she was doing it again. She laughed and said it was a joke. He didn't speak to her after.

Lena's children, her cousins, came for a week. Calum crashed into her consciousness and she forgot Billy Carson. Fifteen years old, in his school blazer and cricket flannels, he was a god. All tanned limbs and athletic fervour, he spent the days bowling and batting against a wicket he had chalked on the privy door. His black hair fell into his eye, and he flicked it back in a gesture that was totally his. The two younger girls, Angela and Thelma, did not share her view of their brother's charms. They were made to bowl endlessly, all the summer afternoon, while he hit boundaries into the Dodsworths' garden.

Sarah would have liked to bowl too, but didn't know how. She watched. She didn't like to ask if she could use the privy, and the warm liquid she was retaining gushed down her legs. Angela screamed with laughter. Calum pretended not to notice. Her hero.

She and Angela played a game called 'The Fortune Strip'. You wrote a list of things on a long strip of paper, and the other person pulled. You found out about the future that way – husbands, favourite flowers, film stars, colours, everything. Everything was on the Fortune Strip.

Angela had:

Imogen, red, Tyrone Power, Sweden, George, a sailor, Irish stew, and a kitten.

Sarah had:

Clare, rose pink, Charles Boyer, Switzerland, David, a poet, fish and chips, and a pony.

They screamed and squealed. How could it be so correct?

'That's because you wrote it,' said Calum. He wouldn't do his. 'Girl's stuff,' he said.

15

The third of September 1939, unless you were Gran, Ellie and Sarah, was notable for the fact that Britain declared war on Germany that day. They noted that, but it was also the day they moved out of Rathmines Avenue, to two unfurnished rooms, a little way away.

It was an irrevocable decision, like Chamberlain's – and one it had taken Ellie almost as long to make. Fear was in the air, and muted excitement – Sarah didn't know if this was for their fate, or for England's.

The measured tones on the wireless gave out advice and instructions. Gran and Ellie had for weeks been filling Sarah's doll's pram with pots and pans, and getting her to wheel them over to the new premises. This made her feel like a spy. Eric seemed to be the enemy, the Other Side. They were removing only small necessary objects; Gran was providing most of the furniture, from her Yorkshire cottage.

'Can't we take the wireless?' Sarah asked. It seemed it was to be left for Eric, in case he was lonely, or wanted to hear war bulletins. It was his, as were the furniture, the parrot and elegant lady picture, the good china, and the books. Sarah wondered what was Ellie's. She secreted Ibsen's plays in the pram, along with a frying pan. She regretted only the loss of her radio friends, Uncle Mac and Ronnie Waldman, who did Puzzle Corner on *Monday Night at Eight*. Gran had let her listen more lately. Sarah didn't regret Eric; she never saw him these days.

'You have to make sacrifices, now there's a war on,' said Gran. Sarah hoped Gran wasn't going to make the war hers, the way God had always been, so that no one else got a look-in. The war would suit Gran.

The new place was Gran's too – her dark, heavy furniture, mahogany chests and wardrobes, her large bed and an awful night commode, which, when you lifted the lid, revealed a chamber pot.

'I want nothing from Rathmines,' said Ellie, her mouth turning down like Gran's. 'He can have it all. They chose it, they can come and pick over it, if they want to.'

Sarah thought that silly. The aunts would not need it, their own house was filled with gate-leg tables and ornate chairs and little pots of plants. She thought of Eric, sitting alone in all this furniture, like a character on a stage. Would he care? She thought it would not make much difference to him. He wouldn't get shouted at so much.

Everyone seemed to be springing to life suddenly because of the war. They would all have to decide what to do, take in evacuees or join up, or do special work. Ellie was to go into an aircraft factory and spray Spitfires.

Eric met Sarah on the street one evening, while she wheeled some stuff over. She tucked a cover over it, feeling guilty.

'Out with your dolls at this hour?'

'Just visiting a friend,' she lied. She went past quickly, wondering how she had delivered the line. She felt sorry as she saw him weaving his way back. He wasn't even drunk, she could tell. Would he be able to live on mushy peas?

When she got to the rooms, Ellie was putting up blackout curtains over the pretty ones they had hung earlier. Sarah had already done the brown sticky tape in a diamond pattern to stop the windows shattering in the event of an air raid.

'Who will do father's blackout at Rathmines?' she asked Ellie. It seemed to Sarah he was too cut off to know about these things.

'That's no longer our business,' said Ellie. 'His sisters will get their handyman to do it, no doubt.' She sounded bitter. Sarah wondered why it had all suddenly changed – why they had not gone on the way they were.

They heard Gran's heavy tread, up the stairs. The house was bright and modern; the young couple who owned it, the Rosenblooms, had not got a stair carpet. They hadn't been married long. They had a small baby, Joseph.

'What do you think of it? We'll be all right here, won't we?' said Gran.

'I suppose so.' She saw from the arrangement she would be sleeping with Gran again. Ellie would sleep in a Put-U-Up in the main room, because her hours would be erratic, night shifts, etc. There was only a kitchenette and a paraffin stove. Sarah thought it all fun. She was impressed when she saw Ellie in her overalls, like a man. She even had a tin hat.

'I'll decorate your gas-mask for you,' Sarah offered. She had done her own, with Walt Disney characters. Gran didn't want hers done, she thought it frivolous. Sarah did flowers on Ellie's. The two women seemed happier, thought Sarah. They sent her back for things they had forgotten, occasionally. Eric was never there. She worried about his gas mask – had he got one? 'Of course, you silly girl, everybody has one. Even him,' said Gran.

Walking back from the old home to the new, she wondered why their lives always seemed different. A lot of families had rows, but it never came to this; the living in two rooms. She knew that Nora in *The Doll's House* had left, but that was the end of the play. What happened to Nora? Ibsen hadn't written that one. Perhaps *they* were acting it out – but this stage was real, and more muddled.

With the war, everyone would be in a play too. All living altered lives. Perhaps everyone would be living altered lives, and she and Ellie (and Gran) would not stick out so much, as odd ones. She certainly hoped so.

If she had been asked whether she would have liked to stay in the old house, the old life, the way it was – or have this new excitement, she would have chosen the new. This gave her a fresh insight into Ellie and for the first time she began to admire her mother for what she had done.

Sarah had fallen in love with the Rosenblooms.

He, Paul, was a bus driver; sharp-featured, with curling black hair under his cap, and crinkly laugh lines around his eyes – the kind of young father she might have chosen for herself, but of course, she had Eric. Paul was always joking with her, or he would kick a ball around the crab-grass-filled garden at the back. He taught her to bowl overarm in case

81

Calum should ever return. He was like something from the Fortune Strip or the cards in the slot machine on the pier – 'Your Future Husband'. Except that he was Jean's husband, of course. Jean was eighteen, a girl herself, rather like the older girls Sarah saw going to the grammar school. She had long legs and large glasses. But she was already a mother. Joseph was six months old, all dribbles and smiles. He smelled more new than anything Sarah had ever smelled before; a mixture of soap and flesh.

The house was as new as the marriage, as Joseph. Ordinary, uncomplicated, sunny and still very bare as they hadn't much money.

The furniture was lightweight and pale, bought on the never-never. 'Gimcrack stuff,' sadistic Gran remarked, already getting her talons into these two innocents. But Sarah preferred it to Gran's heavy sombre pieces. Gran's articles of furniture, uncompromising as herself, had scraped off bits of the new paint on their progress up to the top floor, but the Rosenblooms had not complained. Sarah supposed they needed the rent to help them buy the rest of the things they wanted.

She thought that if she were them she would not let Gran, Ellie and herself in, with their dark view of life. Sarah peeped into their bedroom, with its white, gilt-knobbed dressing table and matching wardrobe. The bed had a padded headboard, and it seemed all light in there, unlike Rathmines Avenue. On the dressing table was a corded silk scent spray, and a powder bowl made of cut glass.

Joseph's cot, with its blue-painted rabbits, was in the corner. It didn't seem long ago that she occupied a similar one. What fun it must be to be them, Sarah thought.

Ellie was permanently in dope-spattered dungarees. 'Dope' was the orange-red stuff sprayed on the planes before they were covered in camouflage. One of Ellie's co-workers made Sarah a tiny Spitfire brooch, and camouflaged it too.

It seemed everyone had forgotten Eric. Sarah decided it was easier to join in with other people's ready-made lives. It was better than having one's own, because it didn't hurt, you were not part of it, really. She breathed on the edge of the

Rosenblooms' existence.

'We won't ever go back to our own house, will we?' she asked Ellie. Ellie's face was sour.

'Do you want to?' she asked, finally.

'Oh no. I like this better.'

Sarah had been surprised at Ellie's hesitation. Wasn't she sure she had done the right thing?

'Will you ever see *him* again?' Now even she was calling Eric 'him'.

'No.'

The starkness of that 'no' haunted Sarah for a while. How could Ellie say that? It was how people were about the Germans, suddenly every German person was bad. In Germany, did they think every English person was, too? Eric was no different from what he had always been. Was that true of the Germans? How could anyone be sure?

Gran said Rosenbloom was a German name, and why wasn't he interned, or in the Army. She sniffed. Sarah never knew why Gran didn't like people – she always criticized them, whoever they were. Ellie told Gran to stop it – they didn't want to lose the accommodation.

The history of the marriage break-up went on when they thought Sarah was asleep.

'I always knew he was no good. No good for Lena and no good for you.' Gran would be lisping, having taken out her teeth.

'Forget it. It is all in the past.' Sarah could hear Ellie striking matches for a cigarette and then coughing.

Sometimes Sarah was mentioned.

'You are giving up your life to her and what will she do? Run off and get married.' Sarah was hurt that she too was under Gran's line of fire. She hadn't any intention of getting married yet. What was she supposed to do then? Not marry? To be with Ellie always? – she would shrink into her pillow then. She had not asked Ellie to give up her life to her – anyway, she never saw Ellie. It seemed unfair to be blamed – she had not been asked. She decided that one day she would throw herself on the mercy of the Rosenblooms and live with them for ever and look after Joseph.

The mornings were always more cheerful than those miserable whispering nights. There would be the smell of the paraffin stove, the hot tea and bread and marmalade. Gran often made porridge, and sometimes there was a bit of dripping when they had eaten a tiny beef joint. She went off to school; Gran had got a job as a housekeeper to two maiden ladies near the park. Ellie had been gone for hours.

This time was known as the phoney war; nothing much was happening. Everyone waited for the Germans to do something. At school there were air-raid drills instead of just fire drills. You must carry your identity card at all times, in case they thought you were a spy. Also your gas mask. You read posters which said: 'Careless Talk Costs Lives' and 'Dig for Victory'. Sarah didn't really know what careless talk was. Was it like when Gran talked about people?

Then France fell, and Dunkirk happened. Sarah dreamed of Nazis coming to get her, and wondered if she would stand up to torture. Ellie had admired Hitler once; did she still? Sarah daren't ask. It was possible Ellie was a spy. She hadn't, after all, told Sarah about leaving Eric. She didn't tell secrets.

Sarah found it strange that here were the three of them, like refugees, really, yet in their own town.

But she felt safe in these rooms, on top of the Rosenblooms – three women together.

Saturdays were best; she watched Jean fill the baby bath and together they immersed the struggling child. He lay, chuckling and splashing, he loved the water. Jean said it was because babies felt at home in it because of the womb. Sarah didn't know what she meant: she had not bothered to wonder yet where babies actually came from.

The slippery object was lifted out on to a towel laid on the kitchen table – dried, and liberally sprinkled with talcum powder; it was like when Gran powdered the board for pastry making. They then put a tiny Chilprufe vest over his lolling head, then a jumper and a matinee coat. A towelling nappy covered his red rear; Jean kept the pins in her mouth while she restrained his flailing limbs. Then he acquired leggings, over his waterproof pants. His sparse hair was brushed over his bare

84

pate, like an elderly gent concealing baldness. Then a bonnet, and another outdoor coat, and he was ready for the great outside world.

'He looks like Winston Churchill,' said Sarah.

'All babies do,' said Jean. They put him out on the front porch, where he snoozed and made little cries like a bird, until he was hungry again.

Sarah helped Jean clear up, wiping out the bath and hanging it on its nail; putting the jellied soap in its dish. The whole kitchen seemed filled with damp love. Jean made mugs of tea, and they made sandwiches to take to Paul at the bus station for his lunch.

Sarah liked all of this, it seemed like the games of mothers and fathers she and her friends had played in the garden of Rathmines, but in this case the family was a real one.

Why was it so peaceful when Rathmines had been so anguished? She and Jean sang together:

> Whistle while you work, Mussolini bought a shirt,
> Hitler wore it, Chamberlain tore it,
> Whistle while you work...

They went to the shops, wheeling Joseph, stopping off at the terminus to give Paul his lunch box. He looked dashing in his uniform, Sarah could imagine him in the airforce blue, or the khaki of the armed forces. But she hoped he wouldn't have to go. An intense anguish filled her at the thought that he might be one of those who would be killed. An officer passed. Sarah had noted that the officers wore better, more elegant uniforms – she couldn't understand why this was so. Was it fair that all those risking their lives should do it in different uniforms? Some things she would never fathom – like when Gran said the lonely little girl across the road would not be allowed to play with Sarah, because they went to different schools. 'You go to a rough school, you see,' Gran said, as if that was a natural thing. Sarah had never thought of school as anything but just school.

Sarah felt some invisible cord bound her to baby Joseph. She

85

felt close to Jean and Paul too, but it wasn't the same. Joseph was, in a sense, hers.

She liked Jean for her seriousness, the way her glasses steamed up when she bathed the baby, and the methodical slowness of her, as if what she was doing was the most important thing in the world. She seemed to be learning as she went along, and Sarah learned with her. It was like the boy at school who was good at the violin: each week he was better at it; you could see him getting confidence. Sarah knew she couldn't be trusted with Joseph yet, but she would be, one day. She was allowed to hold him, feeling the wet imprint of his bum on her navy blue gym slip. She wanted desperately to be like Jean, to have a bright little house, a husband like Paul, and a sweet baby.

Sarah met Eric. He was formal, as if they were strangers. You didn't see many men around, now. Even Eric had a job – he told her proudly he was a civil servant. You could see he was pleased.

'Be sure and tell your mother I'm working,' he said. He didn't mention Gran. 'How are you getting along?'

'All right,' she said, wanting to be off to see what Jean was doing.

'I offered to send you away to school, you know,' he said. She frowned at him. Then she could have played with the little girl across the road, she supposed, in the holidays. On the whole she would rather play with Joseph.

'I'm happy where I am,' she said. 'My mother is in the aircraft factory, you know. She sprays Spitfires.'

'Does she?' he said. 'Fancy that.'

'Well, goodbye.' Sarah wished he would hurry away. 'I expect we'll see each other again sometime.' She had never found it easy, talking to him. He said he wasn't at Rathmines Avenue, but at the aunts' house. She watched him walk away. He seemed different, more responsible. Why couldn't he have been that way before? Adults were so silly. He seemed old. She thought of him having scrambled eggs on a willow pattern plate; it was what the aunts had always given her for tea.

It was so dull at school that she wished Hitler would drop a stray bomb on it – then she always got cold feet and prayed that he would not. She closed her eyes and imagined it; Miss Tattersall would go, flying off into space, mouth open in a scream – the girls would go up too in an explosion of black stockings and gym slips, all sent hurtling over the Blackpool Tower.

'Sarah Shand, what have I been saying? You were miles away.'

But any time she was not with her ready-made family was wasted time. Around them she never had such destructive thoughts.

On Sundays, she, Paul and the baby would go to the park. Sarah, who had never before gone on walks with a young male, would hang on to Paul's arm, making it difficult for him to wheel the pram. She chattered on, about school, about Eric – he would point out to her the way the ducks and drakes were always in pairs, and the male more colourful; the way they dipped their heads in and their tails up, to get food from the bottom of the pond. Or he would get Sarah to find out the names of the roses in the Rose Garden: she would crawl and scramble through the thorns to read the yellow labels for him; he wished to have a rose garden of his own when he got rid of the crab grass.

Sarah wore her best shoes, got blisters, and swung the new handbag made of imitation patent leather that Paul and Jean had bought for her birthday. The aunts had sent a ten shilling note, with a card, and Eric's name had been added at the last minute.

While the Sunday walks took place Jean would flop out on her bed, reading the *News of the World*, with the fading smell of Sunday lunch filling the house. In their own rooms Gran and Ellie too would be napping, giving Eric the once-over.

Jean had a beauty treatment, a Yeast-Pak facial mask in the bath, and then did her toe and finger nails with rose-pink Cutex. '*My* afternoon,' she called it.

Sarah thought Jean might have been wise to come along on the walks; she and Paul seemed to get on so well, you never knew, he might begin to prefer her. She had grown her hair, and she released it from its plaits, and wore it down her back, with a velvet headband, on Sundays.

But then, thought Sarah, she was probably exaggerating the relationship with Paul.

Gran always said that she was so crazy for attention that she went mad when she got any. Gran was right on matters like that – they always rang true, her dreadful, accurate comments.

Paul sometimes let her wheel the pram home. After, she fed Joseph his 'pobs' – rusks mashed in hot milk. Paul went up to see what Jean was doing.

Sarah loved the way the baby lapped from the spoon. She then gave him his bottle, testing the heat of the milk on her inner-wrist, from the teat, as she had seen Jean do a million times.

Jean and Paul, looking flushed and happy, always emerged later. Sarah thought the walk and the beauty ritual must do them good: they were always cheerful on Sundays. Which was more than you could say for the other couple upstairs. They would be raking over the past like two tramps in a dustbin when Sarah went up.

Ellie would have washed and set her hair, and would be lying, smoking and reading her women's magazines. Gran usually dressed for tea, after doing some darning and mending. She would try a new recipe for supper; a cake from carrots, or a new way of doing dried eggs. The paraffin stove would reek. Gran usually went to the evening service at church. When she got back she would continue criticizing the Rosenblooms.

'They are like animals – those two. It is disgusting.' She was always holy, after a hymn or two.

Sarah thought about it. They were like animals. He was a black panther, and Jean, just because she was so sweet and shy, was a rabbit. She told Gran and Ellie. They laughed until the tears ran down their faces, she didn't know why.

'You might well laugh,' said Gran, wiping her eyes. 'But you want to watch that child – she is man-mad. Comes of having no father.'

'I have a father,' said Sarah. What did man-mad mean? That she liked Paul?

She went to the windowsill and read her favourite book. Her second favourite was *The Doll's House* by Henrik Ibsen, but her first was *Mr Galliano's Circus* by Enid Blyton. It was about a boy who had run away and joined a circus. Sarah would have liked to do that – but they had already run away, from Rathmines Avenue.

Ellie had stolen that possibility from her.

16

It was the second Christmas of the war. The schoolteachers Gran worked for had invited Gran, Ellie and Sarah to an evening party.

They took it in turns to primp in front of the cheval glass; Gran had on her spotted silk with a real lace 'front', and her peach stockings taken out of the tin trunk, where they nestled next to the laying-out nightdress. 'Might as well wear them while I am still alive,' she said. 'Who'll see them when I am a corpse?' She gave her teeth an extra brush with Vim, and they shone as luminously as her Woolworth pearls.

Ellie looked lovely, Sarah thought, in an old dark-red dress, her hair brushed out, wild and free. She had got used to Ellie in overalls, with her hair in a turban; with a shock she realized her mother was quite beautiful. What a waste it was: no one ever saw her like this. She hoped there would be someone at the party who would appreciate her.

Sarah herself had a mole grey velvet frock, made from one of Ellie's old opera cloaks, with a lace collar made from one of Gran's fronts.

They walked through the snow to the big house on the edge of the park.

'Why are we invited, anyway?' Ellie said, shivering in her tweed coat. 'Are they short of people?'

'It's a party for lame ducks,' laughed Gran. 'They collect them, my ladies.'

Lame ducks? Sarah looked at the frozen pond where, earlier, she and Paul had walked. She skipped in her bar-button shoes.

'I hope it isn't too boring,' said Ellie. 'I don't like do-gooders.'

'At least the food will be a bit of all right,' said Gran. 'They don't exactly approve of the black market, but I think they are a bit grey in some areas.'

'I'm a lame duck,' said Sarah, 'quack, quack.'

'You won't say that there?' asked Ellie.

'Of course she won't. She'd not do that, would you, Sarah?' Sarah shook her head. Why were they spoiling it, already?

Sarah hoped that Gran had not made the food, for Gran liked plain fare, as she was always saying. She hoped it would be more like children's parties had been before the war, before rationing, with cakes and jellies. She was not disappointed. The table was laden with colour. Jellies were done like little sailing boats, the sails were made of rice paper, and you could eat them. There were pink hams and darker pink tongues and saffron rice and salads. To top it all, a Christmas cake, dark fruit, with a white swirling icing on which little gnomes and tobogganing elves cavorted in little red siren suits. Sarah thought it all very fine. She seemed to be the only child there. Was she the only child lame duck in the world? she wondered.

She fell in love at the party with another lame duck, a real one with a limp – Kingsley by name. He had a profile like a hero in the *Girl's Crystal* magazine. He was aquiline-nosed, with curly hair and a sardonic smile. Kingsley was shy; he sat in a corner and did not want to join in the games. When he got up to help himself from the punch bowl she saw how bad his limp was. He could not go to war because of it.

Sarah had to choose a team for games and she chose Kingsley first. She saw Gran's eyes upon her. Next she chose Miss Parun who was a teacher at her school; then, out of politeness, one of the hostesses. A fat old man, who had eaten eight mince-pies, was her next choice. It was then she realized she had chosen neither Ellie nor Gran. She would hear about that later.

Out of the corner of her eye she saw Ellie, still sitting at the table, smoking, putting out her cigarettes in the empty jelly boats. Sarah sighed. What could one do with them? Gran at least had drunk her fill of punch, but Ellie looked as sad as ever. There were no men there to appreciate how nice she looked; they were all at the war. The dancing began. The shortage of men was even more apparent now. Sarah danced. The old man nobly and dutifully managed to wheeze his way through, partnering each lady in turn. Kingsley sat turning the pages of an art book. Sarah hoped that he and Ellie would not get together, the odd-ones-out – she would have been jealous. She need not have worried, neither stirred from their solitary place.

Everyone who could be persuaded did a turn. Gran was the star. She sang music-hall songs – 'Down at the Old Bull and Bush', 'On Mother Kelly's Doorstep' and, as an encore, 'I'll Take You Home Again, Kathleen'. The latter was so applauded she had to sing it all over again. Kingsley played the piano for these songs – Sarah realized that Ellie was the only one who would not join in. She herself recited:

> Arethusa arose
> From her couch of snows
> In the Acroceraunian mountains,–
> From cloud and from crag,
> With many a jag,
> Shepherding her bright fountains.

It was by Percy Bysshe Shelley. She couldn't remember any more of it. Miss Emma sang 'They Call Me Mimi'. Sarah looked across at Ellie, who had her eyes closed. Kingsley drank a lot of wine. When he limped to the door to get his coat, Sarah felt it was the end of the world. Her team had one point more than the other team, and so they got prizes. Kingsley looked in with his coat on and said that Miss Emma had told him they lived in his direction, and could he give them a lift? Ellie smiled for the first time that evening. They got their coats and piled into the little car.

'This is the life,' cried Gran, tipsy, with her nose as red as a holly berry. She sang 'I'll Take You Home Again, Kathleen' all the way back, with Ellie trying to shush her.

It wasn't long, it wasn't long enough, thought Sarah, before Kingsley drew up at the Rosenblooms. They got Gran out and she swayed up the path, still singing. Sarah wanted to hang on to the moment. She rushed at Kingsley and hugged him.

'Merry Christmas, Kingsley.' She wanted to say his name. Kingsley. He seemed surprised, and pleased.

'Thank you so much,' said Ellie in her poshest voice. 'I would invite you in for a cup of something, but it is so late.'

'Thanks for the offer, but I must get home. Merry Christmas to you,' he said, getting back into his car.

Sarah stared at her mother. Would she have invited him in, with the paraffin stove and Gran undressing for bed in front of it? Of course she wouldn't. They never invited anyone to see how they lived.

'Will we ever see him again?' she asked as they mounted the stairs.

'I don't see any reason why we would,' said Ellie.

17

Cold as the winter was, Sarah was now entrusted with wheeling Joseph about. She would sit, freezing, by the frost-dusted bowling green, by the unused swings. The other kids ribbed her.

'That your baby, Sarah?'

'Is it your mam's?'

She ignored them. They all stuck their little brothers and sisters in the pavilion, with dummies in their mouths, but she was devoted to Joseph. He could sit up all the time now, and he watched her unblinkingly while she read the *Beano* and ate her way through her sweet ration. Gran was greedy with hers; she bought chocolate with her coupons, and ate it secretly in bed. Sarah used to share hers, but as Gran was so greedy she gave that up. Ellie never wanted her allowance and one marvellous day she came home from the factory with a huge carton of orange-cream chocolate bars – they had, she said, 'fallen off the back of a lorry' – which really meant they were black market. Sarah thought they would last for ever, but they went down in a few weeks.

Gran had a bilious attack, the first she'd had since leaving Rathmines. After that she seemed bad-tempered and was always complaining about the rooms, saying Jean was a slut, and that there was something suspicious about Paul's still not being in the Forces. She always got morbid at this time of year; it was when Grandfather had died, had lain corpse-like for two years up in the Yorkshire cottage. Sarah remembered him as a yellow, rigid figure, one toe sticking out from the sheets that covered him. Paralysis, it was called, when you didn't move. The district nurse came in once a day and helped Gran turn him; it was like lifting a statue. It was typical of Gran to mourn

94

him, said Ellie, though they'd been miserable. Still, thought Sarah, they had spent their life together. 'Spent their life', was a funny phrase. Did you *spend* life? Were they spending theirs? She liked other people's lives best, in books. If you plunged into their lives it made your own better.

Ellie got moved to another factory, miles away, and had a train journey there. She worked nights. She left at teatime and got back for breakfast. She slept all day, it was as if she lived on another planet. She and Sarah hardly saw each other.

Then life became like a novel – Dickens, perhaps. Ellie, tired from the turning of night into day, and travelling in unheated trains in the blackout, became ill. She lay, spitting blood. Gran put kaolin poultices on her chest and back. The reeking odour met Sarah as she came in from school; it was like the smell of death. The dope had got to Ellie's lungs, said Gran. That and the constant cigarettes. Ellie moaned, delirious. Sarah thought she was pretending, it sounded silly and too dramatic. She told Gran Ellie should see the doctor.

'He'll have her in hospital, and then where will we be? The poultices will do the trick.' But they did not, and the doctor told Gran off, and Ellie was carted down the stairs on a stretcher, with a red blanket over her.

Ellie didn't get her sick pay through, and money was short. Gran ate lunch at the schoolteachers' house and brought back bits of food. Sarah was always just empty enough to be suspicious that they might be, like characters in a Victorian novel, starving.

'We're not starving, are we Gran?'

'Of course we're not. Don't be dramatic.'

It was hard, paying the rent and feeding themselves on Gran's pension.

'People can't starve these days, can they?'

'Of course they can't. We're just a bit hard-up.'

Sarah thought it must be their fault. They had done something wrong. They must be more foolish than most. A lot of girls took money for National Savings, there was a chart in the class, and a lot of competition between forms. Sarah hadn't taken any.

'If I asked the aunts, would they give me my birthday money

95

in advance?' she asked Gran, unwisely as it turned out.

'You must be mad. If they gave us money we'd use it for food. You could go along and ask them for a pound or two – they'd never refuse.'

Sarah said she couldn't. She said Ellie wouldn't like her to do that. 'Beggars can't be choosers,' was the reply to that. She went along, past the bowling green, with a note. She hoped Eric would not be there. It would be like confessing that three women could not manage, on their own.

The aunts sat her down and gave her a cup of tea and a piece of madeira cake, which seemed as full of butter and eggs as a pre-war one. They read the note from Gran, went away, and came back with another envelope. She opened it on the way home. A pound. Twice a birthday. Gran was well-pleased. 'If you don't ask, you don't receive,' she said.

They went off for their rations, and after stocking up there was enough for a bunch of flowers for Ellie. They took the bus up the hill to the hospital.

Ellie was sitting propped up at the end of a long, polished ward. She had lost the yellow look, and was cheerful. Sarah had got permission from the matron to go in; she felt very grand. She clutched the flowers, feeling very shy, as if she didn't know Ellie.

'I thought you were going to die,' she whispered.

'Not me. They've got me on some new wonder drug. Saved my life.' Ellie fussed about where Gran was to sit. Gran was subdued in front of the starched nurses. Ellie had a snood on her frizzy hair, and she behaved in a shrill manner as if she were a celebrity.

'We got a pound out of those mean buggers,' Gran said, and clapped her hand over her mouth. Ellie didn't look pleased, she began a paroxysm of coughing. When she had ceased she drank some barley water, and smiled at Sarah.

'Never mind. They can spare it. It doesn't matter.'

'We are getting on all right, aren't we, Sarah?' Gran nudged her.

'Oh yes.' It was a lie. They argued all the time, even had physical fights. Gran was a terrible pincher. Sarah's arms were black and blue.

'How are the Rosenblooms?' asked Ellie. There were gaps in

the conversation, as if they didn't know each other.

'Fine,' said Gran, sniffing. Really the Rosenblooms were not fine, they were not speaking now that the rent was owing. Gran didn't help, with her arrogance.

They left, in the beginning Spring sunshine. They turned to wave at the end of the long ward.

'She's lucky. It's like the Ritz in there,' said Gran.

'She won't get ill again, will she?' Sarah had been very scared, and was only now beginning to let it out, like air from a balloon, slowly.

'Not until next time,' said Gran, winking at her.

As it was the Easter school holiday, and she was no longer spending all her time with Joseph, Sarah went off with Gran in the morning to the villa near the park. She sailed her toy yacht in the park on the still lake, where the ducks still dived for weeds down at the bottom. One day she found the girl from the house next door to the schoolteachers' one, looking out at her from an upstairs window, with binoculars.

'Hello,' she shouted. 'Why don't you come over? I'll open the gate.' The garden gate between the two houses was in a wall covered with honeysuckle. Sarah waited while the girl undid the lock from the other side.

'I'm Hermione,' she said, holding out her hand. Sarah shook it, feeling a bit silly.

'Sarah Shand,' she said.

'SS? Are you a member of the SS?' Hermione grinned at her. 'Hey, Oliver, come here. I've met a member of the SS.'

'Shut up,' Oliver said. He was obviously her brother, but older, almost a man. He had a silk scarf tucked into his open shirt neck, and he wore riding breeches. Sarah didn't really know what they meant.

'Have you just moved in? We haven't seen you around before. Where do you go to school?'

'Cut it out, Hermione. Leave her alone. You are like a large bloody puppy, leaping all over people.'

'She's so quiet,' said Hermione. 'Are you always so quiet?'

'I don't know,' said Sarah.

'Would you like to meet Poppet?' asked Oliver. 'Do you ride?'

'No,' said Sarah. 'I mean, I would like to see Poppet, but I don't ride.'

Poppet was a Shetland pony, tethered to a post further down the garden. Sarah was entranced.

'Who does he belong to?' she asked.

'To-whom-does-he-belong?' sang Hermione. 'Why, to me, of course. Poppet is mine, and Oliver had a real horse because he was jealous.'

'Take no notice,' said Oliver. They walked down to the stables at the rear of a sloping lawn. There, nose out of the stall, was a chestnut horse, stamping and snorting.

Sarah couldn't believe that there were such wonderful things in the world. How could one *own* a horse?

'Of course, we have to leave them here – we are going to America. Are your parents sending you to America?'

'To America?' Perhaps they were both mad.

'There's a war on, silly. A lot of people we know are going. I may become a cowgirl. Do they have cowgirls?'

'I don't think so, just men,' said Sarah. She was overwhelmed with all this information.

'Why are you staying next door? Are you a niece, or something?' Hermione pulled out a sugar lump from her pocket and gave it to the chestnut horse.

'Yes,' lied Sarah. 'My father has just died in the war; he is going to get the VC. They invited me to stay, to get over it.'

'What's his name?' asked Hermione. 'We must look out for that, mustn't we, Oliver? You'll probably have to collect it yourself, if he is dead, from the King.'

Sarah knew somehow that they did not believe her.

'Who is the lady I see you with? Is that your Nanny?'

'Yes. Dear old Nanny,' said Sarah. 'She's been with us for years.'

Oliver came out with a tray of lemonade.

'I see you are a sailing person,' he said, smiling at her, pointing at the yacht.

'That belongs to my little brother, Joseph,' she said, sipping a glass filled with ice cubes. She was getting quite good at this; she might take it up permanently.

'I think she's been telling little white lies, don't you, Oliver?' said Hermione.

'Stop it,' said Oliver. Sarah looked at him in desperation. Was he on her side, or was he playing with her, like Hermione was?

'Where do you go to school?' Hermione asked.

'Tanner Road Elementary,' she said.

'We were having a bet that you were an evacuee. You aren't, are you?'

'No,' said Sarah. 'I've lived here all my life.'

They let her through the garden gate again, to the teachers' garden.

'Come again,' said Oliver.

'Thanks for the lemonade,' she answered, politely. She couldn't make out why she felt so unclean, unless it was that lying made you feel that way.

'How much would it cost to buy a horse, Gran?' she asked, as they walked home.

'God knows. We'll be eating horses before this lot is over. The French do, you know. Just look at this little bit of scrag end I got from the butcher. And Ellie coming home on the weekend.'

Sarah wanted to ask Gran if rich people's lives were more important, but she knew she wouldn't get an answer, because people like Gran lied about that. They pretended that God treated everybody equally. 'His eye is on the sparrow,' Gran used to say. But to Sarah it seemed that unless you were an idiot that wasn't possible to believe.

Not only did girls like Hermione have horses and houses, and a sense of their own importance, they made you ashamed you didn't have them too. It was that feeling, a hard hurt around the heart, that made Sarah swear she would find some way, when she was older, to make all those people pay. She didn't know what people. She wanted to beat the world.

Sarah told Ellie about her encounter when she got out of hospital.

'Are people sending their children to America? I didn't know that,' she said, looking worried, as if she had committed some breach of behaviour. She always looked lost when faced with

99

other people's actions – she found most people incompre-hensible, as she had Eric.

'Don't worry about it. I only told you for a joke,' said Sarah. 'I mean, one of those boats full of rich kids was sunk in the Atlantic, you know. They are all at the bottom of the sea, now.'

It must have been the relish with which she said it; Ellie looked at her strangely. She seemed more worried than ever. It was as if she were seeing Sarah for the first time.

The final outcome of the meeting with Hermione was very strange. Ellie decided to send Sarah for elocution lessons. Sarah had no idea why it had had such an effect.

'She wants to make you posh for one and sixpence a week. Hoity-toity, ain't we grand?' Gran said, having the habit of hitting the nail on the head.

Sarah loathed going for the ridiculous half an hour of mouthing and breathing from the diaphragm.

'I liked the way I spoke before,' Sarah attempted to say to Phoebe Ackerman, ex-actress, who was a busty blonde lady with a large chest produced by correct breathing.

'Nonsense, my dear, you were breathing from the wrong place entirely, and slurring your words.'

She demonstrated, puffing out her mammoth mammaries.

'How now brown cow. And, after me – AY-EE-AYE-OWE-YOUUUU. Round the rugged rocks the ragged rascal ran...'

What a bore it all was, thought Sarah. She was worse than Miss Jeanne of the Dancing Academy. More of a phoney, even. And, worse, one might get a chest like Phoebe's.

Sarah passed one examination, reciting 'Daffodils' by William Wordsworth. Then everyone seemed to lose interest, and she started to say *Bath* instead of *Barth*, and she felt at home in her language again.

'One and sixpence a week thrown in the gutter,' said Gran. She was right as usual.

18

Sarah said goodbye to Joseph as he sat in his pram, chuckling in his jovial way, gazing fixedly at a string of coloured wooden beads hanging perilously near his eye. Funny, what things people gave babies to do.

'I'll be back, don't forget me,' she said, taking his fat fist in her hand, and pushing it back and forth as if she were arm wrestling with him – it always made him laugh. She saw the curtains move slightly; Jean was watching. Now they were all enemies, Gran's sharp tongue and the owing rent had done their work. Ellie was to move to a factory in Birmingham, and Gran was to go and look after cousin Margaret's baby in Keswick. Sarah was to go to Yorkshire, to Aunt Lena.

Sarah had never been on a train alone before; she sat primly, reading *Jane Eyre* and feeling like her. She took sly looks at the landscape, but she didn't want to attract attention, having had the usual warnings of strangers offering sweets or speaking to her, especially men. But there were no men, except the old ticket collector, and he was busy and cross. An old lady offered her a biscuit and she took it as it wasn't a sweet, but she felt queer after and imagined it might have been drugged – though for what purpose she couldn't imagine, as the old lady got out quite soon.

Sarah felt sentimental about leaving, even though she hadn't much affection for the town. She would certainly miss the raging brown sea – she was used to thinking about its pounding away out there as she went to sleep. And the Tower – she would miss the constant challenge of the Tower, for she'd never been up to the top; all the kids she knew had done it – said it was great up there – but she was too cowardly. There wasn't a day she didn't think about her timidity about the

Tower, and now she was leaving without resolving it. How could she live without the comfort of the sea, the challenge of the Tower?

It was raining as she left and there was a grey pall over the piers and the amusement arcades and the lines of small hotels and boarding houses with their silly names; 'Bide-A-Wee' and 'Linga-Longa'. They all seemed to have faces, and they were the faces of friends. She felt even more like Jane Eyre going to Lowood Institution.

At the station, at the end of her journey, she was met by Aunt Lena, accompanied by Thelma and a large black dog.

They kissed. The dog jumped up at her, nearly knocking her down. Lena regarded her for a minute.

'Well, you are a thin one. We'll fatten you up, won't we, Thelma?'

Thelma grimaced. She was a funny little thing, blonde, unlike the rest of the family's dark looks. They walked from the station down cobbled streets. Ellie wouldn't have walked, she would have got a cab, no matter how hard-up they were.

'Do you ever see your father?' asked Lena as soon as they got in. Sarah smiled: it was like that awful picture hanging in the school hall – 'When did you last see your father?' – but she took the smile off her face and said, no, she didn't see much of him. She hoped she was not regarded as a pitiful character, like Jane Eyre. She did feel sad but she knew herself well; it was only laziness. It had struck her that now she was at their disposal, Aunt Lena's family, she would be much more of a child. It would be a bore, having to put up with the interest shown in her – after the life with Ellie and Gran. Although Gran had been a nuisance, she had been easily avoided.

At least there wouldn't be bombs here – there was no sign of the war. Blackpool had been starting to have a few because of the aerodrome and the factory. Still, rather bombs than humans, thought Sarah. Bombs were predictable – it was just silence, whine, boom. You knew where you were with bombs.

Behind the house the Pennines stood, comforting or menacing, depending on which way the light hit them.

Sarah often escaped up there with Henry, the labrador, freeing herself of the family – who were good to her.

She didn't, funnily enough, connect the moors with Charlotte or Emily Brontë, even though she'd just read *Jane Eyre*. And though Haworth was just a few miles away, they were *her* crags.

'I think it is very boring here,' she said to Angela in bed at night. She had swapped Gran for bony Angela. Thelma also shared the room, but she was the baby, the outcast.

'You are lucky to be here so don't complain,' snapped Angela. She had her sanctimonious side. 'Your mother is a bit of a muddler, you know.'

'Yours has eyes like two poached eggs.' It was true, poor Aunt Lena had bifocals, which enlarged her soft orbs. They giggled, forming a truce against silly adults. Angela had a game, writing messages on Sarah's back. They were usually just film-stars' names. Sarah had to guess what Angela had written, and then it was Angela's turn to be written on. Sarah loved the feel of Angela's cool long fingers on her back. She liked, too, feeling Angela's bony spine when it was her turn to write.

Aunt Lena was strict. The house was run on rigid lines: routine and discipline, like the Army must be, thought Sarah. She missed sloppy Ellie, with her constant cigarettes and make-up; her pessimism. Here it was all too worthy. Angela said the rest of the family thought Ellie a bit of a tart. 'Not me,' she added, 'I think she is lovely.'

Sarah was hurt. Ellie wasn't in the least a tart. She worked as hard as Lena, harder, in fact – she was out in the world, in the war. Lena cleaned and scoured, but just for these people, and that was not important really. She seemed to have some standard she was keeping up with. Sarah didn't want to be like either of them. Down on her knees on the bedroom lino, in her Viyella nightdress, she prayed (praying being a rule of the house) for a better life than she had seen most women getting.

'Why is Calum at a grand school, and you have to leave and get a job?' Angela was going to leave school at fourteen and work in a store as a trainee buyer.

'It's because he is a *boy*, stupid.' Angela seemed to think that explained something. Not that Sarah minded Calum being the family god – she agreed with it in her more dopey moments –

but she resented it for her own sex. Calum even had his shoes cleaned for him by the girls, when he was home, Angela told her that. Sarah actually felt torn by her idolization of him, and the feeling that it was not right to think of him as superior. She could only work it out if he was here, and he was not here. She asked Angela if she minded starting work – why she wouldn't rather go on at school and do something with her life. Angela said: what did it matter? – she would get married anyway as soon as she could. Unless the war went on and on, and then she would join the WRNS. Sarah perked up at that, sensing ambition.

'Would you like to do that?' she asked.

'Yes. You'd meet a very nice class of naval officer,' said Angela. Sarah gave up.

She'd never lived in an industrial town before; you could hear the clogs clattering down the cobbles, and the factory and mill hooters, very early. Some of the children at school wore clogs. The people seemed plodding and dour, after the trippers and amusers of trippers in tinsel town. Lena belonged to the church, and the events were all connected in some way with that; jumbles and amateur theatricals, and the odd Gilbert and Sullivan operetta.

The hills were the only splendour. For the first time *words* actually meant something to her: 'I will lift up mine eyes unto the hills, from whence cometh all help'. She did that, often. But no help came in the relentless routine. She used the moors, as otherness – just as she had the sea.

No chance here, either, of faking the odd illness and going off to see Barbara Stanwyck at the local Odeon. Ellie had been good for a false sick note, always. She wouldn't dare try that on Aunt Lena.

Aunt Lena. Sundays, she would enter the room filled with girl-sweat and dreams, bearing a tin tray full of cups of tea and ginger-nut biscuits. With her blue dressing-gown flapping around varicosed legs and her greying hair in a pigtail, she was truly Gran's child, a thought that struck Sarah as odd.

She squinted at them, glasses off, revealing soft brown eyes like Ellie's.

Sunday they had real breakfast: bacon, eggs and coffee.

Uncle Alaric had his soft shirt on, and sat reading the papers. It was less rigid than usual, although there were two religious sessions to get through, Sunday school and the evening service. Back from Sunday school, the girls collected rhubarb and cabbage from the kitchen garden, for the massive late lunch. Rationing didn't seem to affect eating here; there was a barter system – everyone grew food, or knew a local farmer.

Sarah would stare at Lena. Had she ever been a girl, a bride? Uncle Alaric must have loved her once. They snapped at each other now. They never went out together, or even sat together in the house. Lena was always busy. Poor Uncle Alaric, they could hear the arguing through the thin bedroom wall between their room and his and Aunt Lena's – they would stuff the sheets in their mouths to stop giggling. Married love.

Monday was wash-day; Lena was up at five, possing the clothes she had soaked in barrels, with the copper posser. The clothes were boiled then, sending a smell of carbolic and ammonia up to the waking children. They could hear her, beating the evil dirt out of them, hear the sound of the mangle being turned, as they themselves turned over for an extra five minutes.

Tuesday was ironing day – after the garments had blown in the wind from the moors, and hung on the kitchen rack they were starched and ironed and put on the rack yet again to air. Wednesday was baking – the whole week's bread and cakes and pies, and Thursday was church social night. Friday the whole house was cleaned thoroughly, not the dusting and tidying that went on each ordinary day, but a scouring and polishing for the weekend. Saturday was market day, when Thelma and Sarah accompanied Aunt Lena for the week's shopping. Sunday rolled round again. There never seemed to be time to breathe, or read or play. It began all over again. Sarah thought it was not enough.

'Send me an adventure, God,' she prayed. 'Why not drop a bomb? It would at least wake them all up.' Then she would feel guilty. They had, after all, taken her in. Not that she wanted to be taken in.

Uncle Alaric, sandy-haired with streaks of grey, pernickety, was not inclined to take much notice of Sarah. He was a cabinet maker, specializing in coffins. He brought home, for Thelma, little bits of pastel satin, samples of coffin linings – peach, blue and ivory – and Thelma, aided by Angela, had clothes for her dolls made out of this eerie material. Sarah found it morbid. She watched his freckled, pale fingers at the table, thinking of their carving someone's last abode. He was, in fact, rather a melancholy man, not given to talking much, except to admonish Thelma whom he adored – the last, late flower of his life.

There were two lodgers, as well, up on the top floor with the rooms that had fantastic views of the Pennines. Aunt Lena had taken them in years before, and now their rent was essential to help with Calum's school fees. Mr Max, a plump old bachelor, gave Thelma and Sarah his sweet ration every Saturday. It was a little ritual, going up, knocking, being admitted and given the sweets, and saying thank-you. Mr Max had been part of a very rich family who manufactured the little pink pills Gran bought, and he had quarrelled with his father and taken rooms with Lena. He never went back. He had trays of food in his room, went for a brief walk every morning for the *Manchester Guardian,* and during the cricket season he made excursions to Old Trafford and Headingley, but the war and gout had put a stop to this. Sarah worried about his life and that of Miss Swift who played the church organ and who lived in the room opposite.

Angela said Miss Swift was dying of passion for the local vicar, but Sarah thought that unlikely, looking at them both. It seemed to her more logical that Mr Max and Miss Swift should fall in love and marry, but Angela scoffed, saying life was never like that. Sarah should not concern herself over those old has-beens, said Angela, they'd had their lives. But Sarah thought, no, they haven't – that was why she worried.

The problem of being unable to eat came over her. It was because of the gargantuan feasts that were provided. She was not used to provincial eating, having lived on the meagre rations for three back at home. At the table she began to feel displaced, the room would spin around, the sound of the voices waver and blur – she dreaded mealtimes, knowing she would be forced to eat large portions of fatty meat or things she was allergic to, like tomatoes. Aunt Lena would not tolerate faddiness, as she called it. Sarah would pass a piece of meat fat or a tomato to Angela, who would stuff it in her knickers. Sarah did not dare do this herself. The fear of the whole occasion made her feel sick, even before the eating began. If she left anything she had to come back and eat it, even if she had rushed out to vomit.

Aunt Lena told her she should be grateful for what the Lord provided in a time of shortage.

'I wish the old bastard didn't provide quite so much,' she said to Angela. Angela ate like a horse and yet was very skinny. Sarah was putting on weight in spite of the fact that she tried to eliminate what she ate in one way or another. Aunt Lena thought, probably quite rightly, that Sarah's rejection of the food was a rejection of her and the family. Sarah thought she must be the only person in England praying for less food and more excitement.

As a sort of travesty of the walks in the park she had taken with Paul Rosenbloom and young Joseph, she now walked with Aunt Lena and Thelma. Angela, to do her credit, refused.

Thelma and Sarah, as starched as two Edwardian children, paraded slowly, meeting the neighbours. It was important to Aunt Lena, obviously. It even gave Sarah a sense of identity, to be introduced as the little niece from Blackpool. And she would hear, frequently, the magic name of Calum, the local star turn.

'How is your Calum? Still singing?'

'Yes. He sang in front of King Leopold of the Belgians, you know.'

The neighbour would smile and pass on, hating Aunt Lena's superior smile.

Yet she realized this performance had some meaning for Lena. It made her work worthwhile, like an exhibition for a painter or a concert for an artiste. She, Sarah, was slotted in now to a family, a real group – it wasn't unpleasant. It made her, in a sense, able to rebel against it, in the way she never could rebel against Ellie. That's why Angela was more confident – Angela had received all this and was now able to dismiss it. Sarah was too easy, she knew that – it came from not being sure enough to hurt anyone. Their own little trio, back in Blackpool, were fighting the rest of the world so that disloyalty was impossible. The structure here, made and held by Lena, was so *there* that she would, in time, be able to reject it. They would expect that; it was what children ideally did. Margaret, the eldest, had done it, marrying her soldier and moving to Keswick. Calum, the golden boy, had done it. Angela and Thelma would in their turn become independent and leave. But she – owing Ellie – would she ever be free?

The trouble was these considerations were Sunday considerations, brought on by the solemnity of the day. The trouble was it was more real, living with Ellie.

19

After the Sunday walk it was time to write letters home. This always seemed stupid to Sarah as she didn't know what kind of life Ellie was living and was unable to visualize it – and was unable to say what life was like at Aunt Lena's as the letters were censored, benevolently, of course, by Uncle Alaric. 'We don't want to upset your mother, so keep cheerful' was the usual advice. This left Sarah sitting in the study, chewing on the old wood pen, spattering ink on her fresh Sunday dress, writing rude words on the blotter which she would hastily ink out. She looked out at the Pennines: they looked back. She would imagine a German parachutist dropping, oh so slowly, out of the sky of scudding clouds, until she sometimes thought it had happened. The Germans must have known how boring it was here – they were leaving it alone. Henry would scratch at the door and come in and flop at her feet. When she had finished the letter Henry and Uncle Alaric would take it to the post. It was like writing in water – there was no truth in what she wrote to Ellie – there couldn't be.

She would have liked to write to Calum also, but Angela said she shouldn't be such a drip, and that she better stop thinking of Calum – they were cousins. Sarah retorted that cousins could marry. Angela said they bred idiots if they did. There were many in the village where Gran had lived, she said. Even brothers and sisters had offspring – they were all idiots. Angela got a lot of information out of 'Believe it or Not', by Ripley, in the *Reynold's News.*

'Letter ready?' Henry leapt up at the sight of Uncle Alaric in overcoat and walking shoes.

Sarah, seeing he was ready to go off, added 'HELP' at the bottom of the innocuous letter, and sealed it.

'Here you are,' she said, all innocence. Ellie might get the point and come and rescue her and take her back to the real wartime world.

'Naughty girl, I wanted to add a little postscript,' said Uncle Alaric. 'You haven't been worrying her, have you? She's on important war work, you know.'

'I know.' Silly old sod, she thought. She watched him go, making sure he didn't go into the kitchen to steam it open. He strode off; so unlike her own father, she thought. He never drank, except for sherry at the occasional celebration. He was a bit of an old lady, really. She decided to write a story about him, to remove the venom from her heart. It was a method she had found, to get even. You wrote the thing down and it seemed better. It got it out of your system. She always stayed in the study for a while, concocting her tales. She decided that if she had to stay there she might as well start being herself. It began by telling Aunt Lena that she was really an atheist and that when she prayed, it was only for presents, or to put a spell on somebody. She thought it a kind of joke; to Lena it was incredible. She went very white. Uncle Alaric had a talk with Sarah.

'You mean you are agnostic,' Uncle Alaric said, patient and grim. 'That means you don't know if God exists. Atheism means you believe he doesn't exist.' He shut his thin mouth, as if that were the end of it.

'I do mean that,' said Sarah. 'I don't believe. And what is more,' she added in a burst of inspiration, 'I haven't been baptized so I don't belong to the church at all.'

Aunt Lena had hysterics.

'Just what I expected from those two,' she said. 'Freethinkers. All that Bernard Shaw and Bertrand Russell. I said they would come to no good. Well, we'll soon settle that.'

Sarah wondered what she meant. She did not have long to wait. Next Sunday she was to be baptized, along with new, squealing babies of the parish.

Angela was in fits. 'I can be your godmother,' she said. Sarah said she was not going through with it. She would refuse.

'There is no way out,' said Angela. 'I've seen them like this before.'

The vicar stood simpering. He was just as embarrassed as Sarah. The family, dressed in their best, were in the second pew. They were waiting, as it was the turn of some poor infant to be given the name George Formby Jones. The Jones was a family name but the George Formby was not. So said Angela to Sarah.

'Could I change my name? Could I be called "Barbara Stanwyck Shand"?'

Angela giggled.

'You could, I suppose. But she'd never let you. Ask her and see what reaction you get.'

Sarah didn't see the point of being christened if you couldn't change your name. Poor old George Formby Jones was dolloped with holy water and given back to his proud parents. It was Sarah's turn. She hoped the vicar would not sweep her up into his long sleeved arms.

He didn't. He sang through the preamble. Mr Max was to be her godfather, and Miss Swift her godmother. This had caused Angela some amusement – she said Sarah had brought them together at last.

Sarah tried not to listen, and crossed her fingers so it wouldn't take. She didn't want to join the God brigade. When he got to the bit about 'I name this child', she said, loud and clear, 'Barbara,' but she never got to 'Stanwyck' because his voice overrode hers, from years of experience, she thought. Lena, anyway, had said, 'Sarah,' in her loud tones. So Sarah it was, again.

The vicar came back for sherry and the usual spread. Margaret, from Keswick, looked strained. Sarah thought of her with sympathy – staying with Gran. Lena kissed Sarah gravely, as if she were now recovered from a long illness.

'Do you feel holy?' asked Angela, winking at her. 'Try some sherry, *Barbara*. I have. All you can do at a function like this is to get drunk.'

Sarah took a bit. Angela's face was very red, and she was giggling even more than usual.

'So you are no longer a little heathen,' said Mr Max. 'Well, well, well.'

She thought she'd shock him with the information that

111

godparents were supposed to provide presents all their lives to the baptized one; but he was such a sweet old thing, she resisted. Miss Swift was overcome at being in the presence, socially, of the vicar, and had to go upstairs.

'It was a shock, that cold water on my head,' she said to Alun Foster, who was Calum's local best friend, and an admirer of Angela's.

'*Holy* water,' he said. She stared at him. He, too, then believed. She looked at the clenched hands of the vicar, around a delicate sherry glass. Suppose those white fingers had magic powers, and she had been, unwillingly, given to God. She shuddered. Perhaps that was the way they netted you.

'Why were they so keen on having me done?' she asked Alun.

'It's important to them,' he said, sipping his sherry. His eyes roved the room for Angela, who had disappeared.

'But there are people being killed by other people all over the world,' she said to him. 'It is daft to worry about whether I'm baptized.'

'I expect they think every soul is important,' he said, after long thought.

'Angela's up in her room, drunk, and you won't be allowed up,' she said, trying not to make it sound triumphant. He was so 'good' he wouldn't even try, she knew. He didn't. She saw him collect his coat.

She and Angela smoked a couple of Woodbines, up in their bedroom.

'Your first sin as a Christian,' said Angela. Sometimes she was a real tonic.

'I dare you to call me Barbara,' said Sarah. But Angela said it wouldn't be worth it. She knew Lena.

Thelma said she must be older than Sarah as she had been christened first. After that, things were back to normal.

Angela and Sarah decided to start a magazine, to liven things up. Sarah Shand (Barbara Stanwyck) and she became the editors of 'Sophisticate', a magazine for glamorous young Yorkshire women. They tried to sell subscriptions, then single copies, Angela at the store and Sarah at school.

'They are all too dumb,' said Angela. 'Or too mean.'

Sarah sold one copy at school, to Dorothy Pearson, and she passed it round. The others said it wasn't worth it.

'It's worth it for the beauty hints and fashion alone,' argued Sarah. 'My cousin Angela is very hot on that kind of thing.' It made no difference.

They turned it into a newspaper, timing it for when the local paper did not appear.

'There's no news. Even the local rag has nothing to say,' complained Angela.

'We could make news. Kidnap a dog or something.' Sarah tried to think up something. 'We could ask Calum to send articles about his school.'

'Oh, great, that's all we need.' Angela appeared to be growing bored with the whole idea.

'What's in that red file in the basement, the one that's locked?' asked Sarah.

'Oh, that's secret information for the Germans,' said Angela, sarcastically. 'Your beloved Uncle Alaric, my saintly father, is actually a spy.'

For a moment Sarah half-believed her.

'I wish it was true,' she said finally.

Angela said she was giving up journalism. From now on she was concentrating on becoming glamorous and preparing to find a rich husband.

Sarah sighed. There was no one in the world who felt as she did.

20

UNCLE ALARIC'S COLLECTION
by
'Barbara Stanwyck'

Delphine Jones, woman detective, went down the creaking, dusty cellar steps. She was wearing a white raincoat and a large felt hat. Delphine was the bravest woman on the Lancashire/Yorkshire border. She piloted her own plane. She advised the government about the War. She had been told to find out the Secret of the Red File. Tucked away, in an ordinary family house, was the box which could change the fate of millions. Would it be here? Secret messages were being sent to the enemy from a hidden cave in the Pennine crags – and those messages were in the Red File.

While the family of the house slept, Delphine made her way down into the depths of the cellar. She took out a nail file from the large bag of tools she carried and tried to prise open the lock. It was too difficult. She fingered the pistol she kept in her raincoat pocket. But no, the noise of shooting would be too great; she tried again with the nail file. Just then there were footsteps approaching. The familiar creaks she had heard when she stepped down were repeated. She pressed herself into a dark corner, hidden from view.

The sandy-haired man looked innocent enough. He moved towards the file, rubbing his hands together. He put in his key – she held her breath, wondering if he would notice the lock had been tampered with. But he was chuckling too much to care. He drew out a document, looked at it, put it back. Then he locked the file and went upstairs.

114

Delphine sighed with relief. When the door at the top of the stairs creaked shut, the beam of light she had relied upon disappeared.

Delphine, who was good at seeing in the dark, because she had eaten a lot of carrots in her youth, could see enough to prise at the lock again. With a major effort, she made it.

It was worse than she had thought. For instead of military secrets, the file was full of pictures of ladies in the nude, lying in coffins. Thin ones, fat ones, tall ones, ugly ones, all lying in exotic carved boxes, which were lined with pastel satin. On each white neck, two little holes. Red. 'Uncle Alaric' as he was called by the secret service, was not just an ordinary spy – he was a vampire, too.

Delphine staggered up the stairs, filled with her secret knowledge. Now she had to catch the villain in the act. The only thing to do was to infiltrate his ordinary life and watch him day by day.

Delphine was a master of disguise and by changing her hair and her clothes she made herself look younger and turned up at the house.

'Hello, Uncle Alaric,' she said. 'I am your little niece from Australia.' His eyes narrowed. He licked his lips, looking at her thin white neck.

'Welcome, my dear,' he said, rubbing his freckled hands together. 'I am sure we will get along.'

She pretended to fit in with his life and that of his family. He was a curious man, only interested in coffins. She followed him carefully over the moors as he walked with his huge black dog.

One day she fooled him by letting him see her, making him go out of his way; then she said a cheerful goodbye and concealed herself behind a rock. He went over to a crag, pressed something at the side, and a sheet of rock slid open. She crept along on her belly and just managed to crawl in behind him.

The inside of the cave was·filled with coffins, like drawers, built on top of each other. He pulled them out at random, cackling all the time. 'Hello, my little beauties,' he was saying. 'My lovely collection.'

With horror she noticed that one of the coffins hadn't got

anyone in there. Looking at the brass label she saw the engraved name on it: 'Delphine'. She was so upset by this that her foot hit a little stone and shifted some earth. 'Uncle Alaric' turned towards the noise. His eyes were not their usual glazed blue but were bright red.

Delphine ran, scattering small stones as she went, down the gorse-impeded paths, the icy grass made her slip and slide. He could not go as fast as she did, but she could hear his heavy breathing behind her. Luckily she had made friends with Lucifer, his dog, and instead of obeying his master's instructions to 'Get her, go after her, Lucifer,' the dog just jogged along beside her, hoping for some of her weekly sweet ration.

What was she to do? Now he knew that she was aware of what he was, a vampire who kidnapped women and drank their blood, made coffins for them and kept them up on the cold moors.

She locked herself in the bedroom. 'Uncle Alaric' knocked at the door.

'Yes?' she said, feeling in her pocket for the pistol.

'What's wrong my dear, are you ill?' he said, making his voice gentle and kind.

'Yes, I have a bad cold, maybe the 'flu,' she said. She heard him go down. He didn't like germs.

But that night as it grew dark, she heard him come again.

'Let me in, let me in. I can cure you,' he said. 'I've made a little concoction for you to take.'

'Oh I am feeling a lot better, thank you,' she said. She put a pillow in her place on the bed and she stood behind the door. Not before time. He battered down the door with his inhuman strength.

He rushed past her, his black cloak around him, his fangs gleaming in the dim light. He fell upon the bed, tearing at what he thought was Delphine with his voracious teeth, expecting blood, getting feathers. He choked, gasped.

'Help me my dear. Help your old uncle . . . ' His eyes, like red coals, flashed at her, imploring.

'Certainly not,' said Delphine, cool as a cucumber. 'Think of all those poor women. I have a gun you know. I am not really your niece at all but the chief woman of the Secret Service.'

'You won't need the gun,' he spluttered. A stray feather lodged in his windpipe. He made a strange noise, like the wind in the pipes of the church organ, and then he choked to death before her eyes.

She put the gun back in her raincoat pocket, ready for her next assignment.

She searched the pockets of 'Uncle Alaric'. It was true, he was a Nazi spy. He had been sent on a one-man mission to destroy British women.

Delphine was promoted to Head of the Secret Service after that, the first woman to do so.

The women were brought down from their moorland cave and given a decent Christian burial. Delphine left the grey North and travelled down to London and the King gave her a medal for bravery.

21

It was Calum's eighteenth birthday, and his friends, old chums from before the time he was shipped from their midst to his public school, gathered in the dining room for the celebration.

They were shy, soft-spoken boys, with rough hands. Already the difference between them and Calum was marked. Sarah wished they would not be so subdued; even in her admiration for Calum, she did not see why they behaved that way. Aunt Lena beamed as she welcomed them in, noting, Sarah was sure, the difference Sarah herself noted, but with a different result.

'Come in, Frank, Norman, Alun,' she said, to the boys she and Calum had known from birth, but who now were to be worshippers at the shrine of her upgraded son. 'Come along, it's a long time since we've seen you all.'

Angela and Sarah were in charge of the buffet food. They had been up since six that morning preparing it and were to be allowed in later for dancing, if there were not enough girls. Two large tables had been placed together and covered with a lace cloth, the edging of which looked very familiar to Sarah. She couldn't place it for a moment and then she suddenly remembered Gran's hair-tidy, from what seemed an age ago. The lace was the same.

There was kipper pâté, and cold pork (Aunt Lena just happened to find a neighbour who had killed a pig) and meat-and-potato pie. They had sacrificed a few weeks' butter ration for the cake which stood at the centre of the table, bearing eighteen blue candles.

'Ma says it is probably the last of these big parties, Calum will be called up – it is a sort of farewell to all of them. They'll all be off to the War.'

Sarah went cold. Surely not Calum? But everyone else's golden boy had gone, so why not him? The lads were all talking about it.

'Why didn't Calum have anyone from his school?' Sarah asked Aunt Lena as they put out the silver.

'They couldn't get here with the railway the way it is these days,' she said. 'Anyway, these are his real friends.'

But they didn't seem to be. There were awkward gaps in the talk.

'It's like a morgue in there,' said Angela, leaning against the kitchen door. 'I shall have to put on a heavy jumper in a minute or I'll freeze to death.' Lena told her not to be silly.

Sarah answered another knock at the door and a bunch of girls stood there, giggling. They were not the types she would have associated with Calum – still, they might liven the party up. What about the twin-set and pearls types, like the one on the piano in a silver frame; where were they?

'Hello,' said Angela. She knew most of them – had been at school with them. 'Come on in, we need you. Here,' she said, opening the door of the dining room, 'get cracking.' There certainly was much more noise now, the gramophone was playing dance tunes. 'Thank God for our own sex,' said Angela, putting her arm around Sarah.

They went in with more food and refills for the punch bowl. Angela confessed to Sarah that she had poured in some brandy, to 'make the party go', as she said. But when they entered the room it wasn't exactly a riot. Most of the girls clung to the walls and the boys were chatting together.

'We'll have to do something,' said Angela. 'Let's dance together.' So they did, to a Carroll Gibbons record. The boys applauded and a few of them even asked the odd girl to dance. Sarah escaped.

Calum came out.

'Are you having a good time?' she asked him. He looked devastating in his dark suit, his familiar lock of hair falling over his eye.

'Very,' he said. 'Would you like a dance with the birthday boy?'

She nearly died of nervousness, but he steered her around

the carpet she had vacuumed not so many hours before. It was very romantic.

'Thank you,' she said, overwhelmed.

'That's all right. It's only me, you know.' *Only* him.

She had gone very red. Luckily at that moment Aunt Lena called her to help with coffee and she got out of an awkward situation. She could not talk to Calum for some reason.

A car drew up. Calum was at the door before she could reach it. It was the twin-set-and-pearls girl who was featured in the silver-framed picture on the piano. She slipped out of her coat and Calum handed it to Sarah to hang up. The other girls had gathered in the doorway to view the new arrival. It was odd, thought Sarah; in contrast to their lipsticked glitter Susan was almost plain, in her neat blue-wool dress, her hair simply drawn back in a coil. Brown hair, and, oh yes, the pearls. She did have a touch of lipstick and powder but not like the clowns who had arrived before.

'What's up with you now – jealous?' asked Angela as Sarah stood in the kitchen, looking sour. 'You can't be jealous of her, she's too dull.'

'That's your opinion,' said Sarah, rushing upstairs. She wiped off the rouge that Angela had persuaded her to tint her cheeks with and she tried to comb out her curls and make her hair look like Susan's – but it was hopeless – Angela had done it up in rag curlers for her the night before. She resembled a golliwog.

Sarah scrubbed at her face. Apparently, to Calum, plain was beautiful – she could see it now. There was something intangibly classy about Susan. Sarah couldn't change to a more conventional skirt and blouse because she would have to brave Angela's scorn. She was stuck with this awful floral dress that Lena had told her was a party frock. 'Never forget how she looks,' she told herself, fervently, 'because she looks *right.*'

She peered in to the dining room. Calum and Susan were dancing delicately, cheek to cheek. It seemed more romantic than when she and Calum were doing it, just minutes before. It had been superimposed on their dance, like a faulty snapshot. *Their* dance had been obliterated, disallowed by the fates.

She rushed down to the cellar and leaned her head against

the cool surface of the mysterious file. She could still hear the beat of the dance music from up there. It was possible, from here, to get herself into the old position of hatred. For a moment or two she had been wavering, sucked in by the punch and the music, the dance with her idol, into believing in the whole deal. Now, from the dark, she could tell herself that Calum was a bit of an upstart, a snob – that Angela was common, that Thelma, with her soft eyes and mawkish behaviour, was a silly Daddy's girl – and Lena, Lena was a boring woman, a martyr for *nothing*. Uncle Alaric she hated because she had pinned him in a story, and she hated herself for pinning him. She would never be trapped into gullibility again. This is the true me – Ellie's me, she said to herself.

She wanted to be back among the trivial, the amusement arcades and the strangers to whom one didn't owe loyalty or even politeness. All this family stuff was a sham. She wanted to keep moving, to go into dark, scented cinemas and escape. She hadn't read a book of any substance for months – she had lost the world of fiction in this world of domestic chores and relationships. She couldn't take all this normality. If she couldn't go back to Ellie's life, she wanted to die.

Die, she didn't. She ran off her anguish on the moors, with Henry panting beside her. She flung herself down on the soft earth and watched the sky spin around. She felt herself a small speck on a moving planet. It solaced her. It was great to be alone, to be free.

Calum went back for his last term before he joined the Army. If there had been no war he would have been going to university; as it was, Sarah saw him as doomed. Or, if not doomed, he would marry the twin-set-and-pearls, which was just as bad. He fell short of what she wanted for a hero. What she wanted was for a hero to recognize her.

Aunt Lena had taught her how to be a woman – or female, which wasn't quite the same. How to iron a shirt, doing the collar and long sleeves first, then the back, then the sides, and fold it, and make it look as if the laundry had done it; how to bake, dust and polish – in fact, thought Sarah, to be a doormat. Lena had missed the uniqueness of her, Sarah – to Lena she was just a female who must be taught female things. But the fact that she hadn't seen beyond that had made Sarah feel even more alone; instead of including her in the vast band of women, it had made her feel excluded, for she didn't like those things. 'You aren't the only pebble on the beach,' her Gran had always said to her. But you were. Each person was, to an extent, the only pebble on the beach. And each pebble was unique. That was the feeling she had lost since she gave up living with Ellie.

22

'I've got a date for you Saturday, first house pictures and an early dinner at the Grand,' Angela said. 'It's my fireman.'

'I can't go out with a fireman. I'm only ten and a half. Aunt Lena wouldn't let me. He wouldn't want to, either.'

'I told her you had a birthday tea. And he won't know until it is too late. I'll give you a note, saying why I can't go.'

'Why can't you go, Angela?'

'Because I've got a better offer. But I'll say I'm ill. 'Flu.'

'That's not fair. What will I say to him?'

'Just be yourself.'

'That won't be enough,' said Sarah, looking miserable. 'It never is.'

'He will do all the talking. He's the sophisticated type.'

'Then why are you trying to get rid of him?'

'I'm not. It's just that I want to see what this new one is like and Ian is so jealous.'

Angela's love life was always complicated. But when Sarah met any of the boys, who were described with zeal by Angela in their night-time conversations, they always seemed very shy and naïve, and not at all like she described them. Sarah asked what she should say Angela was doing.

'It will all be in the note. Not to worry.' When Angela said 'not to worry', Sarah always worried.

She stood outside the Odeon. Angela had put up Sarah's hair to make her look older. 'Lucky you are tall,' she had said, lending Sarah a pair of her new silk stockings. Sarah also had on a dress of Angela's that Angela said Ian had never seen on her. Sarah clutched a box of home-made toffee that Aunt Lena had forced on her for her friend's birthday present. She had been going to put it in the litter bin, but it occurred to her it might be good as an ice-breaker. She clutched Angela's note. But when she saw Ian loping around the corner she stuffed it in her pocket – for goodness knows what lies were in it. It was better to do it on her own.

'Angela has a cold,' she lied. 'She's awfully sorry but she thought you wouldn't want to waste the seats and all that, as you've booked.'

He blushed and muttered he was sorry she was ill. Sarah pushed the candy at him.

'Here. Angela made it for you just before she collapsed.' His face lit up again – it was like putting the light on.

For one moment Sarah could see he was contemplating turning in the tickets, so she marched in and stood where the usherette was waiting. Ian fumbled in his jacket pocket. They'd never have traded them in: there was hardly a soul in the place. Upper Circle, front row. That was very impressive.

'Why do you come to the first house?' She realized she was going to have to start all the conversations.

'I'm on duty later.'

'It must be exciting, fighting fires. Is that what you do, fight fires?'

'I haven't been there long. I'm just in the office so far. But I'm training.'

It was difficult to keep it up. Sarah asked him for a piece of toffee, which was a bit rude since she had given it, but he unwrapped it carefully and gave her a piece as if it were gold dust. She realized it must have special value for him because Angela's hands were supposed to have made it. Actually it was just bony old Aunt Lena's hands that had done it. They sucked and chewed.

The film was Betty Grable on some tropical isle. She hoped there wouldn't be much kissing in it, and there wasn't. Sarah sighed. It was heavenly to be in a cinema again – they never went, the family; it was what she missed most about not living with Ellie.

'Did Angela tell you we were going out to tea?' he asked as they left, going out into the darkening street.

'She did mention it – but you needn't bother if you don't want to.' He was well-brought-up, poor Ian.

'Oh, no – I have booked a table.'

The Grand was as empty as the cinema had been. They flapped large menus in front of their shy faces. The waiters hovered. She could see that Ian was put out, they had been given the evening menu, not high tea.

Her eyes lit on the magic words, 'french fried potatoes' – she had not had a sniff of such a delicacy as a humble chip since leaving home.

'Tomato soup, plaice and chips and peas,' she said. She held her breath, not believing it was possible.

'The same for me,' Ian said, handing back the menu.

There was a long silence.

'Betty Grable is supposed to have the best legs in the whole world,' Sarah announced.

'Oh yes?'

'Her teeth are a bit big, though, don't you find?'

'Yes.' Oh, Angela, she thought. What a liar you are. Sophisticated?

The bright soup arrived. Sarah tucked in. This was better than eating at Lena's. It was ages since she'd eaten out. She watched him slurp and blow. Is this why couples had these awful sessions, she wondered, to see how they ate soup – things like that which would become dreadful if you spent a lifetime together?

She would never spend a lifetime with Ian, for instance, because of this blow and slurp.

It had almost spoiled the film, going through this afterwards. She thought she would never like courting. You wanted to go into a cinema and lose youself in the images and the dark, not to be conscious of some oaf beside you.

Still, the chips were good. Heavenly, in fact. She wiped her chin with her napkin.

'Ice cream – coupe Jacques?' the anxious waiter again. Sarah pondered. Well, why not?

'Ice cream, please.'

Ian sighed. He had it too. He asked her if she drank coffee.

'Oh yes,' said extravagant Sarah. Poor Ian. Sarah wasn't allowed coffee at Aunt Lena's – it made you nervous, Lena said.

He actually made a remark as she was putting on her coat, stuffed to the gills.

'Angela is a very nice girl, don't you think?'

'Oh yes,' Sarah said. 'Absolutely.' He didn't seem to hear the sarcasm.

She managed to persuade him not to take her right home. It was difficult, she felt he wanted to get within the radius of wonderful Angela.

'You don't want to get her germs, do you?' she said. 'Just put me on the bus. I've had a wonderful time – I'll tell Angela all about it.'

He looked like Henry when he was deprived of his Winalot. He was still clutching the candy. The bus went up the hill. She saw the sad figure grow smaller.

Angela wasn't too pleased when she told her about the note.

'You mean he didn't get it? Give it to me then.' She tore it up. 'That was telling him to get lost. Now he'll expect to go out with me again.'

'I'm glad I didn't give it to him then. Poor Ian.' For now she saw the cinema visit and the chips in the rosy haze brought on by a filled stomach and satisfied mind.

'*Poor Ian?* – would you like to have to go through that again?' Sarah had to admit she would not.

The upshot of the date was that Aunt Lena discovered about it. Not only that, she found the Uncle Alaric story.

23

Ellie arrived on the coach to take back her erring daughter. She looked wonderful, in a green and black checked coat in the latest style, a green pleated skirt, and wedge-heeled shoes. She whispered to Sarah that she had managed to buy some clothing coupons from a friend who was hard up. Her hair was newly done, her lipstick and nail varnish matched exactly. Sarah felt again as she used to; that life was not quite so dour. Ellie, for instance, just laughed when she heard of the crimes that Sarah had committed.

The atmosphere was cold; Angela came to wave them off at the bus station. Sarah felt sorry for her as she stood shivering in the beginning drizzle, the chimney stacks of the mills obscured by mist. They hurtled out of the dull town. Poor Angela was still there, smothered by the family.

All that had been suggested was that Ellie should take Sarah back to Blackpool for a holiday but once they were released from Lena's disapproval they both giggled like schoolgirls. Sarah was sure Ellie would never send her back.

Uncle Alaric had been suffering from his chronic liver complaint, and was confined to bed for Ellie's spectacular entrance. When Sarah went up to say goodbye, he had risen, like an old prophet in the Bible, in his white nightshirt. Sarah wondered why he had not liked being written about as Dracula – it was, after all, more interesting for him.

'Never darken my doors again if you don't return by the beginning of term,' he had cried, dramatically. 'I shall not take you in.' Sarah couldn't believe it. Now they laughed about it on the coach. Ellie had to look in her little compact mirror to see if her mascara was running. 'Never darken my doors again—' she would intone, and they would both be off again.

Sarah began to feel a little guilty – after all, they had taken her in; had cherished her, in their own way.

'Lena taught me to iron shirts,' she said, looking out at the now flat country. The hills had disappeared.

'You won't need that skill. We're man-less as usual.' Ellie powdered her nose. 'Lena looks a fright. She is not an old woman – yet she behaves like one – why doesn't she make more of an effort?'

'She does,' said Sarah, 'but it's all for the family. All for Calum, really.'

'That dress makes you look like the Wreck of the Hesperus,' Ellie remarked. 'What have they done to you?'

It was true. Since the date with Ian, Aunt Lena had watched her like a hawk, for signs of premature sexual development. She was wearing one of Angela's old frocks, longish, and white cotton knee socks.

'We'll soon have you out of that and into some shorts. That hair style is terrible, too – needs cutting. Long hair saps your growth.'

Sarah smiled. Adults had such contrary views. Ellie had thrown a magazine on the seat beside her, *Life*. All the American girls of her age seemed to have lipstick and bobby sox. Sarah hoped Ellie didn't see her that way.

The coach entered the bus station. The smell of salt air hit Sarah and she felt she could breathe again. This was her natural habitat. Did you only feel comfortable in the air you were born to?

She realized she had forgotten to ask an all-important question.

'Where are we living now?'

'Oh, it isn't half bad. Two rooms in a Victorian house, near the Pleasure Beach. I got you into a school near there. I met this couple in Birmingham; they were fed up with the bombing, so they decided to move here. They are a bit – well, you'll see.'

They took a taxi.

'What was it like in Birmingham?' They sped through the damp, familiar streets. Sarah often longed for this wind, rain and sea when she'd been landlocked. They passed the

Rosenblooms' villa, and the aunts' neat house.

'The money was good, hence the new clobber. The bombing was something else,' said Ellie.

'We passed the Rosenblooms'. How are they?' Sarah asked.

'I wouldn't know. Only been back five minutes myself. He was sent to North Africa. She had a little girl.'

'And Joseph, what about Joseph?'

'Joseph?'

'The baby.' Her baby, Joseph Rosenbloom.

'He died. Didn't I tell you? I'm sure I wrote to you. Pneumonia. Just like I had, you know? That awful winter did it. They buried him in a fruit box, Gran said. Imagine, a fruit box. Gran had something to say about that, I can tell you.'

Joseph dead? But she had known him for almost every day of his life. It wasn't fair. He was the only person she knew who had died in the war. *Joseph.* Joseph Rosenbloom.

The cab drew up. The house was large, falling apart. A decaying privet overgrew the driveway. The windows were dirty and without the criss-cross of tape; perhaps no one cared any longer about air-raid precautions. There seemed to be a lot of people living there; soldiers, the odd staring child.

'We're on the ground-floor front, go along in,' said Ellie, paying off the cab. Sarah went into the sitting-room. A bedroom led off it. She put her case down on Gran's double bed. So Gran was back, too. The furniture was all exactly as it was at the Rosenblooms'. She said hello to the hair tidy and gave the commode a sly kick.

'Oh, I forgot to say, Gran's back.' Ellie stuck a few anemones that were lying on the table into an old honey jar. She put them in the window. They clashed with the curtains. 'What are you doing now?'

Sarah was tying the net draped curtains up with the two hair ribbons she had taken off her plaits.

'I want to see if it looks better like this.' She went outside into the road to have a look. It looked worse, if anything. She went in again and took them down.

'I'd forgotten you were such a fuss-pot. What do you think of it?' Sarah looked at Ellie. She looked like an eager dog. Sarah had forgotten how Ellie was always keen on new things, until her keenness would suddenly wear off.

'It's fine,' she said. 'Not bad.'

For a brief moment she longed for the ordered ritual of Aunt Lena's but it did not last long – there was one thing about living with Ellie, the time passed quickly and you never knew what might happen next.

The couple who owned the house, the Duffells, were unlike the Rosenblooms in every way. He, weasel-faced, about forty, had a heart condition which kept him out of active service. Mrs Duffell, large as a house normally, was swelled up in the fifth month of pregnancy, her stomach stuck out like a large armchair covered by a dust sheet. She slopped about in carpet slippers, the dark roots of her dyed blonde hair giving her a veneer of scruffiness, which, thought Sarah, was unnecessary – she was managing quite well without that extra refinement. Worst of all, Sarah discovered, there was already a little Duffell – Paddy – who had inherited his father's weasel looks. Paddy went to the school Sarah had been newly designated; she realized with horror that people might think he was her own brother.

She was worried about the eleven-plus, the Great Divide – they had lectured her at the school in Yorkshire. If you failed you would be on something called the Scrap Heap, and only get Dead-End Jobs. She had no idea what a Dead-End Job was; it seemed to her that most people did them. One thing was sure, she didn't want to join them. She decided she would like to be a doctor, and she got in ahead of the rush, buying a notebook at Woolworth's and drawing various parts of the anatomy from Ellie's *Home Doctor* book. If she started early she would beat all the others, and the medical schools would marvel at her prior knowledge. She was slightly put off by one of the soldiers living in the house: he was a medical orderly; his fingernails were black as ink and when she asked him about medicine he pulled her on to his knee, and, forcing her mouth open, stuck his large tongue into it, and rolled it around. She avoided him after that. Surely all medical practitioners were not so rude?

Mrs Duffell complained she didn't get enough money from the Government to feed all these young soldiers. Sarah felt sorry for them: they were homesick, most of them, had just left their mums, and landed in this place – to be sent Lord-knows-where, to fight. Were they Dead-Enders too? They seemed like it, with their fags and their beer. They played cards at the dining room table, and read *Lilliput* and *Men Only*, snorting at the naked women.

Mr Duffell ('call me Liam') was always bothering Sarah. He would sit alone in the darkened kitchen, smoking a cigarette, holding it backwards in his cupped hand, like Humphrey Bogart. His hand was stained yellow by this practice. He would call her over.

'Don't tell anyone what you've seen,' he would say, pointing down to what seemed to be a pink Wall's sausage in his lap. He would be moulding it like plasticine. She didn't know what he was on about.

He would stand in his bedroom doorway when she was on her way to the bathroom, wearing just his pyjama top, and this sausage would wave at her. She thought he was daft and knew she should mention it to Gran or Ellie, but she couldn't find the words to describe it. He seemed so proud – it seemed a pity to tell on him. He tinkered with an old motorbike most of the time and was always offering her rides, which she refused.

'Why don't you go off for a nice spin in the country,' said Gran. 'You are a silly girl.'

'I don't want to – he's weird,' Sarah would say.

'You are the weird one.'

Mrs Duffell miscarried. There were bloody rags in a barrel in the back yard. Mr Duffell was distraught. He came out to have a chat with Sarah who was pinning paper flowers on to the dead forsythia bush.

'What are you doing?'

'Making it a bit brighter out here,' she snapped. They could see the bush from their bedroom window.

'I'm very unhappy,' he ventured.

'Oh yes?' she said. 'Couldn't you do something to this garden? It is so drab out here.'

'Haven't got time, have I?' He stood behind her and put his hand up her navy-blue school skirt.

'Get off. I told Gran about you,' she said.

'You'll like that kind of thing when you are older,' he shouted at her, going back in. 'You won't refuse it then.'

She ignored him. He was scared off by the reference to Gran.

Ellie had a mysterious boyfriend. Everyone in the house was suspicious of him, except Ellie. He was Polish and looked like a matinee idol from an early thirties film with his little black moustache and slick hair. He was very correct, almost clicking his heels when he spoke to the assorted women: Ellie, Gran and Mrs Duffell. He didn't do it to Sarah – she assumed there must be an age for heel-clicking and she had not reached it.

'I think he is a spy,' said Gran to Sarah, 'except that he looks so much like one, he'd have to be a fool to be one.'

He took Ellie out to Yates's Wine Lodge, and they drank vodka and Polish spirit, then spent evenings locked together on the rug, staring into the fire, like Greta Garbo and John Gilbert in *Queen Christina*.

'They are too old for all that,' sniffed Gran. 'Still, she needs a bit of masculine company. She has had a rough time, all work and no play.'

The Pole took Ellie and Sarah to the biggest department store in town. He bought Ellie some expensive scent, and told Sarah to choose whatever she wanted from the children's department. She thought he must be mad – some of that stuff was very dear. Serve him right if she chose something that would bankrupt him. She couldn't make up her mind. It was like the celluloid dolls all over again. Deciding to despise his offer, she chose a *Girl's Annual*, which she could have afforded herself.

'You should have chosen something you really wanted,' said Ellie, whispering to her as they left the store. 'He is very fond of you.'

Sarah thought Ellie was losing her marbles.

Marek disappeared one night, taking another airman's expensive flying boots and the contents of Ellie's wallet. Luckily there wasn't much in there, she had not been paid.

'Told you so,' said Gran. But she had not told anyone anything. She was slipping, Sarah thought. She did not have the same powerful effect here as she had at the Rosenblooms'. The young soldiers just laughed when she issued one of her old

132

vitriolic outbursts or her platitudes about life.

Two things happened to Sarah: she passed the eleven-plus, and she was given an old pair of boots and skates by someone who was leaving the house. The eleven-plus was regarded lightly by Ellie and Gran, who, of course, had not heard about Dead-End Jobs. 'We knew you would pass, you're bright enough. What's the fuss?' Gran said. That was that.

Ellie was worried about what school to choose from the list. She fancied a posh private one; all grey-flannel uniforms and good shoes – Sarah hoped against hope that it would be over-subscribed. She could not cope with that kind of thing. Eventually she got a place at the Grammar; Ellie put her down for free dinners and a clothing grant, which made Sarah wonder how they would have managed had she been sent to the other place.

The ice skates were primitive, not serrated on the edges but good enough to learn on. The boots were brown. Sarah whitened them with tennis shoe whitener. They looked a bit odd. They were the key to this new, bright, ammoniac world which had been hidden without her knowledge in the Pleasure Beach, among the papier-mâché laughing sailors and the Big and Little Dippers.

Each Saturday she went to the morning session. The white expanse always thrilled her – it was like a fresh field of snow. Untouched. Then the good skaters came and marked out their practice areas, which meant the others weaved in and out of these earnest characters who had something to work for.

Sarah clung to the barrier, ankles aching. Each week she got a little more confidence, but she wasn't able to do more than skate in a straight line. She realized she was not physically very daring. You needed lessons to get any further. Here, too, there was a hierarchy: the skaters were graded as carefully as animals at the Fylde Show: there were medallists or those competing for medals; there were the ones who took lessons and who made quite a good show, and then there was the crowd, the scattered hangers-on to the barrier, and Sarah was one of these.

Dorothy Gynn, whom she knew from school, took lessons and attempted to teach Sarah. But Sarah was a coward and wouldn't attempt anything difficult, and Dorothy gave up, whizzing out to the centre to do her own spins and jumps.

'You have to forget yourself, like this—' and Dorothy would weave in and out of the crowd, going backwards, trying a spin, or a split jump before she returned, breathless, to the barrier, and Sarah.

'I can't forget myself.' She began to hate the rink, like the old phantom of the Tower. Even when she had sold the skates, and done a paper round, and bought a sparkling new pair of skates and boots, it was still no better. They were perfection, those skates. She would stare at them for hours, running her fingers along the stainless-steel cutting edge; once on her feet they were useless. Then Paddy began to pester her to take him skating and she had an excuse to give up.

Dorothy and Sarah gave concerts in aid of the Red Cross. Dressed in costumes 'borrowed' from the wardrobe of Dorothy's parents, who were professionals, appearing in an ENSA tour of *The Desert Song,* the girls sang and danced for charitable reasons. It was hard to gather an audience; they forced the billeted soldiers to attend, and children from school. Paddy was put on commission to provide spectators, a penny a person. He wasn't good at it and they smacked his legs when he failed.

Clad in men's raincoats and tin hats, they sang, 'We're Sons of the Old Contemptibles' and 'It's a Long Way to Tipperary'; Dorothy then tapped her way through 'Yankee-Doodle-Dandy' and for this she wore tennis shorts, a gold lamé top and a collapsible opera hat (a relic from Eric) on her red curls. Paddy was persuaded, under duress, to sing 'Danny Boy' and then Sarah ended the show warbling 'Land of Hope and Glory' draped in a Union Jack with a tin tray as a shield. She was meant to be Britannia.

'You can't force people to see the show. You are becoming a regular little Hitler,' said Gran, who was seeing it for the third time.

Everyone was getting fraught because the raids had started and, most nights, sleep was disturbed by a trek down to the Anderson shelter. It smelled of dank cement and damp brickwork – they crept there in assorted night gear, curlers in, teeth out. There had been a communal effort to make it comfortable, with cushions and travel rugs, and candles in bottles; but, apart from Sarah who enjoyed it, there was a dispirited air about the gatherings. Ellie didn't bother to go, saying she would rather be blown out of bed than face Mrs Duffell in night attire – but Gran always went and so did Sarah. The people there didn't like each other even in safe daylight; the proximity of bombs and the fear of death did not therefore bring them together in what they had heard, in London, was called the Blitz spirit. Mrs Duffell read her cheap thrillers and hogged the candlelit areas. Paddy whined and moaned. Mr Duffell stared at Sarah and then at Gran; Sarah could see he was wondering how much Gran knew and whether they would all go up in smoke to meet their maker together.

Gran often tried to jolly things up with a sing-song but only got hostile stares. Sometimes one of the more vulnerable soldiers would come down too, but the atmosphere was so bad that they rarely attempted it twice.

'Missed us again, you bastards,' Mrs Duffell would cry as the All-Clear sounded and everyone shuffled back to their beds. No one expressed surprise or thanks that they had been spared. It wasn't dramatic as London must be, thought Sarah; there was just the odd plane, the throb, the silence, the whine and the crash. If your number was on it, it wouldn't matter that it was a single plane. Gradually the raids got fewer and they stopped going down.

Sarah and Dorothy, bored with entertaining for charity, decided to opt out of the war. They wanted to live in the dream world of the Chalet School. This world was fostered by their reading of the *Chalet School* books, by Elinor Brent-Dyer.

At the Chalet School the girls were all exclusive, daughters of European nobility, or rich, interesting people. They were educated, these girls, high in the Tyrol, far from the gloom of ration books and sirens and clothes rationing. There, skis and hot chocolate and torten and black-clothed serious mademoiselles who were expert in literature and languages, and unlucky in love, took their place.

'*Grüss Gott,*' she and Dorothy would say, on meeting to go to the terrors of the primary school – the scoffing boys and the sneering girls. 'We're much too good for them,' they sniffed, fresh from the splendours of Austria. Dorothy was 'Katrine' and Sarah 'Isabelle'. Their father (Charles Boyer) had been a Hungarian Count, but he was in exile. Their mother (culled from the *Tatler* in the public library reading room) was English, blonde and aristocratic. Their siblings came from a photograph of the cricket team at Calum's school. Sarah had pinched it from Aunt Lena's drawer. Dorothy asked if Paddy Duffell could be a cousin as he hung around so much. Sarah said no.

'If you let the Duffells in, you might as well give up.' Sarah was annoyed because she had seen her father in the library when she had been looking for 'mother' and she didn't want reality to break in on the Game.

'Those two are up to no good,' said Gran. 'Whispering and giggling.'

'*Grandmère est folle, n'est ce pas?*' Sarah said. They were practising French, for the Grammar, next term.

Ellie started coughing blood again. Or, as Sarah preferred to think, Isabelle's mother, the Countess, was suffering from her rare hereditary disease. The Countess went off to stay in the country, to recover.

Grandmère also was called away, to attend to Margaret's baby. Isabelle was left to the tender mercies of the old family retainers, the Duffells. Dorothy/Katrine was getting bored with the Game.

Sarah/Isabelle, left to her own devices, read the cheap romances and thrillers Mrs Duffell had around the house. She read all night, eyes popping, all the lurid stories of nice young girls betrayed, of nurse-doctor romances, of strange happenings in magnificent houses, governesses falling for tyrannical owners, of farm girls being kicked in the stomach when pregnant and turning out badly in the big city, of tight-lipped detectives in Los Angeles, solving impossible crimes. The feverish sub-sexuality tired her; she went back to *Jane Eyre*.

The Game, languishing because of Dorothy's defection, died. She and Dorothy ceased to see each other; Dorothy seemed afraid that the Game would be mentioned at the new school. She made Sarah swear to give it up. Sarah swore, feeling obscene about it now. Dorothy had made her feel it was like reading those romances by candlelight.

The mistake had been to include another person in her fantasy – from now on she would not.

The Countess, Ellie, appeared again. They were to move. The new place was the Ranelagh Hotel – which, oddly enough, could have been the family *Schloss* from the Game – standing, as it did, above the town, a granite castle.

24

The proprietor of the Ranelagh was Austrian, originally, but prided himself on being British now. He mentioned it often, not knowing that Ellie had admired the unmentionable Adolf, before his prime, or that Sarah lived in the Game. Sarah tried *'Grüss Gott'* on him once or twice, but he looked around guiltily, and she gave up.

Ellie was the under-housekeeper. The head housekeeper was an elegant Swiss lady, who had a lovely daughter who was not that much older than Sarah. Marianne had left school already and did office work in the hotel, and had many admirers of all nationalities.

The hotel was being done over, after an influx of Army brass who had now departed, leaving it battered and scruffy. Sarah and Ellie were given a grand room overlooking the sea until the staff flats were ready. The beautiful green lounge seemed familiar to Sarah; she couldn't make out why. It had a feeling of being a saloon on a boat. It hit her, suddenly – it was like one of the Astaire-Rogers films, with its marbled florid furnishings, its mirrors, its ornate 'thirties nostalgia. At last she was living in suitable surroundings for fantasy.

Prinz, the German shepherd dog, became her constant companion, in walks along the mined and barbed-wire-covered beaches. She had no sense of danger. It was all up to chance. She looked for driftwood and treasure trove from wrecked ships.

It was all remote and elegant. Sarah felt she was living in a movie. Marianne was the heroine, the blonde glamour of her attracted the milk-fed American officers. Sarah was playing the vivacious younger sister, June Allyson or Jane Powell, except she couldn't sing. She liked the formality of the life in a big hotel. She didn't see much of Ellie.

'I wonder if I will grow up like Marianne,' she said wistfully one day. She was trying on her new hockey gear for the Grammar.

'You'll never be like her,' said Ellie. Sarah couldn't make out if Ellie was disappointed or the opposite. One never knew with Ellie.

Damn – she would have to meet someone who was like a real film star, thought Sarah, as she tried on the ugly tasselled cap and the navy blue raincoat she had thought so wonderful before they came to the Ranelagh. The black stockings weren't bad – the uniform otherwise was awful. She made an attack on her hair, cutting it short, removing her braids for a more gamine look – she resembled Paddy Duffell, with his pudding basin cut. Ellie whipped her off to her own hairdresser who was a trichologist. Ellie had thought for some time that she was going bald and spent a fortune trying exotic medicaments for this condition. They were in pretty containers but they smelled out the bedroom when Ellie rubbed them into her scalp. Percy Harbottle assured Ellie they were doing her some good. He assured Sarah she needed a slight permanent wave for her newly cropped hair. She emerged looking like a Zulu.

'I have to start the new school looking like this. You shouldn't have let him do it,' cried Sarah. 'They will think this is the real me.'

She was worried about the real her. Ellie said it was because she was growing up.

Sarah sobbed at night. If the head housekeeper was Mary Astor and her daughter was like Ingrid Bergman and Ellie was Paulette Goddard, why did she have to turn out like King Kong?

'It will grow out.' Ellie tried to hide her disappointment and her loss of faith in Percy Harbottle. If he had done that to Sarah, who knew what would happen to her? She stopped using the creams on her scalp. She did not go bald.

Sarah prayed that Mr Becker would fall in love with Ellie and marry her (when she got divorced from Eric) and they would be rich and live here for ever. She could smoke a cigarette in a long holder – when she was older – and entertain the guests. She saw Mr Becker offer Ellie a glass of crème de menthe, and crossed her fingers.

The cook, an émigrée Hungarian, was Sarah's best friend.

Sylvia had been away on a shopping trip in Europe when the war stranded her in London. She had, in her private things, pictures of her children and her husband, in silver frames. Furs and couture dresses filled her cupboard. She said to Sarah that she was marking time until she could return. Until she decided to earn her living as a cook when her money had run out, she had rarely even been in a kitchen. She had given the menus to her own cook every day at home.

'This won't last for ever. Then I'll find them again,' she said. She never heard, although she sent Red Cross parcels. Sarah thought her very brave. Why were they different from Sylvia? It was, she decided, because Sylvia was marking time – they were not. What they were doing was *them* – it was the way they were.

Sylvia told her to get a profession – not to be indulgent as she had been.

'Look at me – I am no good for anything,' she said, showing Sarah her plump little hands which were stained from cutting up vegetables for her marvellous soups. 'Don't be like me.'

Sarah knew she wouldn't because she was bright at school, in the fast A stream. Also, she was in love with learning, with the smell of the text books and the exercise books with the crest on the front.

The second week after term started she was ill with a high fever. Marooned in the large double room, overlooking the cliffs, she was driven wild by the fact that they were all there, learning, getting ahead of her. Already she was different enough, living in an hotel – the teachers had asked her about that. And now that she was losing out, it haunted her. She couldn't any longer remember how to find the classroom in the long corridors. At times it seemed as if it was a dream, and she had never been there at all. She would never be able to go back. What was wrong with her and Ellie? They never did anything the right way. Even Sylvia was more at home than they were – and she was a refugee. Was it possible to be a refugee in one's own country?

Sylvia had plans to leave the hotel, get her own apartment, and make a living creating fur hats and handbags from her fine clothes; she said the Americans would lap them up. One evening, when Sarah was a little better, they had a sort of fashion show with Marianne as the model, and Marianne's American contacts bought the lot. Sarah saw that Sylvia would not be among them for long.

Out walking, the week before she was due back at school, Sarah came across a shop window full of little wooden dolls, three inches high, like the ones used for art students to teach them anatomy. She rushed back to the hotel to get some money to buy one or two of them; when she returned, the shop had disappeared. She walked the town, trying to find it. She asked at various antique shops. One man said that the dolls sounded to be like the little mascots that Victorian gentlemen wore in their hats on Derby day. If she could tell him where she had seen them, he would be interested to buy. She burst into tears.

It seemed to prove what she had been suspecting all along. She and Ellie were mad – unlike everyone else. It was why she feared going back and finding her way around the school, it was why they would not ever escape as Sylvia would.

Ellie took her to a nerve specialist. He said she was growing fast and gave her vitamin pills.

On one of her walks with Prinz, she met Eric. She had her autograph book with her and she asked him for his autograph – she didn't know why. Still, he had once been a political candidate. All the other people in it were slightly famous – Rawicz and Landauer, the duet pianists; Sid Field, the comedian, and Vivien Leigh, who had been on tour in *The Doctor's Dilemma*. She hoped Eric wouldn't write his name near Vivien. She was hoping to get Laurence Olivier some time. Of course Eric did write there. He wrote:

'Be good, sweet maid, and let who will be clever.' She was very disappointed. She didn't believe the remark. She intended to be the cleverest woman on earth. He put 'Eric Shand' after it, tipped his hat and was away. She would have torn it out, but the book would have come unstitched.

'He signed his full name, isn't that odd?' she told Ellie.

'I hope you still respect your father,' said Ellie. 'He couldn't

141

help what happened, you know.'

Sarah thought about it. She did respect him, in a way, because he so obviously did not give a damn. From her stay at Aunt Lena's she had seen what family life was like and she could see why Eric and Ellie couldn't stand that. Still, the way she and Ellie lived wasn't much either. What was the answer?

'I hate families. I never want to have one,' she said to Ellie. Ellie looked disturbed at that.

Now it was Ellie's turn to be sick again. It had to be kept hidden from Mr Becker in case Ellie lost her job. So Sarah rushed home from school to slap on the kaolin poultices as she had seen Gran do; all the time saying to Mr Becker that Ellie had a bout of 'flu.

She sat doing her homework in the evenings, watching Ellie rant and rave in delirium. Sylvia said she must call in a doctor. Sarah stuck it out – refusing. Sylvia told her she was hard. But Sarah knew that Ellie must not be sent to hospital or they would be without anywhere to live.

Her school books reeked of kaolin. She wasn't doing too badly there, finding herself good at English and history. Gradually, Ellie's fever went down; she was able to crawl about. Sarah was relieved again.

Marianne celebrated her engagement to a Polish count who had been in the airforce. He was not like the Charles Boyer one of the Game – he had a nose like a paper knife and yellow skin. His hair was thin and greasy. So much for romance, thought Sarah.

'You must leave off these things or someone will notice,' she said to Ellie as she slapped on yet another poultice. The coagulated mass was like chewing gum. 'There's a new housekeeper; you have lost your chance with old Becker.'

'Never had a chance,' said Ellie, coughing. 'I wouldn't marry again, anyway.'

This shook Sarah. Was life always to be like this, then? She thought her mother should make the most of her looks – she was getting old, she was thirty-five or so – and soon she would be past it. She should be taken care of and should be off Sarah's hands.

A thought struck her.

'Did you love Eric – my dad?'

'I worshipped him,' said Ellie.

Sarah couldn't believe it. It was worse than Marianne and the Count; it wasn't remotely like love in the films. Surely what she had seen was not what love was supposed to be. Had Ellie just decided to drift along now that love was over, taking Sarah with her?

Ellie didn't get on with the new housekeeper. They decided to move on. She was going away to visit a sister of Gran's in the country and take the local papers to job hunt. Sarah was to stay at the aunts'.

'It will be better for you – with exams coming up,' Ellie said. Sarah had to smile. Ellie had never even thought of exams before. She would find it awkward having to see Eric. She packed her case. At least it would be quiet by the bowling green.

Before they left the Ranelagh, Sylvia got her flat and invited them to tea. There was kassler, black rye bread and a hazelnut cake. The tea was served in bone-china cups. The flat was neat and pretty. Sarah yearned for something like this. Ellie put the kassler, which she thought was raw bacon, into the potted plant. The trouble with Ellie, thought Sarah, was that she had no curiosity. What seemed like adventurousness was just Ellie being knocked about by fate. Whereas Sylvia was building a possible existence, here, in this town.

'Why couldn't we do that, get an apartment, make our own place?' she asked Ellie.

'Too much bother, we couldn't manage financially,' said Ellie. She means she has to support me, thought Sarah. Ellie left for her week off in the country. Sarah looked for a job for the weekends.

'GIRL WANTED. ARTIST'S STUDIO. WEEKENDS or EVENINGS.'

That would be ideal. Sarah went along after school with a copy of the form magazine in her satchel – she had designed the cover. Perhaps she would be like one of Leonardo da Vinci's pupils, filling in the background while the master worked on the main bits. But was there a Leonardo da Vinci in Blackpool?

The studio was a long shed, where a line of blue-overalled girls sat painting the dots on the turbans of negress wall plaques. Another line of girls did the lips and teeth. A further table was devoted to cheeky little white dogs with panting red tongues. They were ugly, the ugliest things Sarah had ever seen. Examples of them hung on the walls, along with some flying ducks – a little more tasteful, these – she had seen them in houses she had visited. People must actually buy these things.

A girl slightly older than Sarah asked her what she wanted, eyeing her satchel. The girl removed the gum she was chewing and stuck it under the table.

'Are you wanting someone?'

Sarah pulled out the advertisement.

'I came about the job – I'm good at art.'

'Hey, girls – she's good at art.' They all giggled. The girl wasn't even looking as she did the dots on the turbans; they passed by her and she dabbed automatically.

'You don't need to be good at art here, love,' said an older woman, with hair like an angry Brillo pad. 'How old are you, pet?'

Sarah hesitated.

'Fifteen,' she said.

'You don't look it,' said the original girl. 'Ought to wear a bit of make-up if you are going to lie about your age.'

'Leave her alone. I'll go and get Mr Bonallack,' said the older woman. Sarah both feared and hoped that she would be taken on. It wasn't anything like she had expected, but the smell of paint was nice, and you really couldn't expect a real artist in Blackpool.

Mr Bonallack turned out to be an elderly Scottish gentleman.

'You were maybe expecting something different?' he said, seeing her glances at the plaques. 'The main thing here is to be quick, to keep the line moving. These girls are all good, fast workers. They've been at it for some time. Do you think you could keep up with them?'

'I could try.'

'We need someone Saturday mornings when Josie can't

come. She has to look after her kids then. Five bob an hour. Will that suit you?'

'Oh yes.' She had got it – her first job.

'Overalls provided. We'll give you a week's trial, or maybe two – don't forget, it's the speed we want.'

She was a professional artist. She was going to paint for money.

The aunts didn't like her having a job, but she persuaded them that it would help her with art at school. She hoped they would never see one of the products.

Saturday, she put on an overall like the others. They placed her in the middle, doing yellow spots on green turbans. She dabbed persistently, sometimes hitting, sometimes missing. Lois, chewing her gum, did the ones she missed. Sometimes Sarah's dots were square.

'Hurry up, young Sarah, you are not in the art class now.' They treated her with amused affection. She had permanent spots before her eyes.

'Don't worry,' said Lois, 'you'll get the hang of it. It is a kind of rhythm. Who buys the damn things, I'd like to know.'

Sarah liked working with the women; she was intrigued by their lives.

'Do you like doing this?' she asked the older woman while they had a tea break.

'It's better than the biscuit factory, love. And the money isn't bad.'

Josie had a husband who had been reported missing. She was the one Sarah was replacing. Her children were home from school Saturdays, and she couldn't work. But Josie was an exceedingly fast worker; she was nicknamed 'Speedy' – the others laughed about this. They called Sarah 'Speedy 2' but she knew they didn't mean it – the negresses' heads piled up at her place and she needed help to get them along. The second week they moved her on to dogs' tongues. She missed the old crowd at the negresses' table. It was slower, though, with the dogs. Her own tongue rolled out in sympathy as she did each panting red object. It was enough to put you off dogs for life.

'Who buys these?' she asked her neighbour.

'Fairgrounds, mostly – haven't you seen them? Bet you'll never want to win one now.'

The women were good-humoured and nice to each other. They had a collection for Josie's kids because their Dad was missing.

'She used to bring the kids in but they were bored and started smashing the place up,' said Lois. They all knew each other well and covered up for anyone who was feeling ill or who wanted to go out for a quick smoke. Sarah decided she liked the life, working among the women.

Sarah asked Mr Bonallack why he did these particular objects.

'It's modern art, you see. Wall plaques, a new trend. People like to be modern.'

'Couldn't we do different colours? The turbans, I mean.' Sarah thought the yellow on green was awful.

'Ah, but they are my best line. Sell well, they do. Why should we change them? The ducks are more for your traditional-type home – classy. The little dogs are just novelties. But the negresses—'

She could see it was no use. She tried to persuade the girls to do an odd, different one, but they wouldn't.

'Leave things as they are,' said the older woman. 'Mr Bonallack knows best. We don't want to muck about with new ideas.'

Josie wanted to come back on Saturdays. Her mother had come to live with her to help with the children.

They had a collection for Sarah and bought her a negress's head, as a goodbye present.

She couldn't take it to the aunts' house and she had nowhere of her own. She hated it, anyway, so she took it to the beach and buried it in the sand.

25

The aunts had another guest while Sarah was there; a Canadian soldier, a vague cousin, who had had half his face badly scarred by a shell. He stayed in his room as much as she did (she was swotting for exams) and sometimes they met in the neat bright kitchen. He was conscious of his injury and always swung around to thrust it at the recipient, as if his bravery in doing so would negate the shock. Sarah was, after the first dreadful time, prepared for this.

'Sit over here, it's my best profile,' he said, attempting his usual jocular references. He passed her the teapot. 'I find it strange, the fact of you being Eric's daughter. I wasn't even aware he had a daughter.'

'Well, he isn't very aware of it either – as you may have noticed.' She chewed on a piece of toast, trying to remember a few history dates.

It had been easy to work there with her own room, the guest room Ellie had sobbed in, all those years before, overlooking the bowling green where she had sat with Joseph Rosenbloom.

'Did you know you had a Canadian cousin, twice-removed?'

'No,' she said, 'but then – we're not the usual kind of family. Ellie and I just drift about, you know. I'm not here for long. They are very kind,' she finished.

'I *know*,' he said. They laughed. She liked Ivor. To her it didn't seem to matter about his face. But then she hadn't ever seen him before. He grinned at her with his slit-and-patched mouth.

'I asked Aunt Frances what they thought when Ellie walked out,' said Sarah. 'She said "we never spoke of it". Can you imagine?'

'It's a different generation,' said Ivor. 'We are tougher, don't you think? I want to ask you something tough.'

She quaked a bit, inwardly at that. She wasn't good at dissembling.

'What?'

'Do you think any woman will be able to look at this face? Permanently, I mean.'

She swallowed.

'I don't see why not.' She tried not to ooze out of it by being sentimental. 'I like you, Ivor. You are the only person I have been able to talk to, really.' It wasn't what he had asked.

He leaned over and kissed her on the cheek. She knew she wouldn't flinch and she didn't.

They looked out at the neat daffodils and crocuses, all, in their own way, perfect among the white rockery of the tidy garden.

'Are you going to stay in England?' she asked him after an awkward silence.

'No, I'll go back. I have to face all the people who knew me before this. I don't want to start somewhere new – it would be opting out.'

'Did you have a girl at home?'

'No.'

'I don't notice it, now I know you. Everyone will be like that, you'll see. People are like that.'

'You really believe that, don't you, Sarah?'

No, she didn't. But her inner scars were worse than his outer ones, and she was not going to reveal them to him. She hated herself for it because she considered being kind was a soft option.

'I don't want pity,' he said.

'I know.'

'When I get back, they'll be at the station to meet me; my parents, my little sister – how about that?'

She knew he was bitter and there was nothing she could ever do to change that.

'You are lucky in a way because they won't care – they love you,' she said.

'I'm sorry. What a stupid conversation.'

'No,' she said, 'it's fair enough. But at least they will care.

My dad wouldn't even notice.'

'That isn't true.' Now he *did* believe that.

'I asked him for his books. He said "no". Just like that – "no". I think he owes me.'

'Perhaps he feels you chose your mother over him.'

'I doubt he cares.'

'Then you may be wrong about the people who care about this.' He waved a hand over the bad side of his features.

'I'm not talking about people. Just him.'

'He's a bright man. He quotes Shakespeare at me by the yard. He discusses the political situation.'

'Ah, well, he's good at that.' She picked up her satchel. 'I have to go.'

'Sarah—' he hesitated. 'You hate him quite a bit. Let it out, otherwise you'll be in trouble later on.'

'I don't hate him. I don't feel a thing.'

And she rushed out, convinced she meant it, while Ivor poured himself another cup of tea.

26

Ellie was optimistic again after her spell in the country. She had another job lined up – helping to run a small private hotel. A couple had advertised for someone to help train the staff as they themselves had no experience. Fourteen bedrooms, neat and pretty, it stood at the opposite side of town from the Ranelagh.

Mr Bates was a plump elderly man, who was the virtual twin of General Eisenhower. He was recovering from a heart condition. She, Mrs Bates, was an enormous woman, jovial behind her bi-focals. The only drawback as far as Sarah could see was that they had a daughter, also Sarah, aged eight.

'Not another kid, after Paddy Duffell – I can't stand it,' Sarah complained.

'It's a nuisance, you both being Sarah,' said Ellie.

'I suppose she'll be Sarah One and I'll be Sarah Two,' sighed Sarah.

Sarah One was a sweet girl, even Sarah Two had to admit that. She was delicate with a certain solemnity about her. The miracle was that two such lumpen, older parents had produced, late in their life, this flower. She was given everything they could provide, which, as they were hard-working and self-effacing, was considerable. Private school-ing, white kittens, mini-pianos, had all fallen into her lap – and all had made her sweeter, not spoiled. There was none of the steak-and-kidney-pudding-armpit quality Sarah Two had come to associate with schoolgirls in this neat package. But then, the Grammar lot wore serge, the private lot grey flannel; the Grammar girls had holey black wool stockings, the private ones pure silk. The private girls never seemed to get spots, while the others had the lumps and pustules of pre-puberty.

Why, oh why? moaned Sarah Two, in the privacy (comparative) of the bedroom she shared with Ellie. She tried to pretend it was apparent that her lot had more brains – but even that was not true. Sarah One was a whizz at natural history and biology – what was more, she worked at it, collecting specimens, reading. Sarah Two groaned. What hope was there when the cards were stacked against you?

The first few months were bad. Sarah Two was jealous though the kitten got run over on the promenade and the gold and cream mini-piano lay untouched. Sarah Two then realized the difference between herself and Sarah One. Sarah One had been born without hunger. Sarah One saw the world as a benign place. Sarah Two knew her advantages were hunger and the fact she did not see the world as a benign place. She was way ahead.

She bought two copies of sheet music; 'The Blue Danube' and 'Tales from the Vienna Woods' and ploughed through them, seated at the mini-piano. She was as inept as she was on the skating rink.

Summer came and Sarahs One and Two were thrown together in mutual escape from the routine of the hotel. The cook packed them a picnic lunch and they were off for the day, exploring rock pools, making large holes in the sand and lying there, reading, as brown as berries.

Sarah One tried to teach Sarah Two to swim. She was a sinuous water baby herself, daring and graceful – but Sarah Two's cowardice won through and she could not trust the perfect creature to tutor her.

There was a conscious element of sadism in the relationship – Sarah Two tried to suppress it; it was all too easy to dominate Sarah One because of her nature. Her beautiful temperament was a constant challenge. She had sand accidentally, on purpose, kicked at her, or her book dropped in a pool. Her lunch was pinched or her back went red raw because Sarah Two would not rub suntan oil on it when requested. All this had no effect on Sarah One's affection for Sarah Two.

'I wish you didn't like me so much,' she said to Sarah One. 'You want to watch it, you are too good to live.'

'What do you mean?' Sarah One was all eyes.

'I mean the good die young, like Beth in *Little Women*. The good always do.'

'Then I'll go to God, won't I?' Sarah Two couldn't believe it; all that *and* faith too.

They spent a lot of time scrambling over cliffs to collect Sarah One's flora and fauna for her collection. She had them all neatly pressed and labelled. It was like a small exclusive museum, her room. Sarah Two saw that the other Sarah had talent in that direction – she had won prizes at school; and here *she* was, spending her summer as Sarah One's little helper. Sarah One said she might become a marine biologist.

'Great,' said Sarah Two. No doubt she would make it. She'd probably win the bloody Nobel prize.

Sarah Two was suffering the pangs of unrequited love, for the games mistress, Diana Gorman. Diana was a surrogate male for a lot of the girls, Sarah included. Diana looked like Calum, from the lithe tanned body to the lock of straight hair glistening over the eye. Sarah Two could not hope to make any impression at all on Diana because of her inept behaviour on the hockey field and the cricket pitch. She wasn't bad at tennis but Diana never seemed to notice. In hockey, Sarah always feared the other opponents, especially during the dreadful opening moments known appropriately enough as 'bullying off'.

She was tall enough to be good at netball but she dreamed all the time and forgot to mark her partners. There was no way to impress the golden Diana. She was reduced to writing poems to her in the lavatory and flushing them down.

The odd thing was that in spite of being bad at all sports, like Sarah, Sarah's friend Meriel got along well with Diana. Meriel, who was over-developed, and who had begun to menstruate long before anyone and who wore a bra and corset-like thing – Meriel was Diana's pet.

'She is keen on art as well as sport,' said Meriel. 'She likes Dali, just like me.'

'You've got bad taste. If you do art you'll be very commercial and anyway you get on my nerves, discussing rubbish,' said Sarah Two, who deplored the constant carping about fashion from Meriel.

152

'I wouldn't mind. I'll make lots of money. Diana is interested – we often have a coffee and discuss make-up.'

'You are pathetic,' said Sarah. 'She isn't at all like that, really.' But the fact was, Meriel knew the goddess, and she did not.

Ellie was happier than Sarah had ever seen her. She and Edwin Bates seemed to get along well – too well, it seemed. At night, after work was done, they would go off to a pub together. Mrs Bates didn't seem to mind or, if she did, it was hidden through her armour of fat. Sarah One was too innocent to notice the growing affection, even though she was her father's pet. No one except Sarah Two noticed their making eyes at each other. One day she caught them holding hands, looking out to sea at an upper window. She coughed; they jumped apart.

She had to stop this nonsense. She was annoyed by Ellie's silly behaviour. Ellie emitted tiny emanations of pleasure, humming to herself under her breath, smiling a lot. Sarah couldn't stand it. Where was the old, negative mother she knew and loved? She heard the couple nattering on about sheep they had seen on one of their night drives to the Fylde to get fresh chickens. 'Our sheep,' they called them, smiling at each other, like a couple of besotted teenagers. It made Sarah feel sick. Their eyes would interlock over a plate of mince hash made by Mrs Bates. Sarah wondered where it would all end.

'There's something wrong with that man,' she said to Ellie. 'He grins all the time, it is obscene.'

'Perhaps he's happy,' said Ellie.

'Simple-minded is more like it,' said Sarah Two. It was a hint for Ellie which she did not appear to notice. You had only to mention his ridiculous name for Ellie's face to light up and look as stupid as his.

'He's fond of you,' said Ellie 'He said "she didn't know how to smile before she came here!" '

'What's so great about smiling? I'm not smiling now,' said Sarah. She thought it ridiculous because they were both so old.

One night when she was tucked up in bed with Ellie, and

153

presumably fast asleep, he came in. He kissed Ellie on the mouth, lightly.

Sarah froze.

'Is she asleep?' he asked.

'Oh – yes,' Ellie said.

'This is hell, you know. We can't go on like this.'

'I know,' said Ellie.

Sarah twitched, to scare them. He sighed, and took Ellie's hand for a minute, and then he went out, closing the door quietly. Sarah kept still for a minute, wondering what to do. While she was wondering, Ellie got out of bed, lit a cigarette and stood by the window.

'What are you playing at?' asked Sarah. Ellie jumped, turned. 'You aren't going to wreck this family, are you? Think of poor Sarah and Mrs B. You don't want them to be like us, do you?' She hardly knew exactly what she was saying – it was ridiculous to be protecting Sarah One, for a start. But she had to fight for Ellie.

Ellie began to cry.

'It isn't really your business,' she said finally.

'There will be a dreadful fuss,' said Sarah. 'He's a very conventional man, I would think. You haven't a chance, you know.'

It was true, really. She could see Edwin Bates hadn't the guts to let them down, his wife and daughter. But that wasn't her reason. She wondered to herself what was triggering off this reaction. In a way it just seemed automatic, she didn't know why. Could it be that she was more dependent on Ellie than Ellie on her? Was it that she couldn't share Ellie?

'Well, you know me,' said Ellie, coming back to the bed. 'I don't suppose anything will come of it, really.'

They put out the light and subsided, each turned away like a couple who had had a deep and wounding marital argument, making the shared bed an abyss. Ellie still cried, softly, like an animal.

'They are going to buy a bigger hotel – in Scotland,' said Ellie's muffled voice. 'They've asked if we will go. But you know how these things work out. So I don't need you to tell me that I haven't much of a chance.'

154

Poor Ellie. Sarah was ashamed of how she had behaved. But it didn't deter her from hammering a few more nails in.

'How could we go to Scotland – I'm fixed in my school? I'm doing quite well. Can't we just stay still for a while?'

'How can we, if they move? We'll still have to find somewhere else.'

'Yes, but here. That's different.'

Ellie sat up, blew her nose.

'I'll think about it tomorrow.' Sarah didn't laugh. She used to laugh at that, because Scarlett O'Hara had said it in *Gone With the Wind*, and it was something they said too. But Sarah had seen, suddenly that it wasn't enough.

'I think it would be better to end it if they are going to Scotland.'

'I suppose so.'

Ellie was silent and then Sarah heard her soft breathing, regular now. She could always sleep through crises. Lucky Ellie.

Sarah puzzled over the events of the past half an hour. Could it be that all the time she had thought she was the strong one – supporting Ellie – Ellie had really been the one in power? Maybe she could prove that was not the case by her disruption of Ellie's plans. She prayed, a cynical prayer, but meant. 'Dear God, don't deprive Sarah One of her Daddy. She is, after all, Daddy's girl.'

The Lord turned up trumps. Ellie and Edwin seemed to drift further apart from that night. Ellie, fraught, worried, became ill. Ellie, thought Sarah, had become ill to test Edwin Bates.

Sarah Two, nurse in charge, instructed the scared man in the art of nursing Ellie. Poultices, thermometers, drugs – all to save the thin delirious body which sweated out its love for Edwin Bates on the sick bed.

The Bateses had given up their bedroom and hired a nurse, but it was no use. Ellie was carted off by the ambulance men, under the scarlet blanket as before. Sarah had never seen anyone so worried as Edwin Bates; he thought his romance had killed her. She could see that it was dawning in his slow mind, what it would be like living with Ellie. He didn't smile much any more, Sarah noted.

155

As Edwin was doing the worrying for both of them, she went to the cinema a lot while Ellie was in the hospital.

'Dearly Beloved – how clearly I see . . . somewhere in heaven, you were fashioned for me.' Rita Hayworth sang and whirled. What a pity there were no romances like that in real life, thought Sarah.

Ellie recovered. Roosevelt died. Ellie came back, thinner and weak. Sarah Two realized their days with the Bateses were numbered. She taught Sarah One to skate on the frozen park lake. Sarah thought she could see the ghost of Paul Rosenbloom, wheeling Joseph along by the rose garden, a small girl by their side.

Meriel said the lake was like a Breughel painting – it was the kind of remark she had started to make. She hoped to teach Diana Gorman to skate but Diana did not turn up.

It was beautiful, Sarah thought. The ice was not like the ice at the rink, pristine and artificial; it was yellow and had the mystery of the lake beneath it, and twigs and leaves and branches spoiling its surface. When groups of skaters stood, to talk, it would crack, reminding them it was a temporary place, that it would revert back as soon as the temperature rose a few degrees. Others skated out to the small islands embedded in the ice, disturbing the troubled birds. Some timid souls pushed chairs in front of them. A few of the rink stars showed off, spiralling and spinning among the amateurs. Each day they could not wait to lace up their boots and be off, skating under the dark, bare trees.

'You did good, Lord. Top marks,' cried Sarah. Meriel was embarrassed.

Sarah One was scared of the ominous cracks and noises the ice made.

'It's the river god stirring, coming to get you,' said Sarah Two. Sarah One did not like to come out into the centre of the lake. Meriel said she couldn't blame her – it was more difficult than the rink. Sarah Two didn't want young Sarah along anyway. This was a miracle – why should she share it? She resented that. How she resented it.

'My skates are too tight. My ankles hurt,' Sarah One would complain.

'You'll have to put up with it. It is so beautiful, don't you think?'

'Yes,' said obedient Sarah One. Her ankles caved in.

'I'll take her back,' said Meriel.

'No, just hang on, Sarah,' said Sarah Two. And began to get up speed. She went as fast as she dared, weaving in and out of the slow ones, going into the centre where the good ones were. They went as if possessed. Sarah One, hanging on, began to scream. Relentlessly, Sarah went, ignoring the remarks until someone stopped her, sending a spray of ice over them. This skater told her off and led the weeping Sarah back to the edge of the lake. Her knees were bleeding and her bandy, thin little legs were blue from the cold.

'I won't tell because I know you didn't mean it,' she said on the way home. 'You just got carried away.'

'No I didn't,' said Sarah Two. Not even the response she wanted, she thought. Sarah One had won again.

27

BLACK ICE
by
'Rita Hayworth'

There were once two sisters who loved each other dearly. They lived in the Austrian Tyrol. Their father, the Count, who was said to resemble the film actor, Charles Boyer, had been used by his country – a small state in Europe – as a double agent. There was a crisis brought about by a minor war.

The Count, brave and full of individual integrity, 'had refused under torture by one side, what does it matter which? to give information. The sisters, who adored him, were saddened, but also cheered by this, as if it proved that in their veins ran a superior kind of blood.

Michelle and Karen were both blonde and blue-eyed and, like their dead mother, were graceful and intelligent.

Michelle was the eldest, and perhaps the more complicated of the two, though Karen was precocious too, in her own way.

If Michelle had one wish it was that she might have been male, and as talented as, say, Leonardo da Vinci. In the family castle hung endless portraits of their family, painted by famous artists. These had been to some extent damaged by the recent misfortunes. Michelle intended to restore them – it was to be her life's work.

Karen was a docile child, dependent totally on her older sister. Some said she was prettier than Michelle, though Karen thought her sister the most lovely girl in the state.

They had both been at school in a neutral country, but now the time had come to return home, to find out what had happened to their village, with their castle at the top of the hill, overlooking it.

It was going to be difficult to leave the neutral country and get back to their own. Winter, the hardest in years, had frozen everything, including the railway tracks between where they were and where they wished to go.

The only way was to either ski or skate along the river that connected these two lands.

They packed their belongings one night, and crept out of the dormitory they shared with a Yugoslavian princess. They carried all they owned on their backs. They carried the skates that were to take them home over their shoulders, by the knotted laces.

It was hard, sliding along the road to the frozen river. They must not be seen by the many guards who patrolled the riverbank.

Eventually, with Karen almost in tears through exhaustion, they reached the frozen stretch of water that was to lead them home.

Michelle knew she would have to bear the responsibility of the journey, being the eldest, and the stronger. She had not suspected Karen was so frail. As soon as they started the child was whining, saying her skates hurt her feet, she could not see, for the snow was blinding her, covering her eyes.

Michelle sang to her, a song she had learned from an English girl at the school – 'Hearts of Oak'. It seemed to work. Karen moved along again, slowly, but with great courage. She held on to Michelle's coat. But the dead weight of Karen kept Michelle back, and if they did not reach the border before dawn, it would be hopeless – they would be in full view of the guards and would be arrested.

Karen said she could not go on.

Michelle said she couldn't be ill now, it would wreck all they wanted to do. She knew she would be considered cruel if anyone heard her, and yet it was her job to be cruel. It was imprudent to be weak. Only strength would save them now.

A man, old, almost a hunchback, swept up to them, leaning in against the blizzard, as speed skaters did.

'What is your problem?' he asked. 'Can I help you?'

'We have to get to the mountain village. How could you help?'

'My name is Erik,' he said. 'I can lead you where you should go.'

There was something about him that made Michelle pause.

'No,' she said, finally. 'We would rather make our own way.'

At her words, the old man dissolved into a pool of black ice, on the yellow glass of the river. Karen began to howl.

'Be quiet, you fool.' Michelle had to control her sister.

'I want to give up,' cried Karen.

'I won't let you,' said Michelle. She grabbed Karen by the hand again, and dragged her, fast, along the ridged ice.

'My knees are skinned. My legs are breaking.'

'I don't care,' Michelle went on, ignoring the cries.

An old woman blocked their way, in the middle of the river.

'Senna pods, syrup of figs, sal volatile?' she cried. 'Stop me and buy one . . .'

Karen screamed louder at this. She wanted to stop. Michelle went on. By now Karen was being pulled along on her belly, like the horses in Western films dragged the hero along. It must be painful, Michelle knew, but she had to go on.

The couple, fat and middle-aged, sitting by the side of the river, seemed to recognize Karen.

'Karen, Karen,' they cried.

'Can't stop,' said Michelle.

They passed a guard, frozen rigid, with a blasted face. Michelle went on. Twenty kilometres. For what seemed a long while, Karen had been silent. Michelle had not loosened her grip.

'We are nearly there,' she said. 'Sorry I had to be so hard, but if you are not determined, you don't get there.'

There was no reply from Karen.

Michelle looked at the small body, the fair hair flowing out like water, the black stockings torn into shreds. The ankles were broken.

'Can I be of assistance?'

It was a man in a uniform, rather like that of a bus driver.

'My sister,' she said. 'She seemed all right, through the journey, but now it seems—'

160

'She's dead,' he said. He picked up Karen and put her in a fruit box.

'Where are you taking her?' Michelle asked.

'Home,' he said. 'I have a very fine Rose Garden. I'll bury her there, if that is all right with you?'

'I suppose so,' said Michelle. She laced up her skates again. 'I have to get on. I must go on.'

'Good luck. I hope you find it, whatever it is.'

He swooped off, bearing Karen like a dead bird in his arms.

Michelle skated along furiously, across the white ice, which was, because there was no longer any light from the waning moon, turning itself into black ice.

28

Truman dropped the bomb on Hiroshima and everyone seemed to think it a good idea. In the new street where they lived the flags were out for VJ Day. They roomed at night, bedroom only, in the house of a war widow. Her son was actually the boy Sarah had hit over the head in primary school. He had the little pinpoint marks of the stitches near his ear. They laughed about it now. He said the class had thought her mad. She refused to come to the VJ Day party, all jellies and sing-songs, saying she was more worried about the people in Japan – were they celebrating too? He said she was still mad.

The reason they were rooming at his house was that there was not room for them at Gran's. She was in the same street, looking after the house of a Catholic lady, who had a big job in schools administration.

It was a neat little pastel-painted place, with saints in every alcove. Gran said because she was religious she would not complain about Ellie and Sarah descending on them. She said that Miss Mavor had implied Sarah looked like Jennifer Jones in *Song of Bernadette*, and so Sarah tried to look soulful whenever Miss Mavor was about.

Jennifer Jones or not, Miss Mavor resented Sarah's taking long and luxurious baths in her bathroom, with her scented soap. Sarah, who had by this time little sense of personal property, thought her a hypocrite for objecting. Gran said Ellie had better hurry and find somewhere and that is how Ellie fell in with Mrs Encino.

Mrs Encino rented houses in the less salubrious part of town, and it appeared Ellie was to have one. So, while Ellie made her arrangements, it was suggested that Sarah visit Aunt

162

Lena for a holiday and to heal the breach that had existed since her non-return.

'Suppose he did mean it – "never darken my doors again"?' Sarah grinned. Ellie said nonsense. They had been keen to see her again, she had spoken to them on the telephone. They'd had it installed because of Uncle Alaric's illness, so the doctor could be reached.

Sarah took the train as she had before, but she no longer felt she was Jane Eyre. She watched the landscape change from the flat, green, sea-edged sort to the cobbled streets with their hills and springs. Would Uncle Alaric have forgiven the childish story? It couldn't have been nice, realizing one was Dracula to an ungrateful girl.

Retired now, he sat in his chair in the study by the desk where she had written her letters. He read the *News Chronicle* and stared at the moors. Angela was away, engaged to an accountant in Manchester; she had, they said, a good job as a secretary in a law firm. Thelma was outgoing, spindly, older than Sarah, when Sarah had been there. The dog, Henry, had died and was replaced by Bella, a setter. Mr Max was in an exclusive old folks' home and only Miss Swift was the same, receiving her eternal trays and playing the organ, though the loved vicar was long dead and his replacement young and impatient, and not the apple of Miss Swift's old rheumy eyes.

Sarah walked Bella over the moors. She was subconsciously awaiting Calum, though no one had said he might arrive. She knew, or wished it in her bones, that he would. The family, including Aunt Lena, had diminished. She had seen them as so vital, so alive – so much a threat to her, that it was a let-down to see how vulnerable and sad they were now. There was, on the piano, a new girl in the silver frame, but she didn't worry too much about that. No one remembered the brown-haired Susan when she mentioned her – that was a good omen. The time she had spent there was sealed off, a dream time. She doubted it had mattered to any of them, except herself. Now the love she had never felt for them welled up in her; she had nowhere to put it – they certainly would not have known what to do with it.

The routine had died; that was what was so awful. All that

washing and scouring and baking and polishing, and the enormous meals – all had diminished into a bland routine of Uncle Alaric's diet, and a general shutting-off of rooms and communications. She was not asked to help, that was in a way the final, upsetting thing. A girl from a nearby family came in to help and clean. Thelma, the youngest, had escaped Aunt Lena's terrible tyranny of a few years before.

Sarah asked to cook dinner one night; she made vegetable soup and Hungarian goulash that Sylvia of the Ranelagh had taught her. She sensed they didn't like it much and she didn't ask to cook again.

Calum, the rescuer, came. His cowlick of hair had been trained back under his major's cap. It was a defeat.

She could see from his reaction that she too had changed. They walked the dry moors with Bella. They lay and looked at the mackerel sky. His almond eyes, so like Ellie's, looked at her shrewdly.

He didn't want to discuss the Army, saying it was just a hierarchy like everywhere else. He knew where he stood, he said. If he stayed in the Army he would have a good career.

He looked at the landscape, the streams over cobbles, the odd decaying mill chimney.

'I love this place, but it is dying,' he said. 'I can't stake my life here – yet what will they do if I don't come back? You are lucky, floating around with Ellie. You don't have any responsibility.'

'I like roots,' she said, swirling around, Bella barking at her. 'I ought to stop up here. Live here for ever. It's my place.'

'I don't mean *up here*. Up here is fine. Easy. It is down there that worries me. I'm their big investment, you know.'

'I know,' she said.

'I come back and each time they are older, greyer. I'm their great hope. Have you thought how many there will be like me? Let out and having to return...' His voice trailed off.

'I used to pretend I was Cathy Earnshaw and you were Heathcliff,' Sarah said.

'I was never Heathcliff,' he said.

There was an awful finality about the way he said it; he could have been Ellie's child.

'Never mind,' she laughed.

'The trouble with me,' he said as they made their way down, 'I was born old. I'm an old man.'

She looked at him. He meant it and it was true. She felt a terrible pain because she knew she could never persuade him otherwise. It was just like manipulating Ellie – you couldn't get over the doom they had in their souls. Was it in the blood? It could, of course, have been Lena's ambition that had scuttled him – or his own early prodigious talent for music. He was tired.

'It's only a phase,' she said. 'Anyone can do anything, really.'

They marched along the cobbles. He didn't answer her.

He had asked her earlier how old she was as if he could not remember, and she had laughed as he asked and said women didn't like to be asked that. In some obscure way she had supposed the question was sexual, although it could have been just that he found it difficult to think of things to say. She left her bedroom door open that night, knowing he had to pass it; but she fell asleep hearing him playing records in the study and when she awoke next morning her bedroom door was shut firmly.

Sarah, Aunt Lena, Uncle Alaric and Thelma attended the performance of the St Matthew Passion in the church Sarah had been christened in. It was one of the reasons Calum had come home. He was, in fact, Jesus. His voice was not as good as it had been when he was a child soprano – still, he was better than the others. 'O my Father, if it be possible, let this cup pass from me: nevertheless not as I will, but as thou wilt.' It was apt. Poor Calum, she thought; poor Calum.

She took the train home next day – as he did but in a different direction. She hugged Aunt Lena at the station, feeling for her, at last, genuine affection.

She knew she would not be back, except perhaps for family funerals. How could the child-hate have disappeared so totally? (And the child-love for Calum.)

They had watched together the khaki-clad figure get his own train and depart. It had gone out before hers. She wished she had gone first for Lena's sake. But she couldn't help the railway timetable.

'How was family life then? Still as dull?' asked flippant Ellie.

'Different,' said Sarah.

'And how was Calum?'

'Devastating,' she said.

29

Ellie had decided to rent a house from eccentric Mrs Encino who owned lots of property in the town. Sarah could only assume that Ellie had got a pay-off from Edwin Bates and she didn't like to ask. The house was in a bad state of repair like all Mrs Encino's property. Sarah and Ellie would have to stay at Mrs Encino's until their own place was ready. Mrs Encino's was a large decaying villa, almost as big as an hotel, near the sea and a few streets away from where they were to go.

'She's like a witch,' Sarah said after meeting Mrs Encino. Ellie said she was rather beautiful, aristocratic really, in a deranged sort of way. Sarah looked at the gaunt figure, usually clad in clothes that seemed to be from jumble sales or perhaps her own wardrobe (they were tattered but expensive) and covered with a long, motheaten fur coat. There was something strangely attractive about her, with her thin, artistic hands – the fingernails long as a mandarin's – and her long feet encased in gym shoes. She rushed from one of her houses to another in her Rolls, giving out the rations. It was one of the conditions of taking on a house from her; the food was to be communally distributed.

'So we aren't really on our own, after all,' moaned Sarah.

'We are, except for that,' said Ellie.

Tooley drove the Rolls and did odd jobs around the place. Mrs Encino's relationship with Tooley was the talk of the other tenants.

'They do say they are lovers.'

'Someone who knew Tooley before the war says he is a pansy.'

'He used to be a waiter in the South of France.'

'That's where they met. She picked him up. She was married

at the time. No one knows what happened to Mr Encino.'

'Her father was a banker. Don't let the clothes fool you.'

'She's a miser. You won't get enough food to feed the guests.'

Sarah and Ellie didn't know what to believe.

Chickens flew around Mrs Encino's kitchen, perching on chair backs, shitting as they flew. Sarah found that her navy-blue school uniform was permanently spotted white. There was nowhere else to eat breakfast; finally she solved it by buying a bun from the baker's and eating it on the tram on the way to school.

Once or twice Tooley took her to school in the Rolls, which caused a small sensation. Sarah liked him; he was full of funny stories about when he lived in France – he used to hum little café concert tunes as he drove along. She couldn't work out how old he was or if his hair was real or a toupee. The girls nudged each other and giggled when they saw her with him but she didn't mind. He was a bit odd, with his soft voice and gentle ways. His face was lined and dotted with blackheads. Once, on the beach, she was watching him and he suddenly did a back flip and walked along on his hands for a while, like a circus performer. His hair remained on. This convinced her it was real.

The really odd thing about him was his total devotion to Mrs Encino. Sarah was quite touched by that.

They were squatting in a basement room used for storage, tea chests full of crockery and linen, cans of Spam and barrels of pickled eggs.

'It isn't for long. We have to look on the bright side. We'll soon be in our own place,' said Ellie. She had that eager look Sarah knew so well.

'The other tenants say she keeps a hold on you with the food arrangement,' said Ellie when Sarah said Mrs Encino could not be trusted. 'But I think, beggars can't be choosers.'

Sarah thought Ellie was getting more like Gran each day. It seemed Ellie hadn't noticed that her life was moving fast, that soon she would be old. Of course, she was only forty; but then forty was old.

At night they did not dare get out of their camp-beds, for fear of the cockroaches which emerged when the light went off. Sarah had a torch which she beamed around for a few minutes if she wanted to get out and go to the bathroom.

'I can hear the little buggers scuttering away,' she said to Ellie. 'See, they are like people rushing to a shelter.'

They could hardly wait to move out although their own house was a shambles.

'At least it is clean and bare,' said Ellie, scrubbing brush in hand. They painted, using a lot of cream and pink to brighten the place up. Ellie made curtains on an old sewing machine Mrs Encino had dug out of her attic.

'She is a real benefactoress,' said Ellie.

'The word is benefactress. And let's wait and see,' said Sarah.

'I've made a cynic out of you,' said Ellie.

'You have,' said Sarah.

But she liked the house with its little bit of triangular lawn and its large windows filled with sea light, although it was a street or two from the beach. There was a dusty visitors' book in the hall, with a few remarks. No one had filled it in for a couple of seasons. Soldiers had been billeted there apparently and one had written, 'Now this lot is over I can go home and fuck my wife.' Otherwise the remarks were all dull: 'Nice stay. Will be back next year.' Or: 'Very Pleasant Holiday', and the names and addresses. Sarah thought she would write to them all and drum up trade; then she abandoned the idea.

'They may be dead, or bombed out – I shouldn't bother.' Sarah looked surprised at that, from Ellie. It was possibly just a conditioned reflex, harking back to the old days, for Ellie was different now – positive and working hard at getting the place in shape.

There was a slight worry that there wouldn't be any visitors. There was not much money about, now the boom of the soldiers in the town was over. The Yanks had gone. Men in ill-fitting demob suits were filling the pubs, talking about the war, planning a new life now that peace was here.

The women, used to working, kept on their jobs in department stores and offices. They were used to doing something with their lives. But the wartime crèches closed down and the men wanted babies.

Barbed wire was removed from the beaches and mines were defused. Landladies prepared for the onslaught.

'After this we might run a nightclub in London,' said Sarah, carried away. She was finding it increasingly difficult to go to school, involved as she was in furniture and fittings, and the excitement of property-owning. It was as if the house might disappear if she left it.

She'd had a successful year, designing the school magazine cover and coming top in French and English. But she was happier pottering with Ellie.

'Write another note, saying I had 'flu,' she said, on one of her rare attendances at the Grammar. Ellie complied.

Sarah acquired a real illness. She became increasingly claustrophobic, she could not bear being in the assembly hall or in class. Ellie said she was just avoiding school. She would have to get over it. They didn't know what was wrong with her; she panicked when in any sort of a crowd. She couldn't, finally, go on trams.

'It could just be puberty,' said the doctor.

'Puberty?' Sarah could see from her expression that Ellie didn't know what he meant.

Sarah had begun to menstruate; Ellie had thrown a box of Kotex at her and said all women had to put up with it.

Eventually she didn't leave the house except to cycle over to Mrs Encino's house for the food supply. They were stocking up for the first influx of guests. She didn't feel odd now, being at home.

Ellie bought her a dog, a wire-haired terrier bitch.

'Just to keep you company and get you out a bit,' she said.

Sarah felt she was in heaven. She had never loved anything so much as this hunk of canine flesh.

She spent hours training Judy, alone with her on the beach, teaching her to heel, sit and die on command.

There were still no guests although it was May. She had only been at school for part of that Spring term – everyone seemed to have forgotten about her.

At Mrs Encino's kitchen table, covered in bird droppings, she would sit learning from Tooley the gentle art of faking the catering food returns, which all of the tenants had to send in. Tooley taught her to postulate how many possible hot beverages, subsidiary meals and main meals they might have served had there been guests. It seemed an odd occupation, like deciding how many angels danced on the head of a pin. By pooling the actual points coupons received, the combined tenants could give Mrs Encino a larger food allowance, though Sarah didn't know why this was an advantage unless Mrs E. and Tooley were in on some kind of devious practice. Sarah became involved in this fantasy – she became more daring as she went on. There was always the chance of a visit from the man from the Food Ministry but Tooley laughed that off, saying they were few and far between, those visits, and, anyway, a little bribery worked wonders.

'Maybe there never will be any guests,' said Sarah to Ellie. Perhaps all they would do, from now on, was wait for the imaginary trippers and calculate their phantom food.

Ellie didn't believe that. She stood at the door as if ready to welcome car loads of visitors, kids with buckets and spades, fat grannies, men who would roll up their trousers to the ankle and wade into the brine; all this was written on her anxious face.

They advertised in the local paper. The only reply was from the Ministry, that had moved from London during the war. The civil servants who had occupied the better hotels were now being turned out for the expected wave of post-war holiday-makers. They were being returned, slowly, to Whitehall, but Ellie netted a few who were delayed by the inevitable red tape.

Ellie fussed and flapped, thinking their standards would be higher, as they were from London. She had only been prepared for simple souls on a cheap week's spree.

They were an assorted bunch, the civil servants. Clerks, mainly, though Mr Thomsett was rather more important and he had his own secretary, Enid Craig, who was to have the room next to her boss's one. There was Mrs Dempster, a young and merry widow, and the Allens, an Irish couple. The Allens were not on their way back to London but were to emigrate to New Zealand. Sarah took to them right away; he was a tall black Irishman, she was a beauty with long chestnut hair and startling blue eyes. It was soon apparent that Enid Craig was dying of frustrated passion for Mr Thomsett who treated her with cavalier disdain. He had strict principles and an older wife in Pinner.

Enid Craig and Sarah played tennis together on the public courts. Enid wasn't bad; she belonged to a tennis club back home in Morden. Her bottom waggled in her schoolgirl shorts and her legs were diamond-patterned from sitting in front of the gas fire in her room, dreaming of Gordon Thomsett, thinking of his returning to Pinner and demanding a divorce from the waiting Mrs Thomsett. Sarah knew all this mostly by osmosis, but also from the way Enid sighed sometimes and the way she fell apart on the court when Mr Thomsett had been a brute in the office that day. They never mentioned the beloved one's name. Enid was very discreet, thought Sarah. She, in Enid's place, would not have been discreet. She would have been as passionate as Isolde. What a shame Enid didn't know how to act. The Allens looked more likely romantic types but in fact they were as prosaic as Enid. You never saw them holding hands – they were always discussing the sort of jobs they might get in New Zealand and how long they should wait before having children; until they could provide properly for them, said Mary Allen. How sad, thought Sarah, such a beautiful couple and so organized.

Mrs Dempster was the odd woman out. She dressed well and, for some reason Sarah could not fathom, she hated Sarah and nicknamed her 'The Duchess'. How could one be a duchess? thought Sarah, carrying in Ellie's food – Spam salad or the tiniest lamb cutlets in the world, provided by Mrs Encino, or the Creamola pudding. They always looked away as Sarah entered with the tray, fearing to know what was to be inflicted on them.

'They can't grumble, with what they pay,' said Ellie. 'If they knew how hard it was to screw anything out of Mrs Encino, they'd go down on their knees and thank me.'

'You be the waitress and I'll cook,' said Sarah who had the Sylvia recipes up her sleeve and a couple of years' domestic-science training at school.

'Very funny,' said Ellie. 'The whole point of being in the catering trade is to allow so much money per head and make a profit.'

'But we aren't making a profit, are we?' It was true. They couldn't even pay all the rent to Tooley when he called, never mind paying all the food bills to Mrs Encino.

'I think she overcharges,' said Ellie, brow wrinkled, trying to do the accounts. 'I don't like to think it of anyone but she might not be that honest.'

'No? You don't say.' Sarah had to laugh.

'We'll just have to cut down. They aren't at the Ritz,' said Ellie.

'You can't cut down on nothing,' said Sarah. 'And I have to carry it in.'

Sarah thought, after all this, that Ellie had in fact been quite canny, living with and on others since she left Eric. Now they were on their own, running a business, and it was scaring. Just to breathe cost money. There were the household bills and the food bills and the rent – it was like trying to carry water with a hole in the bucket.

Although they were hard-up, Ellie rented a wireless for a shilling a week, from the Rediffusion Company. It stood on its own little shelf in the kitchen. Sarah loved it. It was their first radio since Rathmines.

It was meant to cheer them and it did; they would wash the dishes and peel the potatoes to AFN Munich, where the disc jockeys gabbled all day, or listen on Sunday evenings to *Variety Bandbox,* or the music from the Palm Court. There was Spike Jones and his City Slickers, singing 'Chloe', and a new beanpole of a singer called Frank Sinatra. Sarah spent half her time with her ears pricked to catch the sound world as if it offered some alternative just as she had as a child.

'The only way we'll pay off Mrs Encino is for you to marry into the family – that or get this lot out and some real paying guests in.'

'There aren't any to be had. Have you seen how deserted the town is?' Sarah resented her mother's remarks about marrying. She wasn't sure she wanted to, ever. And the Encino boys were a joke – one a B-picture heavy, who attended to all his mother's

173

business affairs; the other a student – a gangling youth who was a recluse. He jumped out of the way if he saw you in the street, he clung to the walls on his way to Yates' Wine Lodge where he read books on symbolic logic. Some said he was a mathematical genius, others that he was a looney.

Sarah tried to find out about him, David, from Tooley. But Tooley just waltzed her around, singing 'Long Ago and Far Away . . .' He knew of her obsession with the red-haired Rita. Sarah felt she might like David, if she got to know him – at least he could talk about something far removed from boarding houses and food. But Tooley said he doubted David had ever spoken to a member of the female sex – except his mother, of course.

She knew she could go either of two ways. Either she would become like reclusive David, hugging her interest in books to herself and becoming more and more odd. Or, she might try to become Rita Hayworth.

School was not out; she hadn't been back for so long, she couldn't return. Eventually Ellie had gone along and said they were leaving town. She paid the next term's fees to get Sarah out. God knows where she got them from, thought Sarah. But she managed to find them. So it seemed she would have to go the Hayworth way – being an intellectual was out. She wouldn't even get the School Certificate.

Why feel guilty about such freedom? When she saw old school friends in the town she avoided them. She could do what she liked; the possibilities were endless. Except that there were no possibilities.

She tried to write out her thoughts and descriptions of Mrs Encino and Tooley, but she usually tore up these efforts.

Mary and Michael Allen were worried about her.

'What are you going to do with yourself, Sally my dear?' Michael called her Sally. 'You can't just drift along like this.'

Mary said she should find a hobby. Go to evening classes in art. This, for someone who wanted to be the first female Leonardo da Vinci, once?

'What are you interested in?' persisted Michael. She wondered why he bothered – he was on the way to New Zealand, after all.

She couldn't tell these two she wanted to be Rita Hayworth.

'I guess I'm just interested in Judy,' she said finally.

'Well, that's something. Why not show her? She's a pedigreed dog, isn't she?'

Mary agreed with him, as she always did.

'She's a nice little bitch. It's a fine world that, showing dogs.'

Obedient, because of their persistence and because she didn't really care, she started attending the local shows. She got accustomed to spotting the finer points of a champion. She spoke to a breeder of wire-haired terriers, who suggested he look over Judy and keep her in trim. He gave Sarah his address.

She took Judy the next Saturday. His office was filled with pictures of spruce-looking terriers, all with rosettes pinned to the frame. He trimmed Judy, and chalked and powdered her. 'Perhaps you will be the one to become Rita Hayworth,' whispered Sarah into Judy's ear.

There was a snag. Judy's ears stuck up like a rabbit's. Mr Fernald told Sarah to look at the pictures closely.

'Notice anything?' he asked her.

'All their ears fold over,' she said, doom in her voice.

'Nothing you can do about it, it's a fault. You can't show her.' Sarah felt that was too sweeping a statement and when she got Judy home she stuck down the offending ears with Elastoplast. Nature could be tamed, she was sure of it.

After a week she took off the plaster and the ears sprang up like two released springs. Undaunted, she placed tiny pebbles from the beach under the plaster. The weight pulled the ears down into the correct flaps. Sarah felt she had won. But a week later the ears sprang back to defeat her.

'You are being a bit cruel, there, Sally,' said Michael. All very well for him to talk – he was off to New Zealand in a few days. Her whole future depended on this, the descent of Judy's ears.

Eventually she had to succumb to fate and nature. Judy was relieved, her ears had won.

30

Gigli was coming to town. Sarah could hardly believe it. A truly famous person, here? The great Italian tenor would visit her town. Everyone had 'Your Tiny Hand Is Frozen' on the gramophone. She had played it a thousand times. It was their only classical record, apart from Solomon playing Tchaikovsky's First Piano Concerto. The aunts had let her take away the gramophone from Rathmines as they had a superior one but Eric had kept his Wagner and Beethoven. Ellie and she had gone out and bought these two records – although the shop girl had found it difficult to understand they wanted the Gigli, as they pronounced it 'Giggly'.

'Who is he anyway, a fat old Wop, that's all! And what did he do in the war?' Enid asked.

Sarah was surprised at that; she had thought Enid cultured, being a secretary, coming from Morden.

'The tickets are expensive. I don't suppose I will be able to go,' Sarah moaned.

'It's months ahead anyway. You'll be able to get some money.'

Sarah couldn't ask Ellie – she was always worried about the cash owing to Mrs Encino. If she asked Ellie, Ellie would say, oh, go ahead, you only live once, because that was the way she was.

The answer came, funnily enough, through Judy. Mr Fernald happened to mention, blushing, that Judy was about to come on heat. Did Sarah know? Sarah said yes, she did.

'You could breed from her, you know. As you can't show her. I have a good stud dog – I could do it for nothing and take the pick of the litter for my fee. The ear fault shouldn't show up in the pups. You'd make a little cash on it.'

It was like the answer to a prayer.

'How much cash?'

'Oh, it depends. Say, five guineas for a bitch, eight for a dog.' He was fluffing out Judy's beard.

'How many could she have?'

'She might have four – maybe. She's a bit young though. One thing—'

'Yes?'

'You must get someone else to bring her – it wouldn't be nice for you to do it.'

'Why not?'

He didn't answer, just went on chalking Judy.

'Get someone to bring her in within the next couple of days and you should have a nice little litter in six weeks.'

'Why do people pay more for males than females?' she asked.

'That's just the way it is.'

On the way home, with innocent Judy trotting beside her, she added up the dates and the prospective cash. Not only could she take Ellie but they could buy some clothes as well. They never had money for new clothes.

Who could take Judy for the blessed event? The Allens would have done it but, cases packed, they had gone off for ever to the Antipodes. Enid might do it, although Enid was in the depths of despair over Mr Thomsett.

Enid was not keen. She thought it rather indelicate. But she finally said yes, to get rid of Sarah who wouldn't leave her alone.

Enid and Judy arrived back. Judy looked no different. Enid was her usual dour self.

'How do we know it has taken?' cried Sarah. 'Did you watch?'

'No I did not,' said Enid. 'But Mr Fernald assured me that everything had taken place.' Enid was really rather prim, thought Sarah. No wonder she hadn't seduced Mr Thomsett.

Judy seemed to get fat almost immediately.

'You are feeding that dog too much,' said Ellie, oblivious to all Sarah's machinations as usual.

'She's eating for six,' said Sarah.

'She's not pregnant? She is too young. Poor thing.'

177

'Mr Fernald arranged it all,' said Sarah.

The weeks seemed to go slowly. Judy waddled along with her huge belly. At last the day arrived. Three rat-like creatures appeared.

'Come on, Jude, there must be more,' said Sarah, leaning over the long wooden box full of straw, under the kitchen table.

'Leave her alone. She's done her bit,' said Ellie.

Judy lay, wagging and panting, licking the squirming objects which made their way straight to her dugs.

Sarah was fascinated; Judy had become dutiful immediately, washing their little bottoms when they had fed, or even while they were still at it.

'It's like a milk bar. She has totally changed in personality,' reported Sarah.

'Mothers do,' said Ellie.

The pups, two males and one bitch, made their way down to the end of the long box to defecate almost as soon as they were born. Sarah hadn't realized that they were blind until she lifted up one of the squeaking objects. Judy protested at this.

'No one told me that,' she said.

'I expect there is a lot you don't know,' said Ellie.

Mr Fernald looked them over and chose Bill, the largest dog.

'He's a fine specimen,' he said, 'and the ear problem hasn't occurred. We've been lucky.'

'All except for poor Judy,' said Ellie.

'She's a great little mother,' said Mr Fernald.

'But why only three?' Sarah had been adding up the money. Not as much as she'd hoped.

'She's a bit on the young side,' he said. 'I'll be back for the dog later.'

So Ellie had been right. Sarah stroked Judy.

The bitch and the second male dog were duly advertised in the *Evening Gazette.* Ellie and Sarah shed a few tears when they were sold. Then Sarah went down for the tickets and her shopping spree. She came back with a rose-pink crêpe dress with a peplum, and a darker rose of the same material at the hip.

'Good grief,' said Ellie. 'You'll look like a blessed debutante in that. No one else will be togged up like *that.*'

She was wrong for once. The mayor and corporation were out in full force, with their fur-coated wives. There was the constant odour of moth balls and eau de cologne. Sarah had also bought her first pair of high heels, brown suede, with a cheeky little bow at the front.

'You look a curious mixture,' said Ellie. 'With that coat.'

It was true. She only had her school gabardine. Still, when she took it off she was elegance itself.

Enid had declined the offer of a ticket weeks before, so Sarah had bought Ellie new stockings and a jumper and an artificial silk scarf. Ellie had it knotted around her neck; it matched the jumper exactly.

'Better on our own, isn't it?' said Ellie. 'You never know with strangers, how they will react. Whereas *we* know, don't we?'

They did. They were comrades again, as they had not been for a while. Ellie was vivacious as she had been when Sarah was little. She saw how her mother must have been all those years ago, going to the opera with Eric. She was wearing one of the skirts she had bought while at the Bateses'. Sarah remembered then, it was the last time she had looked happy, as she did tonight. It seemed funny – she might have been in love.

It was House Full, of course, and there was an enormous sense of suppressed excitement. Sarah had held conflicting hopes in her mind; that she might be the only one there and would sit in solitary splendour – and the other, that he would be very popular, which had indeed happened.

She was proud of the town for turning out that way, all the bosomy ladies and their spruce escorts, chattering, unwrapping chocolates.

They were in the dress circle, very good seats. The stairs made Ellie wheeze. Sarah hoped she wouldn't have one of her bronchitic spasms. When she did that she sounded like their old Hoover in full spate.

Sarah herself had forgotten that she had claustrophobia.

There was a large black concert grand on stage and a potted palm. The tense audience, silent now, waited. He trotted on, plumper and older than she had expected. The pianist tried a note or two while the applause ascended like a mountain of noise. Then the silver stream of notes began; all the old favourites, the Puccini and Verdi arias. It was heavenly – Sarah could hardly believe it was happening.

Ellie fanned her with the programme as she was twitching so much.

'Are you all right?' she asked anxiously. Sarah nodded. It was just that it was so marvellous she couldn't really bear it.

It was the interval. She wondered how people could go out and chatter and drink at the bar. They should remain quietly and wait for his return.

'Want an ice?' asked Ellie.

'No,' she snorted. Ellie looked at her anxiously.

The second half had some Bellini and Donizetti, and then a selection of light Neapolitan ballads. The audience went wild. There were a couple of encores, and a third, and then Gigli, wiping his brow with a large white handkerchief and bowing in all directions, lifted his hands in a final farewell and left the stage. It was over.

They moved out slowly, among the massed audience. Sarah had waited for this day for so long – she didn't have anything to look forward to now.

The strong sea wind blew in their faces. Ellie shivered in her thin tweed coat. Sarah was still as if hallucinated; she was only just beginning to realize where she was. It seemed impossible that the only thing to do was to take the tram home. She wished it was all just starting – this time she would have concentrated more; she felt she had not taken any of it in.

Ellie asked her if she wouldn't like to wait for his autograph. There was a cluster of people at the stage door.

'Oh, no,' said Sarah. She just wanted to go home.

Then Ellie bumped into this couple. Sarah had never seen them before. A sort of Spanish-looking man and his lady friend who was jolly and Scottish. Ellie chatted to them while Sarah sighed and fumed. They suggested going for a drink.

'Wasn't Gigli wonderful?' the man said to her.

'He was all right,' she said. She wasn't going to spill herself over a stranger.

'I think Sarah wants to get back, she was rather thrilled by the whole thing,' said Ellie. Traitor.

'You go and have a drink. I'll go on my own,' she said.

She was glad Ellie was going out somewhere; she looked so nice, it would finish off the evening for her. She rode home on the tram. Her head was full of music. She pitied the people riding with her; for her world had been transfigured by where she'd been. They looked tired, ordinary, dull.

When she got back she put Gigli on the gramophone. She relived the evening, making it hers.

31

The couple Ellie had met that evening were also tenants of Mrs Encino, or rather, ex-tenants. They had just been thrown out for non-payment of rent; they had suffered the same difficulties as Ellie, in filling their not-too-salubrious boarding house with guests. It had been a bad season all round.

Mrs Encino's heavy son had been around a few nights before and had had an argument with Lev; the result was that they had booked into a cheap hotel and were deciding what to do. They had blued the last of their money on Gigli. This amused Ellie and, without really thinking it out, she asked them to stay, saying they could owe her rent until they found their feet. Lev could help her do the place up a little. Anna had already got herself a job in a pub.

Sarah was furious. She thought Ellie had been carried away by the glamour of the evening. It was true to a certain extent, Ellie admitted.

'But it might be nice,' she said, 'having some congenial people around.'

'Mrs Encino won't be pleased,' said Sarah. She could be very condemning as Ellie knew. 'We'll be out on our ears, too.'

'She won't know. You can go for all the food and Tooley won't come.'

'She'll know,' said Sarah.

'Lev said he gets on well with Tooley, so it will be all right.'

Sarah could see Ellie's mind was made up. Sarah was beginning to feel like Gran. She wondered if the puritanism and severity had skipped a generation, and she was like that fierce old lady. She looked in the mirror. There was a resemblance.

'Anna has her job as a barmaid and Lev is going to work at

the Pleasure Beach,' Ellie said, as they unfolded the Put-U-Up they both shared in the alcove off the kitchen.

'I don't care – I'm not worried about it,' said Sarah, feeling older than Ellie at this point.

Sarah, after her first doubts, had to agree that Ellie was right – it was better with others around. For one thing, Anna and Ellie got on well; and it left Sarah to her own devices. She began to draw again, going out with her sketchbook and attempting to master oils.

Lev and Anna slept in the downstairs bedroom that had been Sarah and Ellie's. They were keeping the guest rooms empty, in case Mrs Encino's spies came and thought they were not taking it seriously.

Anna had followed Lev down from Scotland when he had got out of the Merchant Navy. He'd been a chippie, a carpenter – he and Anna had met in a bar. Anna had left her two boys and husband to live with him. Sarah found that intriguing. Lev and Anna seemed like a couple from a story; he was about forty and looked foreign, but wasn't – except in the distant past there was French blood in his family. Anna was a plump Glaswegian, a little older than Lev. She had great teeth and was always laughing. She was slightly matronly, much more than Ellie, for instance, and her brown curly hair was streaked with silver.

'She's given up a lot for him,' said Ellie. 'He is a lucky man.' Sarah didn't see it that way; did not fathom what Lev could be attracted by in this rather ordinary woman. She was surprised to hear that Anna's husband was a doctor and even so had been quite brutal; had beaten her up when he heard about Lev and had forbidden her access to her children.

Sarah realized she categorized people too much. That is, she could not see why Anna had followed Lev, if she was such a middle-class matron, and he – well, just a handyman, really. At the same time, she had little patience with Lev's choice either – surely he could have done better. She felt she and Ellie, because they had floated about, drifted, could not be judged in any social context – and yet this was not true, either.

They got a few late summer guests – a crippled girl and her brother, and their old father. A family, a young couple with a baby. And suddenly there was a lot to do.

Enid and Mr Thomsett had left, on different trains.

'Forget him,' said Sarah, as they hugged each other, she and Enid, at the station.

'I can't. I'm still his secretary you know.' They cried a little, promising to write to each other always.

Mrs Dempster was the last to go. She tipped Sarah a pound to make her feel small. That was, then, the end of the civil servants, thought Sarah.

The crippled girl, her brother and Sarah went to the beach together, with Judy trotting along, newly slimmed down.

'Who is your favourite film star?' Sarah asked her. It was always a good ice-breaker, she thought. But the girl was too shy to say. Her brother was not shy. He and Sarah tried French kissing in the promenade shelter, while the girl looked out to sea, and pretended not to notice.

Sarah decided to try out her nightclub act on them.

> 'When tearing off
> A game of golf –
> I may make a play for the caddie
> But if I do
> I don't follow through –
> 'Cause my heart belongs to Daddy . . . '

The girl's brother said it was 'teeing off' not tearing off. He had laughed uproariously all the way through. Sarah was very offended. She thought she was very like Mary Martin.

Kay and her brother left at the end of the week. The couple with the baby remained.

An ex-Indian Army officer and his leathery, tired wife took the front double room. He was looking for a post-retirement job.

'The Brodies are very genteel,' said Ellie. 'God knows what they are doing here.'

Mrs Brodie had migraines all the time and Sarah was asked to turn down AFN Munich.

'I don't know why she has migraines all the time – the colonel is such a gentleman,' said Anna.

'That's why she has migraines,' said Ellie.

'The colonel's lady and Rosie O'Grady are sisters under the skin,' Sarah heard Anna say.

'Not in this case, my dear,' Ellie said. And they both laughed like schoolgirls.

Sarah liked Mrs Brodie. She wasn't like any other woman Sarah had known. She was beautiful in a battered sort of way like her leather suitcases which she had not yet unpacked. Her voice was strong and clear; she strode across the beach on her morning walks, a scarf tied over her dark hair, her raincoat collar turned up. She only changed when with the colonel – then she was timid, anxious and eager to please. Sarah did not think that right. Perhaps he shouted at her constantly because he had no one left to command.

Sarah wondered why they had landed at their place; they were obviously used to better things. Posh. Port out, starboard home. Lev had told her that was what it meant.

Ellie, who always got the residents' life histories out of them within minutes of arrival, announced that the Brodies had grown-up children, a son in Canada and a daughter married to a farmer in Suffolk – and neither of them had shown any interest in what the colonel and his lady were going to do with the rest of their lives.

'It is sharper than a serpent's tooth to have an ungrateful child,' she intoned, sounding like Gran.

Sarah wondered if the remark wasn't intended for her. It was the kind of thing Gran used to do. Perhaps they were both getting like the old lady. If Gran was anything to go by, Ellie should now be changing from a colourful butterfly into a large, comfortable moth. Sarah did not see any signs of that. Nor was that happening to Anna. Perhaps each generation was different?

Anna told Sarah she should not have done anything so drastic as to leave school. She said the claustrophobia was just her hormones playing up; it happened in puberty. All the dizziness in the hall and the feelings of non-existence were, said Anna, just a sign of female changes, of growing up. Your body went a little crazy. Sarah said she wished she had known that.

It was odd, the ravages time made on women, thought Sarah.

For instance, Mrs Brodie was one stage on from Ellie and Anna, her carapace was toughening, her neck was wrinkled with circular rings like those marking the age of a tree – her body was getting the sexless armour of old age. There was something in her that Sarah respected; a kind of stoicism. She was, Sarah supposed, a conservative, with a small 'c' – a dying breed in the new era of post-war Britain.

Sarah could see, in Mrs Brodie's eyes, a shrinking fear of the Old Country of which she had dreamed for so long.

Mrs Brodie liked Sarah and would walk with Judy and her along the dun beaches. She was not unlike Aunt Lena, one rung up the social ladder.

Mrs Brodie questioned her about Lev and Anna. She was not surprised when Sarah revealed they were not married.

'They don't look married,' she said with a wry smile.

Sarah did not know what she meant by that.

32

Sarah found a new tennis partner now Enid had gone. Lev. They went over to the deserted public-park courts in the evening, before going to collect Anna at her pub. Sarah found she could take a couple of sets off Lev; it boosted her morale. He was out of condition. She discovered also that she could talk to him. She told him what it was like, living with Ellie. Among other things she told him about Enid and Mr Thomsett, and the sadness of it.

He recited to her:

> Let me tell you a little story
> About Miss Edith Gee;
> She lived in Cleveland Terrace
> At Number 83.
>
> She'd a slight squint in her left eye,
> Her lips they were thin and small,
> She had narrow sloping shoulders
> And she had no bust at all.

'Did you *know* Enid?' she cried. He shook his head and grinned at her. She had never got on with anyone the way she did with Lev.

'Why are you like this?' she asked him as they sat by the rose garden (oh, Joseph Rosenbloom), talking, talking.

'Like what?'

'I don't know. Free.'

'I'm not,' he said. His mood darkened and he said it was time to get Anna. She deplored her habit of breaking a mood by asking a pertinent question, yet she never could resist it.

'I wonder why Ellie invited you two to stay. It isn't like her, up to now she has avoided people.'

'It's my fatal charm,' he said, winking at her. She didn't know if he meant it or not. 'I'm a poet. People like a bit of poetry. Even Ellie.'

Even Ellie?

She wondered about his claim to be a poet. He wasn't – at least, she didn't think so. He never wrote poems, as far as she could see. But she wondered about the 'even Ellie' remark. It was very perceptive.

'Anyway,' he said, 'money brings freedom and I haven't any of that. You are pretty free yourself, it's the way Ellie has brought you up.'

'Is it?' Privately she thought Ellie had not brought her up, not in the usual way. She had just scraped by.

'You don't make moral judgments about people, and that's good.'

Little did he know, she thought. It was not true. Decidedly, part of her liked him and admired him for his ease and charm; but there was another side which almost despised him, as it despised Ellie and herself, and that was the side which was often uppermost these days. This side told her he was something of a layabout – like Eric – and something of a romancer, and possibly dishonest. She made judgments about Anna too, swinging from romantic approval of what she had done, to wishing she did not plaster lipstick on to her homely face and go off and work in a bar – and to wondering why she didn't seem to miss her boys more. But she tempered her views on Anna, because she supposed she was softer on women; and it could, after all, be stoicism rather than lack of moral fibre.

She didn't judge herself much – but Ellie did it for both of them. Ellie said she spent too much time with Lev. Said he didn't do enough around the place to justify their having a cheap room. Of course, Ellie being Ellie, she did not say to their faces she resented this, she just moaned to Sarah.

'What are you doing anyway – taking a course in poetry?' She could be sarcastic when she liked.

'He knows a lot about it. Has read a lot.'

'All men have read a lot,' said Ellie. 'Much good does it do them.' Sarah knew she was thinking of Eric.

With uncanny insight, and though there was nothing remarkable in their relationship, the two women tried to prise them apart, as if in conspiracy. It didn't work. They were drawn together as if magnetized.

'I have a vision of the world as it should be, men and women walking about, free – naked – in the woods,' Lev said.

She looked at him, in spite of herself a nasty cynicism leaping forward, however she might have liked to push it away.

'Oh yes?' What could one reply, to that? 'Didn't D.H. Lawrence say something like that?'

'You've read him?'

'A bit. From the library.'

He lent her many books after that, from his big navy sack with his initials stencilled on the side. She read Whitman, Auden, Shelley, Rilke and a funny man called Kafka who had written a strange story about a man who thought he was a beetle.

'You remind me,' he said, 'of a girl I met once in America.'

That sounded to her like poetry, the way he said it. A girl in America. He told her about the girl. They used to sit on her fire escape in Boston, Massachusetts, and read poetry.

'What did you read?' she asked him.

'Whitman, mostly. "I am the poet of the body and of the soul" – isn't that marvellous?'

'Yes.' She shivered.

'I never touched her.'

What did he mean 'touched'? *Touch.* It was a strange word. He didn't touch Sarah, either. Who were they, these untouched girls? Everything he said seemed to have a hidden significance which she thought she would only understand later. Nothing he said seemed accidental, like other people's words. They just talked rubbish really.

'You must have touched her,' she said, with false bright innocence. 'To hand her a cup or something.'

He knew what she was doing. They were sitting on the beach; Judy digging for pebbles. He said they must get back, the others would wonder where they were.

'They know where we are. Out with Judy,' she said,

deliberately concealing the deeps of the conversation as usual.

She got up, brushing the sand from her skirt.

'You are getting to be quite a nubile little package, you know. That's why they worry.'

The crudity of it shocked her. She hadn't expected that of him.

'You have to learn to pull in those tummy muscles, they stick out like a little girl's. Then you'll have quite a good figure.'

'Does it matter?' she said, annoyed. Surely her soul was enough for him?

'It will – you'll see,' he said. 'You'll compare yourself with other women.'

She felt her heart pound, at the same time as she despaired. Had she then joined the sisterhood of women – and did he see her as *other?* She was torn between wanting to be his comrade, as they were; and this new feeling which made her guts ache. Women. A woman.

'Why are you called Lev?' she asked him, walking in his footsteps along the sands.

'I'm not. I'm called Leonard.'

'Leonard?' It wasn't the same.

'My family called me Leo. Then when I was at sea, a young man, I read some Tolstoy. He's Leo, you know, but the Russian is "Lev". And then when I read *Anna Karenina,* I liked the character – so – I was Lev.'

'Oh,' she said. Why did it seem idiotic? She wished she didn't find it so. Leonard. *Leonard?*

'You must read it. You'll fall in love with Levin, too.' Too? Did that mean he was in love with Levin – or that she was in love with him?

She began to run, with Judy. She would get a copy of the book to see what he meant. But first she had to get back to safety, to the gloomy women.

33

There was a crisis back at the house. Mrs Brodie was shut in her room, refusing to come out. The colonel had telegraphed her from London – he had gone to job-hunt there – and now he said he was not coming back. Neither was he about to send for Mrs Brodie.

'It seems he had a Rosie O'Grady tucked away all the time,' joked Anna.

Sarah went up and tapped on the door.

'It's Sarah.' The door opened a crack. The room looked as if a bomb had hit it. Mrs Brodie looked as if she were packing for a trip, until Sarah saw that she was in fact unpacking all the trunks that had lain dormant in the room since they arrived. Clothes were piled on the double bed: army uniforms, cocktail dresses, Indian shawls – all the debris of a life together of a man and a woman.

Photograph albums spilled out their contents on to the floor. Mrs Brodie pushed Sarah over to the bed and sat her down. She thrust a snapshot into her hand.

'Scotland, 1929. Very good at golf, the colonel was.' She pronounced it 'goff'. She used the past tense, as if the colonel were dead. 'And here, Sandhurst, wasn't he handsome?' Sarah saw the sepia-tinted young man, squinting into a past sun. Certainly he bore little resemblance to the ruddy-faced man who had left a few days ago. The one who had usually inhabited the Tootall robe Mrs Brodie now sported on her thin frame.

Mrs Brodie was sipping what appeared to be water from a tooth mug, but by her general demeanour Sarah guessed it must be gin.

'Have you any pictures of your wedding?' Sarah asked. Mrs

Brodie's trembling hand got out a white album from the drawer of the trunk.

It was all there, as Sarah expected: radiant bride in white; pages and tiny bridesmaids; arched swords; uniforms – a 'twenties pastiche. But this was real. Had been real. Was now history, and only meaningful to Mrs Brodie.

'Lovely,' she said.

'It wasn't easy,' said Mrs Brodie. 'Army barracks, married quarters, then a house, then India. The children had to come home to school, and then...' Her voice trailed off. She went over to the washbasin and got the green bottle of Gordon's gin.

'How many children?' asked Sarah. She knew, from Ellie's probings, but she thought it might help.

'Only two. Robin is just like his father, while Olivia—' she didn't finish, but pulled out a sheaf of snaps – prep school boy, a fat baby, a tall slender youth with glasses. Sarah supposed they were all Robin. 'A scientist,' said Mrs Brodie, and shrugged.

Sarah noticed that in the pictures that had more than one person – the family groups – the frocked little figure of a girl had been decapitated, the head cut out, so that the black from the album page showed through, like in Ellie's old silhouettes. Sarah wanted to ask about the missing child – whether she, Olivia, had cut herself out, or whether Robin or the colonel, or Mrs Brodie herself, had done it. The awful thing was, Mrs Brodie didn't seem to notice this. It was as if the photographs were normal. Perhaps she no longer noticed the mutilation, she had grown so used to it.

Sarah felt ill from the scent of gin. She knew it wasn't supposed to smell on the breath, and that is why ladies chose it – but it seemed to her sickly-sweet in the hot room. She asked if she might open the window.

'No,' said Mrs Brodie.

Sarah asked if she might bring up tea, and toast.

'No,' said Mrs Brodie. It was as if she never intended to do anything normal again.

Suddenly she took a handful of photographs and started tearing them. They were tough. It wasn't easy.

'Don't do that,' said Sarah. 'You'll regret it later. You will

192

want to stick them together again, you'll see. Please stop.'

It was dreadful to see her. She had lost all control.

'You lived all of that. You can't destroy them in one evening.'

'He did. So can I.' She tore less quickly, though. She was beginning to sort them out, keeping some.

'I'll make some tea, shall I?'

Mrs Brodie grabbed Sarah's arm.

'Don't leave,' she said. 'Please stay with me.'

'What will you do if the colonel comes back and sees all of this?' Sarah was a bit scared. 'Say he came in now? Wouldn't you like me to get some sellotape and try and mend them?'

Mrs Brodie smiled.

'It's all up here,' she said, pointing to her dishevelled hair. 'All in my head, better than any snapshot. If it isn't in his, that is his loss. You remember the past more when you are older – it is yesterday I have trouble with. I can't remember what I did yesterday.'

Not very flattering, thought Sarah. They had changed her book at Boot's library and gone out for tea. Mrs Brodie had eaten buttered toast and Sarah had demolished two éclairs. She supposed she had remembered because she was young, and she didn't have tea out that often.

Mrs Brodie had been abstracted and nervy, eating her buttered toast. Perhaps she had known, instinctively, then.

Sarah wanted to get away from the ginny breath and the atmosphere. She saw, for the first time, how brave Ellie had been in similar circumstances. It had never occurred to her that Ellie was brave. Perhaps Ellie should have made more fuss.

'Will you get a job?' she asked.

'A job? I have never worked. He can support me to the end of his days with every penny he has.'

Sarah closed the door. So that was the way other women were? She wanted to say to Mrs Brodie that perhaps it would be better to become her own person, like Ellie had. But she knew instinctively that Mrs Brodie would not ever compare her situation with Ellie's. It was sad, seeing her crumpled leathery face like that, tears and gin running down it – it looked like an old glove. Sarah thought to herself that she would never

193

pin her life on a man, like Mrs Brodie had, or Anna seemed to be doing.

What was so wrong about working, she thought, in Mrs Brodie's eyes? After all, most of the human race did it. Except Lev, who seemed to be reading the *Guardian* on the triangular lawn, Judy stretched out beside him.

'How is Mrs Brodie?' asked Ellie.

'Not good,' said Sarah.

34

'What is wrong with women?' she asked Lev. 'Look at Mrs Brodie – she is destroyed. It isn't fair.'

'She's the generation to whom marriage was everything. Yours won't be like that. The war has made a difference.'

Sarah thought about it. It seemed to her that women were still devious. She herself was. It was something to do with the passivity that came with the package, the biological deal. Walking the beach with Lev, talking to him, she was totally happy. She was an appendage to his personality. The message of Ellie's life, and now Mrs Brodie's, came through to her loud and clear. It must not be so. The big double-bind of the big double bed was not for her. Yet only his presence fulfilled her. Ellie's remark, 'I worshipped him', rang around her brain. Ellie had evolved a life to shelter that remark; she had been paralysed ever since. Why was it so difficult? Was the female machine so powerful or was it a fiction, put on women from outside themselves – Sarah couldn't make up her mind.

Gran had only been filling in her life since Grandad died. But hadn't she been doing that before? Wasn't it just money, really, and not the tyranny of sex? Had they had a choice? Would she have one?

'Is Anna older than you?' She and Lev were on one of their walks. She sat on the sea wall, swinging her legs.

'A couple of years. Why?'

'I don't know. She seems it.' Anna's position worried her because fundamentally she didn't trust Lev. Anna had sacrificed so much. 'Do you find Mrs Brodie attractive?' she asked quickly.

'No. She's a bit over the hill. But I never liked that type, those stiff upper-lip ladies.'

She smiled. She'd known he would make some excuse. It was just that Mrs Brodie was old. Older, but not much, than Ellie. Than Anna. And, just a little bit older than himself.

'I think it's sad, about Mrs Brodie.' She stood up, suddenly wanting to leave him.

'It is, but that's life.'

She looked up at his lined, sensitive face (that wasn't really so sensitive after all) and thought how different it was for a man and a woman. If he had been a woman he would be old already. As it was, he seemed young. It was a trick of nature. He wasn't even aware of it, she was sure. Anna was. That is why Anna did not like her walks with Lev. Anna knew that she, Sarah, was a new package of flesh. I'm a new design, thought Sarah, and he can't resist it. It is just there, a fact. Ellie, Anna and Mrs Brodie, they all had their feelings written over their faces – they were losing out and their mouths were turning down, their brows were frowning most of the time. They were saying goodbye to the secret, lost girls within them. Even the colonel had chosen Rosie O'Grady over his old lady. So what did they expect of a poet?

It was unfair and the most unfair thing about it was that she didn't care, not in the core of her. She would be old too one day. But now...

'Race you to the pier,' she said.

She ran like the wind, Judy barking behind her. He caught up with her and, as she knew he would, kissed her. It was a kiss that only caught the end of her mouth, it wasn't like the French kisses of Kay's brother – those experimental probings. But it was as if he were trying to catch something elusive that he needed.

They went in, flushed from the run, and she could see the faces of Ellie and Anna, the losers.

35

Sarah followed both Lev and Anna around, rather as Judy followed her, with dog-like devotion.

'Don't get too wrapped-up in them,' Ellie warned. 'They will be off soon. They are looking for employment in London, you know.'

Sarah was stricken. Lev hadn't mentioned it to her. She decided that she must cultivate him even more; perhaps go off every evening to the pub where he went to wait for Anna.

She drank shandies, listening to the men in the saloon bar fantasize and boast. Is this why Eric had spent so much time in these places? They provided at once an atmosphere of artificial cheerfulness and a feeling of brotherhood – it was an illusion, she knew, but it was all-pervasive. It was always there, too, for those who needed it.

'Remember your father,' warned Ellie. 'Don't get used to drink.'

'I hardly drink.' She did not respond to the hidden probe, that she was there only because Lev went.

She enjoyed the walk back those evenings after the pub had shut, and Anna and Lev weaved, a little tight but no more, along the cliff walk back to the house. Back to the house and Ellie's disapproving look. This must be the way it had been for Eric. She was getting an insight into him although she and Ellie seemed to have forgotten him.

She did not dare think what life would be like when those two had gone. She asked Lev what she should do – she didn't want to return to any form of educational institution, now she had been free.

'He told me not to waste myself,' she said to Ellie, as they lay together on the Put-U-Up in the kitchen. 'He asked what you thought.'

'I think you'll sort yourself out,' said Ellie, stubbing out her cigarette, sounding bored. She knew it was wrong to ask Ellie. Ellie the dreamer, the naïve – Ellie thought you could get by with fate giving you a hand.

'I asked Ellie,' she reported to Lev. 'She hasn't a clue what I am on about.'

'Ask your father.'

'I wouldn't ask him anything.'

'Don't become like me,' said Lev.

She said to him that she couldn't ask her parents anything, because it seemed to her that they were a prime example of what not to do – they were casualties. The only thing she admired about them, when she thought about it, was their negativity. If you had given up, they were the models to choose. She shivered. She might be like that – it could be in her bones.

'You'll be all right – you are full of life,' he said. Adults were infuriating. She wanted to be handed a book of instructions, a key to the universe.

Walking with him along the beach, her dreaded dark tower looming, she knew she would have to break this endless nothingness. She couldn't drift forever.

Lev had stirred in her some feeling of her potential as a female. She couldn't work out why his opinion was so important to her, when she thought him less clever than Eric, or less of an erotic image than Calum. He was becoming too necessary. She was moulding herself to him, and she had never allowed herself to do that before.

'Here are our two philosophers,' said Ellie as they came in. Sarah felt a twinge of guilt, though the reason was more complicated than Ellie knew. For every time she felt the reinforcement of her tie with Lev, Ellie moved further away, out of her thoughts entirely.

Later, Ellie started her pinpricks of sad, lost, possessive instinct turned angry.

'He's a wastrel. No use to you. Let him waste his own life, not yours.'

198

'I'm not doing anything in particular.' Thanks to you, was the hidden, unspoken reply. 'He is the best thing that ever happened to me.'

'That's what Anna thought, and look at her life.'

'It seems about the same as ours.'

'She threw away her family for that.'

'I thought you didn't like families,' said Sarah. It was the first time they had faced each other as women. 'I think Lev is unique,' she said, finally. 'A poet.'

'Funny sort of poet. Poetry doesn't get you far.'

Oh yes it does, thought Sarah. Poetry is the only possible reaction to life. Organize it, order it, through words; the only thing to do with the chaotic mess it all was. And the poetry was within, you didn't have to write it down – it didn't matter if Lev never wrote a word.

She'd just read 'Bride of the '30s' by Auden. That was Ellie. If you showed it to Ellie, she would say that wasn't her. But Auden knew and Lev knew, and now Sarah knew.

Poetry held up what you knew and defined it. You had to see it that way, clearly, definitively, and then judge it, and if you didn't like it, change it. The defining helped. Lev knew that, most people she'd met didn't want to know. Most people crawled through their individual tunnels, trying to reach the light. Some of them didn't even know about the light at the end of the tunnel.

Lev and she knew.

He recited to her:

> I was a child, and she was a child, in that Kingdom by
> the sea,
> And we loved with a love that was more than love, I
> and my
> Annabel Lee.

He never had to tell her that's what they had because he knew that she knew; and that is why they had it.

36

Hamish and Toby, Anna's two sons, came down from Scotland for a visit. They were frightening (and frightened), Sarah thought. Frightening, because they were so boisterous and noisy – and frightened because she could see they both wanted and hoped that they had not forgotten their mother. Lev, she noted, kept well out of the way. He had a temporary job at the Pleasure Beach, running the rifle range, so he had an excuse to avoid the stress.

Toby, the younger boy, was bullied a lot by Hamish. Toby was a bit of a cry baby. Anna was upset, feeling it was her fault.

The boys telephoned their father each night from the booth on the corner. After the call they were always morose. Sarah thought it might have been better if they hadn't come at all, although when she looked at Anna with them she revised that thought.

'What do you think of Lev?' Sarah asked the lads.

'We've hardly seen him,' said Hamish. 'My dad says he's a cunt.' He looked at her to see if she jumped. Sarah doubted his father had said that.

'My dad says he's a pansy, Lev,' chimed in Toby. 'What is a pansy?'

'It's a flower,' said Sarah, before Hamish could speak. She doubted that their father had said that either. They had a photograph of him; he looked an ordinary solid middle-class man, slightly balding, and he was staring at the camera with only barely concealed impatience.

'Lev is running the rifle range at the Pleasure Beach,' she told them. It was her trump card in the defence of Lev. Their faces shone.

'When can we go?'

'Tomorrow.' Sarah the peacemaker.

The next day, with Anna's hard-earned pounds bulging from their crammed schoolboy pockets, they set out with Sarah. They tried the lot; the Big Dipper, the Small Dipper (Sarah refrained), the Octopus, the Big Wheel, the Ghost Train and the Fun House. Candy-floss, doughnuts, Blackpool rock and dandelion and burdock.

They had kept Lev until last.

'I hope they don't shoot me,' said Lev as he handed them the rifles. They didn't do badly. Hamish, particularly, had an eye for a target. Toby was a bit scared. Finally she took him off to the Hoop-La. She noticed that the cheeky dogs she had once painted were prizes. Maybe one was hers.

'Don't win one of those,' she joked to Toby.

'Why not?'

'Oh, just a private joke,' she said. He didn't win anything so she bought him an ice cream.

Hamish had won a goldfish. Toby cried because he didn't have one. Back at home, Sarah ran them a bath.

'You aren't going to see us naked,' said Hamish. 'That wouldn't be right.' She left them to it, splashing and screaming.

Once in bed they were subdued. They had forgotten to telephone their father. Sarah offered to do it; but they said it wouldn't be any use. He'd be very angry. She was amazed how scared they were.

'Where's ma?' asked Hamish, pyjamas on, hair slicked down with water.

'She's working – you know that.'

'She shouldn't work when we are here, should she, Toby?'

'No.'

'Then how could she give you all that money to spend, eh?' Sarah folded up their shorts and shirts. 'She's going to buy you some football gear as well; and that's a secret, so don't let on.'

They grinned at that. Mercenary devils, thought Sarah. Later, when Sarah was reading Auden, they shouted for her.

'Toby has puked all over the bed,' complained Hamish. 'It was all that stuff at the Pleasure Beach.'

'Never mind,' said Sarah.

'I'll clean it up, if you like,' said Hamish.

'No, I'll do it. Don't cry. Everybody is sick sometimes,' she said to Toby, giving him a hug. She changed his pyjamas and the sheets, and mopped up. Toby cried quietly.

'He often cries at night. He wants his ma,' said Hamish. 'Just leave him, he always stops.' He turned over, in preparation for sleep.

She sat on the edge of the bed until Toby fell asleep too.

Anna asked how they had been all day. Sarah didn't tell her about Toby – what would be the use?

Anna, as promised, took them off for football stuff the next morning. Sarah watched her go down the road to the tram, escorted by her two tough, brave boys.

'They are a strange pair. I really like them now. They aren't rough at all – they are just defensive,' she said to Ellie.

'All kids from broken homes are like that,' said Ellie. Sarah stared at her – no, she didn't mean them. Ellie always thought what they did had no connection with her remarks about other people. That was what 'they' did. It was endearing. No. It was not endearing.

The boys were back, trying on their striped jerseys and socks and new boots. They were so elated, Ellie said there would be tears before nightfall. It was one of Gran's homilies.

'Take no notice,' laughed Sarah. She took them on to the beach, and they kicked the ball around for a while. Sarah was in goal. Then the ball hit a sharp pebble and burst. It was a major tragedy, Sarah could see that.

'She tried to bribe us with all that stuff,' she heard Hamish say as they left the beach.

'But she isn't too bad, is she, Hamish?' Toby's voice was anxious.

'The ball burst, didn't it?' said Hamish, shrugging. 'That's it.'

Sarah saw a tall, raincoated figure on top of the cliffs. The boys ran towards him.

He shook hands with Sarah. He had worried because of the lack of a 'phone call the previous evening, and as the boys were due back, he'd come a day early to get them. They hugged him and seemed pleased.

202

Sarah dreaded the walk back to the house but he was nice enough, rather shy, in fact. She hoped Lev would not be there.

He looked around the kitchen, frowning. Sarah tried to see it as a stranger might – it was rather squalid. She went for Anna. The boys went upstairs to get their gear together. Thank God, thought Sarah, Lev is at the rifle range.

Ellie peeled potatoes at the sink; having been introduced she nodded at him and went on peeling, sensing danger.

Anna appeared, looking alarmed.

'We had one more day.' She was tearful. 'You have come early.'

'I didn't hear from them last night.'

'That was my fault,' Sarah rushed to say. 'We went to the Pleasure Beach and we were late getting back. We forgot.' They both ignored her.

'He knew they would be all right,' said Anna. 'He just wanted to spoil it.'

'As their sole parent—'

'I'm still their mother.'

Sarah indicated at them that the boys were standing in the doorway with their cases. Ellie went over and took them out. Sarah followed.

They heard his upraised voice.

'Is this what you gave up your good life and family for – this?'

Then there was silence. In the hall Hamish and Toby were quiet as two mice.

Sarah looked in and saw he had hit her two or three times across the face. Anna's mouth was bleeding. He rushed out past Anna and went out of the front door, slamming it. They could see his shadow in the glass of the door.

Sarah led Hamish and Toby in to kiss Anna goodbye. They each clung to one another, and cried. Then Sarah took the boys out. She watched them walk down the road with their father.

'Get the TCP, Sarah,' said Ellie, 'and the cotton wool.'

She attended to Anna's cuts.

'Don't cry, Anna, they love you – they told me,' said Sarah.

'And where is the bloody poet, when he's needed?' asked Ellie.

She dabbed at Anna with the antiseptic.

'They forgot their goldfish,' said Sarah.

37

Lev and Sarah took Mrs Brodie to the pub one night but she sat avoiding everybody in the lounge bar. She watched the loud girls and the jolly men with an expression of distaste. She reached occasionally under the table and patted Judy, who was avoiding the trampling feet.

'What a couple,' whispered Lev.

'Don't criticize Judy,' said Sarah. She had hesitated before inviting Mrs Brodie but Ellie had said if she didn't get out soon, she'd have to call in a doctor. Sarah sacrificed her time with Lev, which might be limited if they were going away. By helping others you lost out and often didn't help them anyway. Mrs Brodie sipped her gin and didn't seem to know you were supposed to buy a round. Lev tried to charm her. He had even been to India. You could see that Mrs Brodie felt her India and his were two different places.

Seeing Lev despair, Sarah suggested she and Mrs Brodie should take a walk before turn-out time which she knew would upset her.

'I can't stay here, in this town,' said Mrs Brodie's tremulous voice. Her voice, since the colonel left, had been the thing that had changed most. From the ringing tones of command learned at Roedean or a similar establishment, she had declined into almost a whisper. She waved her Jaeger-sleeved arm, describing in an arc the Tower, the low-lying amusement arcade, the ridiculous giant china teapot, saying 'TEAS' on its side – all the things Sarah loved (and hated too). Sarah's heart rushed to the town's defence – so it wasn't Paris, or Bombay, or London but it had its own integrity and charm.

'It isn't a bad place,' said Sarah. 'It is a bit of a joke, I know, but I am quite fond of it.'

'Ah, yes.' Sarah realized it was like Lev's India. The town was all right for her, no doubt, but it was inconceivable that Mrs Brodie should remain there. What would her friends say? Except, as Sarah knew, she really had no friends. It was all too sad, really.

'Come on, Judy,' she said. She was ashamed, pulling poor Judy along like that, without her usual stops for nice smells – but Sarah wanted to end the ruined evening. The walks back with Lev and Anna were the nicest things they did together – she had given it away for nothing, because Mrs Brodie didn't even know.

'Ellie says women should be independent – run their own lives,' she said.

'Who is Ellie?'

'My mother.' She didn't even know that. She became fierce. 'My father was a political candidate here, before the war.'

'Which party?'

'Labour.' What did she think?

Mrs Brodie didn't care, she realized. It was strange to Sarah, because as yet she cared a lot about other people. She could see that when you got older you didn't so much – perhaps it was because you had learned that it had no effect. Or perhaps some people always cared and Mrs Brodie was one of the ones who never had.

It began to drizzle and Sarah asked Mrs Brodie if she could run back, but she swayed along like a camel and they all got very wet.

Drying Judy, she thought of Lev and Anna, laughing in the rain.

It wasn't even ten o'clock yet — it would be ages before they came in, the barmaid and her companion. Ellie had made cocoa which Mrs Brodie refused. Ellie had been doing the accounts in the corner of the kitchen they had made into a little office. Sarah could see she wanted to get on with it.

She offered to escort Mrs Brodie upstairs. Really, Sarah wanted to get on with *Anna Karenina* which she had got from the library, but having wasted most of the evening, she might as well finish it properly.

I hope I am never middle-aged, she thought, as she mounted the stairs.

Once upstairs, it wasn't so bad. Mrs Brodie got out the gin and said she had something to show Sarah. She pulled out a small trunk that Sarah hadn't seen before and out of it she pulled material so lovely that Sarah gasped. Mrs Brodie draped it around Sarah.

'We'll make a little Hindu out of you,' she said. 'Strip off.'

Sarah took off her Ellie-knitted jumper and her pleated skirt and stood in her knickers and vest. Mrs Brodie put tan make-up on her face, arms and neck, then outlined Sarah's eyes with kohl. She put a dot of lipstick in the middle of Sarah's forehead and put her long dark hair behind the nape of her neck. She knotted it. She then gave Sarah a little sort of jacket to put on, and wound the green material around her, sari-style. She showed Sarah how to do it.

Then Mrs Brodie said the pink would be nicer and she got out some even lovelier material, and this had silver threads in the transparent rose colour.

'That's the one,' she said. 'You look lovely.' She seemed to have forgotten all her troubles, so absorbed was she in this new game. 'Now, we must do your feet.'

She took Sarah's reluctant foot and traced around it with red stuff, and then Sarah held out the other one and she did that too. It tickled.

'You can look now,' said Mrs Brodie.

Sarah saw a stranger in the glass. She did not recognize herself. It was like the feeling she used to have, which she called the 'not-Sarah' feeling, a feeling that she was on the dark edge of her own identity and if she let go she might be lost forever.

This was a better feeling. It was as if she had suddenly found a dozen different Sarahs inside herself. Potential Sarahs. This was one of them.

'Oh,' she said, 'thank you. I do feel funny. Different. I like it.' She kissed Mrs Brodie. 'Can I go down and show them?'

'Of course, but walk slowly, gracefully.'

She walked down. Ellie jumped when she saw her.

'You look peculiar. Where's the carnival?' she said. 'No, it's very nice, really. Did she do all that?'

Sarah smiled gravely.

'It's authentic,' she said.

'I'm sure.'

Sarah sat waiting for Lev and Anna. Her heart was beating fast. It seemed like hours.

She heard them shaking out their raincoats at the front door. Anna was complaining about her aching feet. Lev came in.

'You look incredible,' he said. She thought he meant *silly*.

'It will wash off. Mrs Brodie did it,' she said.

'Leave it, as long as possible,' he said, smiling at her. 'Who would have thought it. *Sarah—*'

'It will get all over the sheets,' Ellie broke in, destroying the moment.

Anna came in and laughed.

'Where's the fancy dress ball?' she asked. Then seeing Lev's face she added, 'Oh, you do look pretty.'

Lev and Sarah exchanged a glance.

'I'll go and take it off now you've seen it,' Sarah said and went upstairs, still walking slowly, gracefully, as Mrs Brodie had told her to do.

The voices of the two women rose up, a lot of laughter, probably at her expense. She heard Lev's voice cut in, then there was silence.

It had been worth it, to see herself, what she might be. It had been worth it to see Lev's reaction.

The others didn't matter. They would never matter.

38

Ellie had not finished the food returns or the accounts the night before. She was no good at fiction. Sarah took over. She secretly admired Mrs Encino for all this, her edifice of imaginary beings, guests, tenants and her uncanny air of mystery in what was, after all, a banal existence.

In this world it was better to be an eccentric like Mrs Encino. She deplored the conversations she heard between Ellie and Anna, women's trivia mainly; they felt themselves victims, even martyrs, yet Sarah didn't see them trying to do anything about it.

'There is no way he could interest himself in my problem,' said Anna, 'because men don't feel the same about losing their children.'

Who asks them? thought Sarah. No one had asked Eric. But they weren't discussing Eric – they rarely were.

'He doesn't see her much, does he?' said Ellie. 'But then, I don't ever think of Lev as the fatherly type.'

Sarah froze. Lev?

'He visits her about once a week. Of course his mother has always looked after Carrie. Lev is more like a big brother to her.'

It couldn't be true, Lev would have told her. A daughter. It was worse that it was a daughter. Did that mean he had a wife somewhere? She felt sick. She was damned if she would ask *them* for information. They felt she knew, obviously. After all, why wouldn't she know – when she spent so much time with him?

Why did the daughter upset her so much? she wondered. There was about as much chance that Lev was a besotted father as there was that Eric would have been. Yet it did worry her. She hadn't known.

Ellie, Anna and she went off to the pictures that afternoon, a rare treat. It was said to be so that Anna would have her mind taken off the fact that Hamish and Toby hadn't even written to thank her for the nice week – but Ṣarah didn't think she had worried over-much about that. Family relationships, thought Sarah – what a mystery they were. Perhaps one could avoid the whole deal. Become a nun or something. If only they had an order for atheists, she'd join.

Anna and Ellie sat there in the cool dark, smoking and chewing sweets. They watched Joan Crawford twitch her black brows and open her giant lips. Sarah saw a tear glisten on Anna's cheek and run down on to her Elastoplast, which still littered her face, a present from her ex-husband.

Ellie exuded a mixture of the scent Sarah had bought her for Christmas and the bleach she had used to scrub the pine table. Sarah was imprisoned between them. Why should she be here, pretending to enjoy this drivel, on a fine afternoon?

She wriggled out and whispered to Ellie on her way, that she had just got the curse.

She was free. Females – I *hate* you, she shouted, on the beach. She wanted to be sexless. She wanted not to have to be interested in the flow that was in her, in the tribulations of Joan Crawford, the long-suffering symbol; in the wrongs done by imaginary men to unimaginable women. She didn't want knitting patterns and baby talk, and knotted relationships.

She plunged into the shallows of the glassy waves, her still-hennaed feet feeling the hard ridges of sand beneath. At least it was all pure here. One could be like a bird. This was the Irish Sea. Lev had read to her a description of a girl standing in the water, over there, in Ireland; he said it was by the best modern writer, Mr Joyce. It was about a young man seeing this girl standing in the water like a sea bird, and about his soul shouting for joy.

Sarah thought, there is always this; but one forgets it. It is always here – the new-washed sand, the empty sea. It gets covered by their messiness. I must not forget it.

She took the tram home.

Lev was there in the kitchen, working on something. A

large wooden object. It was a doll's house. He looked up, surprised.

'Is that for your daughter?' Sarah asked.

'Yes,' he said. He had nails in his mouth.

'I might have some furniture for it. I still have a lot of junk. I had a doll's house once.' She waited for him to tell her.

'That would be kind. If you don't want it.'

'Well, you might as well make use of it.'

He wasn't going to tell.

'How old is your daughter?' she asked.

'Nine.'

'Why didn't you tell me about her?'

'I thought I had.'

Oh.

'No, you kept it a secret.'

'Not really. You could have learned it from Anna. We don't talk about those things really, do we?'

'No,' she sulked.

'Does it make a difference to you?'

'No, of course not,' she lied. He should have known. He should have known she would now lie. They were becoming like the others now. She had always been able to cope with the thought of Anna; but this mysterious challenger, that was different. She could defeat Anna; she could not defeat an unknown child. 'What is she like?'

'She's a bit like you. Bright. She looks like her mother – her mother died when she was born. She's the image of Mary.'

There did not seem to be anything to say.

'My mother has always taken care of Carrie. They live over by the park. Carrie goes to the convent.'

'Is she – are you a Catholic?'

'Yes.'

Something else she didn't know about him. He went on hammering the white wood.

'I thought you were all at the pictures,' he said.

'We were. It was such a nice day I couldn't stand it, all that messy dramatic stuff,' she said.

He began to pack up his tools.

'You might make a cup of tea,' he said. 'I'll clear this lot

211

away — they will be back soon. Does Anna still seem upset about the boys?'

'I don't know. No, she's all right.'

For the first time with Lev, she felt constrained. She could hear the loud ticking of the clock.

'You didn't come back to see me, did you?' he asked, brushing the wood shavings from his clothes.

'No, not really. Why?'

She had filled the kettle and now sat on the table, swinging her legs. There was another awkward silence. She could smell his familiar odour of wood, shaving soap and a slight tinge of sweat.

'You are a very sweet girl. Did anyone ever tell you that?' He leaned forward and put his arms on each side of her body.

She frowned. What was this? She was not sweet at all. 'Be good, sweet maid, and let who will be clever' – that was what Eric had written in her autograph book. She despised sweetness. She was not good, she would have stolen the affections of Joseph Rosenbloom from Jean, and Paul from Jean. She tried to prise Calum for herself and she would do her best to pinch this one from Anna, and even from Carrie, if she got the chance. She didn't know why – it was from some inner need. It was strong. She looked at the tanned line of his neck against his blue shirt. Sweet.

'What we have is very precious, I don't want to destroy it,' he gabbled, and took her head in his hands and kissed her on the mouth. 'I didn't want this to happen,' he said, doing it again immediately.

This time his mouth opened, like a sea anemone, and so did hers. There was a whole different universe revealed by this, she noted.

She stretched herself and got down from the table. She stared at him and he smiled. You feel you are pushing, but you are being pushed, she thought. She'd read it somewhere.

'Better get out of here, before the two of them get back. They will know somehow. Women do.'

What could they know? That what they had been expecting was being carried out? They would be delighted. He little knew women.

212

'I'll take Judy out. Come on, Jude.' Judy got up from where she had been lying, surveying their activities.

'There's nothing to worry about, is there?' he said, seeing her frown.

'Oh no.' She was learning from him that what one said and what one did were two separate things. 'See you later.'

She left him making his tea. She and Judy went seawards.

She saw, coming towards her, the two women, laden with shopping bags – Anna in her bright cotton dress, Ellie in her best blouse and skirt.

'Poor old things,' she said to Judy. 'Poor old things.'

39

Now it seemed they were in different positions, a new line-up – Sarah and Lev, Ellie and Anna.

The women had joined together in some sort of conspiratorial despair. They lived it, she had been right. It was like Gran and Ellie whispering together about Eric.

Lev and Sarah hovered on the edge of sensual awareness. Sarah found herself looking at him constantly, and for him when he was not there.

She asked if she could now meet his daughter; he said no. She regarded this as a defeat. But she saw also that it was difficult for him, with his smudged and fudged view of morality, to introduce a fifteen year old to his own nine year old. So he did not defy all the conventions either?

The thing that worried her was whether she could risk all on Lev; on that throw of the dice, his 'poetic' view of the world. Or would her underlying conventional sense tell her that this was impossible?

There was a side, a side of herself she despised, which fell for the consumer images, the girls with engagement rings, given by bank clerks, the neat house and mortgage – the advertising-agency world. It was one she believed that she believed in only as a reaction to living with Ellie.

There were times, in spite of her fascination with him, that she despised Lev, too. His life was such chaos – wasn't she capable of judging failure? She was an expert. Wasn't that the way it should be? Chaos. Why did she crave the other, the ordered, the sure?

The lure of the lax, the lazy was great; the lure of the ordinary was almost a greater temptation. Go back to school, get on, go to university, become one of *them*.

Lev asked her one day, lying in the hot sand, if she could see living in London with him – they'd get a room together, she could study, he write. It would be fun. She had put her arm over her eyes and seen the room: brass bed, a kitten, books, an Indian rug, lamps made out of Chianti bottles – it all shimmered in the beach haze. It was an illusion, like a desert mirage. She was not that stupid. It was at that moment she realized she was older than Lev.

About then, the telegram came from the colonel. He had found a job, and a flat in South Kensington, and had given Rosie O'Grady the boot. This last was not in the telegram. Mrs Brodie got a confirming letter later in the week. Sarah read it when Mrs Brodie was out, buying herself some new clothes for London. Sarah found the letter nauseating – full of self-pity and bathetic sentiments. It didn't seem to affect Mrs Brodie. She handed Sarah the sari-material as a goodbye present.

'A little thank-you gift for keeping me company,' she said. She was a different woman, her voice restored. Off on the train she went, first-class for Euston, the *Tatler* and *House and Garden* in her gloved hand.

'Come and see us,' she cried, but she had not given Sarah the address.

'She's got no pride,' said Sarah to Ellie. Ellie was slumped in the chair. In some ways she seemed older than Mrs Brodie but then she had no colonel to rescue her. Anna too looked strained. They had been having one of their awful conversations.

'You look tired, Anna,' Sarah said. 'Why don't you give up the job for a bit?' She felt a little disloyal although she had not suggested that Lev work harder.

'We'll both be working in London soon,' said Anna, 'out from under your feet at last.'

Sarah hadn't seen her so muted, so resigned before. Could Anna dislike her? There was no real reason, was there? Ellie got up and went out. Whatever had happened, it was serious. Sarah toyed with the idea of discussing Lev with Anna and then thought better of it. She had obviously jettisoned any relationship with Anna because of her infatuation.

Lev had lost his job at the rifle range. But that wasn't what was bothering them all. Whatever it was, they were not revealing it to her.

Ellie hung out the VACANCIES sign. Lev and Sarah painted the Brodies' bedroom. Anna retired to bed, feeling unwell.

Sarah painted, Lev assisted. Overcome by lassitude, they lay down on the Brodies' bed, covered in dust sheets now; appropriately, Sarah thought. There, Lev put his hard body over hers and disarranged her skirt and put his hand into the soft, warm place between her legs. It seemed to her the inevitable end to all the talking of poetry. He tried to get some reponse from her but she lay, staring into the space over his shoulder. She liked it when he kissed her but she did not like this. It recalled Mr Duffell, in the dreary garden, with the dead bush and the paper flowers. She remembered he had said she would like it, one day. She didn't like it.

He gave up, saying she was a green bud, unopened, not ready. He asked her for the first time, surprisingly, how old she was. She said fifteen but she wasn't yet that.

'You still have a chance to get back, join the rat-race,' he said, shoving his shirt back into his trousers. She didn't understand his bitter tone because she hadn't really promised him anything, had she?

'Why do Anna and Ellie leave us alone together so much?' she said, angry at them in a way for not protecting her better.

'Who knows why women do what they do? They are giving us – me – enough rope, I expect. Ellie, perhaps, doesn't know.' He slapped on some white paint, letting the drops spatter where they may.

'She knows,' said Sarah. 'And Anna?'

'Anna knows.' He looked so miserable, she didn't speak for a while. She knew what Ellie was doing, she was opting out as usual, leaving Sarah to cope. Sort it out yourself, she could hear Ellie saying; she knew her so well. Nothing to do with me.

I am on my own, thought Sarah. She felt older than all of them sometimes.

Lev, from that moment, tried to persuade her to go back to school, as if in some kind of atonement for what had not happened.

216

He said she should either do a secretarial course or try and get into an art school.

'What about the men and women walking naked in the forests?' she said. 'Have *they* all got their School Certificates?'

'Probably,' he said, for him rather grimly. 'You just don't understand what I mean.'

But she did, well enough. She hadn't come up to scratch, for whatever reason, as a free being. She knew she would rather rely on instinct; all her – funnily enough – instincts told her that was the right way. But they always let her down. It was like the fear of the Tower. When she had lain there, for Lev, like a mute animal, her instincts had deserted her, just as her courage always had at moments of physical daring. The one girl in the gym class stuck halfway down the rope, the one not able to leap the horse. Perhaps failure was inbred like success. There were successful families and failed ones. Eric, for instance, Eric had had a dream like Lev, not of men and women naked in the forest, but of bettering their lot – and Eric hadn't even coped with his own family. That didn't negate his dream; in a funny way it made it stronger. Lev's too. What she hoped was that her own dream of herself as free, instinctive and brave was not just as illusory as theirs.

'You haven't finished the doll's house. Won't your daughter be disappointed?'

'I never told her about it. I bought her something else.' He said he would finish it before they went to London. She didn't know which 'they' he meant.

She began to see the enormity of what Anna had done, throwing in her lot with him. Anna had given up real boys, with skinned knees and hurt eyes, for this. And a husband who still cared enough to hit out at her in rage. Lev seemed to ignore Anna. The whole thing was a myth, another illusion. What women did for affection – it was ludicrous.

And she was still not immune herself. A day with him was not a day like any other. It was transformed. 'I am the poet of the body and of the soul.' You couldn't dismiss that lightly. It might not be offered, ever again.

It was shattered a little when Anna came into the kitchen one

217

evening, red-eyed from weeping. She gave Ellie the thumbs-down sign.

'It appears I am to be one of Mrs Encino's young ladies – or a damned fool,' she said.

Sarah had no idea what she meant, but she could see that Ellie had.

40

Lev appeared in the kitchen. It was late. Anna hadn't been at work for some days; Ellie had stood in for her at the pub, while Sarah managed to provide and serve the evening meal for the few remaining guests.

'Is Ellie in?'

Sarah looked up. She was reading, lying on the Put-U-Up. He craned to see the title as all readers were apt to do – it was one of his books, *Civilization and its Discontents*. Freud. She saw his wry smile.

'Anything wrong?' she asked.

She closed the book, but kept her finger in the place.

'Just a woman's problem – you know,' he said.

No, she didn't.

'Ellie is having a bath. Shall I call her?' He nodded. She put the book down, and went and disturbed Ellie. She heard the water run out, and Ellie pad along to see Anna. Lev was still seated on the Put-U-Up when she returned. He looked very down. She almost put her arm around him but thought better of it. She picked up the book again.

'You wouldn't consider sleeping with me?' He mumbled this at her – she wasn't even sure she had heard him rightly.

'What? Now? Don't be daft.' He looked so anguished she added, 'You know what a coward I am – what about Ellie and Anna?'

She wished she could be miles away, in some monkish cell, reading in peace. She knew she had sounded too flippant. She saw there was a tear emerging from one eye; it remained there, there were none to follow. What was up? She had no idea. He pressed the palm of his hand in his eye socket, like a small boy, like Toby. She took no apparent notice.

Ellie appeared in her dressing gown, a towel wrapped around her head. She was hiding blood-stained rags behind her back. She looked like an actress in a school production of a Greek drama. Sarah wanted to laugh.

'You'd better get on in there,' Ellie said to Lev. 'And also call a doctor.'

'No doctors, she insists,' said Lev, and went.

'What is going on?' asked Sarah.

'Never you mind.'

'Want me to go for the doctor?'

'No, she's old enough to know what she is doing,' said Ellie.

'Is she very bad?'

'She has had a miscarriage. That's a polite word for it, anyway.'

Sarah didn't question her further; Ellie's mouth had assumed its Gran effect, the cynical turn-down of disapproval. Suddenly, Sarah realized, Ellie had grown old. Well, middle-aged really. When had it happened? Little pin pricks of it must have been undermining the young Ellie, the mother she knew. She had been ageing all the time, throughout the changes, the jobs, the moves – from the Rosenblooms, through the Duffells and the Bateses – the fine girlishness of her exercising at the windows of Rathmines, the jaunty girl in overalls – all these had gone and left in their place this woman whom Sarah hardly knew.

Adolf the admired had changed the world and was dead, Ellie had gone on, and nothing had happened to her. She had just endured.

'You look tired. You should get out more, meet people,' she said.

'Why are you saying this, just now?' Ellie began to rub her wet hair in the towel.

'You aren't old, you know – there's time for you to even marry again.'

Ellie stared at her.

'What brought this on? Anyway, I told you. Once was enough. Eric was enough for me.'

'It isn't good enough. You can't just – not live.'

'I am living, thank you very much,' said Ellie. 'What you are talking about is men – what do you think, that I want one like him in there?'

'Don't you think him attractive?'

'No. But I can't say the reverse.'

Did she mean that Lev had, to use the awful phrase her generation, had, 'made a pass' at her?

'He didn't?'

'He did, just after they moved in. I told him to bugger off. Not that I wasn't tempted.'

Sarah was shocked, both by the revelation, and by Ellie's swearing.

'Why?'

'I refused because he is Anna's – and one doesn't do that kind of thing.'

Sarah didn't believe Ellie had been tempted. It was Ellie's passivity that had ruled her. Sarah never made the mistake of regarding inaction as a moral choice; she was not fooled by Ellie. Inaction was always Ellie's choice in the emotional game. Sarah could not really know what had gone on between Eric and Ellie but she knew this must have been at the root of it. They had both become inactive at the same time – it was like a blight.

Perhaps when they were old, she and Ellie, they could go over the past, like archaeologists on a dig, prising up artefacts from the debris. But not yet, it was too soon.

Lev appeared, bearing a parcel wrapped in newspaper.

'Can I burn this on the stove?'

'Go ahead.' Ellie was drying her hair.

Sarah could not believe this was happening. The silence was shattering.

'Now get out,' said Ellie. 'And as soon as she is fit, you can both leave.'

He went.

Anna was up early the next morning, fresh as a daisy.

'Are you all right?' asked Sarah.

'I'm fine – just a touch of 'flu,' said Anna.

'Hope I don't catch it.' Sarah had looked in the grate that morning. She didn't know what she expected, but there were just the usual clinkers.

'I'm thinking of going to town,' said Sarah. 'Want to come along?'

'No – we're packing. You know we are going, to London?'

'Yes, I heard.'

Sarah went to the account box. which was marked 'Mrs Encino' and removed what was in there; about twenty-five pounds in all. She stuffed it into her raincoat pocket.

'Cheerio,' she said.

41

When Sarah returned they were all standing in the kitchen, like characters in a stage set. Anna was wearing her coat. There were two suitcases at the door.

Ellie's face was highlighted by the two spots of red on her cheeks – a definite sign of anger. Lev's sack of books, with his name stencilled on the side, was spilling over in the middle of the floor.

'You can leave them just for security – you owe me quite a lot, you know.'

'No need to mention it – we intend to pay.' Anna blew her nose vigorously. She may or may not have been crying. 'Let me leave something else. My tailor-made tweed suit, you like that.'

'It was tailor-made for you,' said Ellie. 'What would I do with a tweed suit? At least the books will be useful for Sarah.'

'Don't bring me into it.' They all turned to the door and looked at Sarah. Ellie squealed.

'What on earth have you done to yourself?'

Sarah shrugged. She'd had her hair tinted; she had bought a feminine floral dress and a pink linen coat, high heels, and she reeked of scent. She had been sure what the effect was. By their faces, she knew.

'I thought I'd become a real female. Isn't that what we all want to be – what everybody *likes*?' There was no answer.

'Where did you get the money for all that rubbish?' asked Ellie.

Sarah took no notice. She was looking at Lev's reaction. He hadn't spoken. He pushed the bag of books with his foot.

'Keep them then. For Sarah.'

She looked at him quickly.

'I won't be doing much reading. It's a waste of time really, isn't it? Who likes clever women?'

'Quiet, love,' said Anna. 'You hang on to them, and you send them on when we are settled. All right?' She put her arm around Sarah.

Sarah removed herself from the gesture. Lev went out.

'You'd better go,' said Ellie to Anna. The two women embraced like boxers in a clinch.

'Goodbye Sarah, don't forget us. Come and see us in London.' She went out. The front door slammed.

'Just like Mrs Brodie,' said Sarah.

'Not quite. Anna did leave the address,' said Ellie.

They both listened as the cab started up. Sarah wondered how she could stand there, with Lev moving out of her life. A terrible lethargy had taken her over. She would do nothing now, just let things ride. Things were going to be on her terms and those were going to be limited. No reaching out for anything.

'I'll make a cup of coffee,' she said, moving like someone in a slowed-down dream. 'Why did you do that, about the books?'

'I didn't see why they should just walk away,' said Ellie. 'They owe me – and not just money either. They nearly made me double-jail-bait.'

Double-jail-bait? Sarah's mind was moving as slowly as her body. That would be the 'miscarriage', she supposed – and the almost-seduction of herself, as she was under-age. How strange that those innocent actions were criminal – and triggered by love. Was that the way of it? The stretching of what seemed normal, which hit against laws you were not even conscious of? And all everyday, normal – were they then *evil* . . . ? She wanted to shout, to laugh, it was all so stupid. And what had that to do with her or Lev? The books spilling out were a symbol of what they had really intended.

'I'm glad you kept them,' she said. 'We can sell them, if we like.' She felt quite proud of that remark, knowing it would shock Ellie.

'I'd never do that. He will want them and I only wanted to make a point,' said scrupulous Ellie. Sarah sighed. No wonder she had never taken anything from Eric. She was, after all, a moral person.

After coffee, she went up and surveyed the new Sarah in the long glass in the Brodies' room, where she had been changed by Mrs Brodie.

'Hello tart, freak, moron,' she said, pulling a face. She hated the new Sarah. That was a good sign. She was going to function on hate now, for a while, and see how it worked out.

Ellie was behind her.

'I'll never know why you did all that.' She began to laugh. 'It really is awful.' She couldn't stop. Sarah was drawn to her hysteria as if it was infectious and she began too. It was like the old days, when they were really together. They couldn't stop. Ellie paused, suddenly.

'Where did you say you got the money from?'

'From the tin marked Mrs Encino,' Sarah shrieked. Ellie went down to check. Sarah wiped her running eyes.

'You've done it now,' said Ellie, sober as a judge, as Sarah came down. 'We owe about fifty pounds back rent. I was going to persuade Tooley to accept twenty-five. Now we don't have that. We had better sit down and think.'

They sat and thought.

'I could try and sell the clothes back—'

'They wouldn't take them. They were lucky to sell them once. They couldn't shift them again.' Ellie was off again, laughing in terrible agony, the tears running down her cheeks. It wasn't despair, noted Sarah, it was a kind of relief. The real Ellie was making a reappearance. It was nice to see her.

'There must be something we can sell.'

'But what – none of this is ours. Thank God,' said Ellie. Sarah looked at her with admiration.

'Lev's books are valuable, particularly the Freud. It's a collected edition—' She could hurt Lev that way, in the most cruel way she could think of.

'No,' said Ellie.

'I could sell my tennis racquet and hockey gear. I can't see I'll be doing those again.'

'How much will you get?'

'Not much.'

She was right, she got five pounds. She bought some lamb

chops, apples, *Picturegoer* and some chocolate. She got a bunch of flowers for Ellie.

'What's this – a funeral?' asked Ellie. They munched the apples and shared the chocolate. There was a certain freedom in the air. Ellie had not seemed so happy for ages.

'I feel as if we had already left,' she said. 'We'll do a bunk, tonight. We'll be on the road again.'

Judy jumped up at them, liking the excitement.

'We've got her,' Sarah pointed out.

'That doesn't matter – anyone who takes us will have to take her.' Ellie was almost drunk. The adrenalin had made her so. Sarah.looked at her with guarded admiration. It was all right now, in the hilarity of the moment – but what were they to do? Ellie was filled with thoughts of freedom, there would be no holding her.

Sarah thought of Lev speeding towards London. What did it matter? Ellie and she were on the move, too.

42

Ellie, from excess euphoria, turned fearful. It was the other side of her nature. Sarah had seen this coming. Ellie scrubbed and cleaned the place, as if to placate the absent authoritarian figure of Mrs Encino. 'We're poor but we're honest,' Sarah could hear Gran saying. Sarah mourned the quick decline of vivacious new Ellie, which had so quickly slipped into the touching-the-forelock one, the mute conformist of late.

They had packed their belongings and were camping out in the Brodies' bedroom. It was as if Ellie expected her marching orders hourly. They were waiting for the visit of Tooley and Mrs Encino's heavy son; meanwhile Ellie did the chores and Sarah lay on the bed – scene of her failure with Lev – and read the situations-vacant column in the evening paper.

The trouble was, she could do nothing – was qualified for nothing. The advertisements were dull for one like her – clerks, shop assistants, or domestics. Why hadn't she taken notice of what everyone had been telling her over the past year or so? She read the 'Rooms to Let'. That was even more depressing. And most of them were too expensive for her and Ellie.

Ellie came up and read the advertisements too, putting on her reading glasses. They made her look efficient which, thought Sarah, she was not.

'We ought to stay, put up a fight. They can't chuck us out,' said Sarah. But Ellie wanted to move on, she knew that. Ellie had been there a long time, by her floating standards.

'We are leaving. I feel it in my bones,' said Ellie, looking in the paper for a sign. She had always felt herself psychic though, Sarah thought, if that was so, why did she never know what she was letting herself in for?

'Something will turn up,' said Ellie. Sarah's heart sank.

Psychic Ellie said that they would be along that evening for the rent and that Sarah should stay in the bedroom with Judy tied to the bedpost. Sarah opened her mouth to argue, feeling that if she were present, the situation might be at least ordinary, and not filled with that heightened sense of the dramatic that Ellie resorted to in crisis. But she gave up; she felt they were going to move anyway, Ellie was willing it, and Ellie's negative will was stronger than her positive one.

She could hear the raised voices downstairs and the door slam, and the Rolls start up. She would have liked to have seen Tooley, Tooley the mysterious, Tooley the acrobat.

'Well, that's it,' said Ellie, trying not to look pleased. 'We have to be out by the weekend.'

'But that is ridiculous,' said Sarah, 'I would have done better than that.'

'I know,' said Ellie.

Sarah tried to get Mr Fernald to find Judy a home. But Judy was overweight still, from the pregnancy, and she had eczema of the coat.

'She's not in good condition, you know,' he said. Her son, Bill, had won the best-dog-of-the-show award, at the Fylde that summer. His picture was on the wall with a red rosette pinned to it.

'I couldn't take her on, my dear, not the way she is. Try and find her a good home. Advertise.'

How could she advertise? They would have no address soon.

Ellie fixed them a job for the Christmas period. They would have to get a room and do odd jobs until then.

'I've rented somewhere. No dogs allowed,' said Ellie. Sarah knew what that meant. She heard someone in a pub needed a dog, and she and Judy trekked off to see if Judy would do. The landlord took one look and said she wouldn't be much use as a guard dog, now would she?

Sarah had three pounds left from the sale of her hockey gear. Ellie pawned her wedding ring to pay the advance rent of the room. They were set for their new life – except for the Judy problem.

'We could hide her in the room,' Ellie said. Then she refused to think about it.

Sarah set off to find a veterinary surgeon who would do the deed. Eventually she found one, but both she and Ellie had to really break down before he would agree.

They left the surgery, tears streaming.

'For two pins I would have asked him to do us as well,' said Ellie. 'They should have it for humans.'

As they waited for the tram Sarah swore she would never be put in that position of vulnerability again. Not ever.

'Do you realize that Princess Elizabeth got married today and we didn't even notice?' she said to Ellie.

'You are a hard bitch,' said Ellie. 'I hope you realize how hard you are becoming. You are capable of anything. Anything.'

Thanks, thought Sarah.

43

The room overlooked the railway. Sarah spent most of her time lying on the sagging mattress of the double bed that almost filled the room. She was reading her way through Lev's sack of books. Through the thin walls she often heard the voices of children singing. Sometimes she thought she must be imagining them, for she never saw one along the dim passages of the dank house.

From Lev's books dropped mementoes; old quotes in his unmistakable hand on scraps of paper, the odd bus ticket, shopping list, or bill from a New York bookshop. It made her feel close to him though she knew time was carrying them further apart each day, so that now their destination, which not so long ago had seemed to be the same, was getting to be miles apart. Even if, at some future date, they were together, he and she already would have changed. Time was changing them now, each boring hour she spent was making a different Sarah, and no doubt the same was true of him, wherever he was. She had spurts of obscene contentment, chocolate bars, a rare visit to the cinema. Filling in time was what she did, simply counting the hours until it was official sleeping time, allowing herself, even, a nap in the afternoons, the dreary, endless afternoons. She had not even tried for a job – there was only a month to fill in before they went to work for Christmas and New Year in the small private hotel. Ellie was working. She couldn't understand Sarah's lethargy.

'I just don't feel it is worth it,' Sarah said. 'I don't need any of your hard-earned money.'

'You eat, don't you?'

'Not much,' said Sarah, truthfully. They were allowed to use the landlady's kitchen but didn't bother. Ellie got her main meal at the department store and Sarah bought a pork pie and ate it at the dressing table, staring endlessly at her miserable face.

Ellie treated her as if she were recovering from some illness; that way it was easier for her, Sarah suspected. She would ask how Sarah was.

'A little better today, thanks,' Sarah would say, laughing. Ellie said she was getting a bit peculiar.

The novelty and general scrappiness of the new life suited Ellie quite well. She became quite glamorous again, making up and dressing well, going off for an evening with some of the other women. Sarah hardly bothered to dress, she wore her candlewick robe most of the time. Once she went down for a chocolate bar to the corner shop wearing it. No one stared. She made cups of coffee from the hot water in the bathroom. That place smelled of bodies and vomit. She surveyed it all as if it were not happening to her. It could have been a field study in biology. Isn't that interesting, she would think, seeing the dirty lavatory or a spider scuttling along the windowsill. She wondered how the Biology Princess, old Sarah One, was getting along. She toasted her silently with Camp coffee. She must surely be a success by now.

She no longer bothered to pinpoint people by her stories. They were either all interesting, or of no interest, it seemed to her. Neither way did it matter whether or not she recorded them. They were as exotic and indescribable as tropical fish at the bottom of the sea. Maybe if light struck them they would reveal themselves as colourful, worthy of attention, instead of floating in the grey-green deeps – but she wasn't going to be the one to turn on the light.

The landlady, a dyed blonde ex-Variety artiste, cheered her. The house was filled with her posters, she had appeared in all the music halls and variety palaces of Europe, at one time. She talked of her career to anyone who would listen. Sarah listened. She heard the lewd stories again and again – how Buttons couldn't undo his buttons when she was Cinderella. How she had carried on with two clowns – one sad, one merry. Sarah thought her the most vital person she'd ever met. She wanted to be like that. The trouble was, you had to live the life first.

231

Sarah wanted to be like her now, without doing all that.

Vera had a lover, an ex-Polish airforce pilot who put his hands over his ears when she started on her tales. They drank; Polish spirit mainly. It made him wild. Sarah had some too, on the afternoons when she couldn't stand her room and Franz Kafka and Walt Whitman with his muscular rhetorical windbag poems. Sarah studied the pilot with interest, his long yellow face with teeth to match, his dead eyes, his violence, which came after two or three vodkas or the stuff – as he called the colourless liquid fire. He never committed the indiscretion of any personal remark, or judgment on life, he never asked her who she was, or why she was there, or why she didn't work – or why she had such a good head for alcohol and was drinking the afternoons away.

He was the epitome of nothingness. She liked that. When violent he would break furniture and smoulder in the corner until he went upstairs to vomit. He came down, his hair slicked down with water; the perfect gentleman again. He never spoke of his indulgence or explained or excused it.

'Come on, love, come and have a tipple.' Vera would be at the door, most afternoons. Sarah would sometimes say no, but rarely. It filled the worst part of the day.

Ellie discovered they had lost one of their bags, the one with all their family records, marriage certificate, birth certificates, posters of Eric in his hey-day, photographs, and cuttings of Eric's speeches and articles in the *Guardian*. She was very cross when Sarah said it didn't matter. Sarah said you could get duplicates of the certificates.

'That's not the point.'

'What was it? My heritage?' asked Sarah.

She was sorry to leave the room. It had become like the carapace of her soul. She looked into the pilot's dead eyes and Vera's bloodshot ones. She hated parting with them both.

The small private hotel was quite near that old haunt, the Bateses'. They, of course had gone to Scotland. The young couple who owned this one had unusual ideas, said Ellie. Fine cooking, open fires, the continental style of things. I hope they make it here then, Sarah said.

Alison the young wife ('do call me Alison') told Sarah she

might like to do a Cordon Bleu cooking course later. Why didn't Sarah do one too? Sarah said she was not interested. 'You ought to do something like that, if catering is going to be your trade,' the officious Alison suggested. Sarah said catering was not going to be her trade.

Sarah had got so used to floating in Vera's disorder, she found it hard to put up with the soft green carpets and the tasteful linen, the dreadful preparations for a Northern Christmas. There was a twenty-foot tree in the lounge that Alison and Tony, her husband, were going to trim entirely in silver.

'She's got good taste,' said Ellie. 'Have you seen her clothes?' Sarah had. They were all little jersey dresses and high-heeled shoes. In their twin-bedded room they had lying on the chair a copy of *The Art of Living* by André Maurois. Dear Lev, how are you? said Sarah, spraying herself with a dollop of Arpège she found on Alison's dressing table.

Tony, the husband, had not got his wife's democratic ideas about the staff. He was the one who took them to the annexe at the back, where their bedroom was, owing to the hotel's being fully booked for the winter season. His attitude suited Sarah better, she knew how to respond to it. Alison got on her nerves.

'What a dump,' she said to Ellie. 'You'll get pneumonia here, it is that cold and damp.'

'It's only temporary,' said Ellie. 'You should see the other staff quarters – not bad at all.'

Ellie was taken in by Alison's charm, Sarah could see that. The daughter she might have had. Would have liked to have. Of course, Ellie was always like this at the beginnings of things, and they would not be here long enough for the novelty to wear off.

Sarah helped Alison and Tony trim the tree. Alison was ecstatic, 'I can't help it – I'm a fool about Christmas,' she cried. Tony smiled at her.

Sarah couldn't analyse why Alison was so disgustingly pleasant all the time. It must be a nervous tic, she decided. Alison had pre-Raphaelite hair, which all the time escaped from the demure roll she tried to make of it. Sarah respected

233

Tony much more when she saw the hair at its wildest – otherwise she would have despised him for his choice. The fact that Alison could not control her hair was her saving grace.

She knew Tony disliked Alison's friendly attitude to her; he was right, it was degrading. He had got her number – he could see through her. He was even more upset when his younger brother, Will, came for the holiday. Will thought Sarah the wittiest thing since Dorothy Parker – he was too naïve to catch the true malice, especially when she spoke of Alison.

Will haunted her, no wonder; there were few guests under fifty. Rubicund men, mainly, with their plump over-dressed wives, they had come for a good festive session of gluttony and party games.

'What will you do when you leave Oxford?' she asked Will. He was doing PPE, but he said to her with a wink he was really only there to row.

'I don't know. I won't do what Tony's done,' he said. 'He has collapsed since he married her. Not that Alison isn't the sweetest girl in the world – but he wanted to write. Now look at him.'

'But I'm asking about you.'

'Ah – I'll go into Dad's firm, I suppose. The easy life.' He didn't seem to care. She liked him – he was so open.

'And you, what are you going to do?' he asked, being a polite boy.

'We are going to open a nightclub, in London. Like the one in *Gilda*.'

She saw his mouth open. He was naïve enough to believe her.

'What's "Gilda"?' he asked.

'Oh, a film. Rita Hayworth. Glenn Ford.' He wasn't a film buff. 'If I don't do that, I'll be a whore.'

'I say, you don't mean that.'

'Well, it's as good a life as any other.' She could see he might mention it to Tony. 'Don't tell Tony,' she said. She didn't know why she had said it.

She took the beach walks she had taken with Lev, with Will. It was a kind of sacrilege. Will noticed nothing – he talked of booze-ups and the rowing eight, and how all the girls seemed to have thick legs, and how his room was freezing, in the cold of Oxford. He talked too, of his father, who had turned up earlier that week. His father had been carrying on an affair with one of the waitresses for years – she had come to this hotel after he sold his own, larger one. They owned many, it appeared. Will would work on the administration side.

'Alma would get her cards from Tony, I think, except that he is scared of what Dad would do.'

'Well, the art of living is very difficult,' said Sarah.

'Eh?'

They ran along the beach each morning, before she started work. It was fine then, with the bare sand uncorrupted by even a mark. It was like the bleak beginning of the world. He was concerned about physical fitness. She was concerned with the way the sea hit the shingle and pounded its guts out, leaving the delicate shells. There was something so comforting about it all.

She got to like his uncomplicated physical presence. He was like a great heavy beast, lumbering along beside her, his blue eyes bright, his cheeks purple from the cold.

She couldn't respond to it the way she had to Lev's devious personality but it was a comfort, just like the familiar sea.

Tony was waiting one morning when they arrived back.

'Just what do you two think you are up to?' he asked. 'You should be getting the breakfasts laid.' He never called her by her name.

'We're obsessed with our physical selves,' gibed Will. 'Any objections? She's in time anyway.' Tony looked angry.

'I'm off to the kitchen,' she said, demurely. She would have liked to curtsey but Tony had no sense of humour. She heard the voices, later – Will's complacent and murmuring, Tony's shrill and hysterical. She heard his last remark:

'She's no good for you.'

'We're not exactly getting engaged. We just get on.' But the runs in the morning stopped.

From morning till night she washed dishes. How could people eat so much?

'I don't believe it—' she sighed, showing Ellie her skinned hands. 'How can they guzzle so much – it must be a reaction to the war.'

Alison was dismayed.

'Look at your hands, Sarah. How awful. You should let me help.'

'Don't be silly. What would Tony say?'

'They are producing some commercial dishwashers now,' she said.

'That's what I am, a commercial dishwasher,' said Sarah.

Sarah secretly thought she'd rather be behind a pile of dishes than in the lounge with the carousing guests. She could hear it all going on, the frenetic games, the sing-songs. Will was good at Northern monologues, 'Clogs' and 'Albert and the Lion'. He was great at parties.

He looked in, on Christmas Eve, a paper hat askew on his black head.

'They are asking for you.'

'Oh no.'

'You must. Tony says so. All the staff are to come in and get a present.'

'Oh well, if his lordship commands, I suppose I will have to.' She took off her greasy apron and smoothed down her hair. Will led her in. The fat guests applauded. It was one of the worst moments of her life.

Tony handed her a wrapped present. It was obviously a book. He looked as uncomfortable as she did. His paper hat was green and was meant to be a clown's bowler with elastic under the chin. There was a red feather stuck into the brim. He looked sadder than ever in it.

'Aren't you going to open it?' Will said. She unpacked it; *The Art of Living*, by André Maurois.

'Thank you very much,' she said.

There was dancing; she danced with the plump males and with Will. Tony excused himself. Alison looked lovely, in a Viyella print dress. She danced with anyone who asked her, and smiled beautifully throughout.

Ellie was missing. Sarah was a little worried by that. But she moved around to soft jazz with Will. A lot of the oldies had gone to bed. It was pleasant enough. Even a little romantic.

'Let's have "Body and Soul" again,' said Will. Now they

were the only two left.

Tony came in and started straightening chairs. She felt guilty, dancing.

'I'll help,' she cried, as they moved past him.

'No, you carry on,' he said. She accidentally brushed against him as they passed, and he leapt away as if burned.

'Sorry,' she said.

'That's all right.' He moved well away.

Ellie, Sarah discovered, had holed up with a waiter and a bottle of vodka to see in Christmas. It could only be an improvement, Sarah thought. She closed the door of the shack, leaving them laid out in state like two Egyptian mummies.

The lounge was almost deserted, the lamps off. She sat on the long couch by the window, hearing the sea outside. The body that had been snoring in an armchair slunk away.

'Merry Christmas,' she said to the dark shape as it left. She took a cigarette from one of the boxes that were littered around, and sat looking out at the silver sea. She wondered if she could play a record without waking anyone. The collection was all dance tunes, except for Will's collection of good jazz; she didn't feel like jazz. There was only one classical recording, the waltzes from *Der Rosenkavalier*. She put it on. Waltzed around to it on her own, happy at last.

'Happy Christmas, Richard Strauss,' she said, helping herself to a little white wine that was left in a bottle on a table.

She half-expected Tony to appear, she didn't quite know why, but the record played itself out and she fell asleep on the long couch, and didn't wake until the sound of the vacuum cleaner in the hall woke her at dawn.

44

They packed. The New Year guests had gone. Will had gone too, promising to write. He wrapped his long scarf around his bull neck. He would, he said, never forget her. He was annoyed when she laughed.

Ellie looked around the shack.

'It will be better than this in London, I promise you.'

Why would it be? thought Sarah.

'It's goodbye to the North, goodbye to this godforsaken town,' cried Ellie. She seemed happy.

Sarah stared at her. It was exactly as it had been when they made their first move, to the Rosenblooms'. Ellie was elated; it didn't matter where they were going. She was full of expectation. What a gift, I wish I'd been given it, thought Sarah. This may be the move that satisfies her. But that was ridiculous, any move satisfied Ellie. Sarah had figured it out; it was because she wasn't trying to *get* anywhere, really. Sarah was beginning to want to get somewhere.

'I'm going to walk around – say goodbye to the town,' she said. After all, it was *her* town. She walked the promenade from north to south, passing the dreaded phallic Tower, still unmounted by her. Passed the beige expanses of sand, the white buildings, the Golden Mile, the Pleasure Beach with the beloved Ice Drome, past the rifle range where Lev and the boys, Anna's boys, had had their confrontation.

She went the two routes to school, which Lev had told her were the equivalent to the Guermantes way and the Méséglise way in that long work of Proust's that he urged her to read one day. She had laughed at him, saying they were in fact only the Rathmines way and the Ranelagh way, and he said it didn't matter, it was what you saw in them. She passed the awfulness of the Duffells' house and the Rosenblooms' neat home.

She said farewell to Joseph, to Kingsley, to the aunts, to Eric, to Mrs Encino and Tooley, to poor dead Judy, to Sylvia of the hats.

She was ready to depart.

Lev's books were a trial, being the heaviest luggage they had. Sarah felt sorry, suddenly, that they had lost the case of family mementoes.

'It doesn't matter,' said Ellie, 'anything one wants to remember is intensified if lost.'

Sarah didn't believe that.

Tony had shaken hands with her. His hands were very cold. Alison had cried copiously.

Sarah and Ellie waited for the coach near the Princess Cinema where they had nourished so many dreams. Ginger Rogers and Fred Astaire, Bette Davis and Charles Boyer, Joan Crawford, Barbara Stanwyck. Rita. Sarah gave her blessing to Paramount, Columbia, RKO and the Warner Brothers.

The coach was half-empty for the winter journey.

'We didn't let Eric know,' laughed Ellie. 'I didn't even think of it.'

'Why should you?' asked Sarah. She had thought about it.

'I guess I am cured.'

Through narrow streets, past sleeping occupants of unlit houses, the odd light burning, but mostly dark – the coach's headlights beamed out. Sarah felt an anguish that she would never know all those sleepers. They went on quickly, to major roads. The Black Country, the Potteries. This was England. She wondered how big London would be.

Ellie had been in touch with Anna. They had the address in Tottenham, and Anna had even sent a few crumpled pound notes to aid them. Lev's books would be returned to him.

Sarah dreamed and dozed, and tried to contain all of the journey which, though not much, was all she had done so far.

She had difficulty imagining London. She had seen British films, and newsreels and postcards of a few famous places.

Her friend Meriel had been to London once in the war on a shopping trip with her mother. They had brought back white shoes. You couldn't buy them at that point in the war. Sarah thought of London as the place where white shoes were always available.

She knew it would have changed from Ellie's London. The Blitz had left holes and craters. She had seen it on the newsreel. She wondered if Ellie's birthplace, Kennington, was still the same. Charlie Chaplin had been born there too – Ellie was proud of that.

'Stretch out, get some sleep. It will be a busy day tomorrow,' said Ellie.

She tried to sleep, watching Ellie's crumpled face reflected in the window of the coach. But she couldn't lose any of the journey, and so she stayed awake, drinking it in.

They stopped at an all-night café used by lorry drivers and coaches. The woman, in an overall over her nightdress and with a few curlers sticking to her hair, poured tea from a large urn. There were pies and sausage rolls. Ellie's scarf trailed in a pool of tea. She lit a Woodbine.

'It won't be long now. *London*,' she said, inhaling.

'Do you know lots of people there?' asked Sarah. Perhaps it would be different, there.

'No,' said Ellie. 'Less than up there, really.' Sarah supposed that from now on, Blackpool would be 'up there'. 'We aren't the kind of people who "know people" anywhere, are we?'

Sarah said she supposed not. Ellie had made it sound as if she meant knowing a lot of Somerset Maugham-like people. She just meant *people*. She had meant friends, roots.

She could see it wasn't going to be that different, really. She was a little scared. She was putting her trust in Ellie, yet again. Suppose Ellie's judgment proved as fatally fragile as it always had before?

She was ashamed of her timidity. Dawn was leaking into the sky. It was better, after all, to be on a coach in the middle of the night, going somewhere.

Wasn't it?

45

I am in Blackpool. Eva has made one of her miraculous recoveries, escaping the grim reaper yet again. I am filled with crazy exaltation. Free, to work – at least for a while.

We sit in the car, Simon's old VW (Gilly has the better car). The rain lashes the windscreen, and foam from the shit-brown sea – sea of my memories – hits the bonnet and us, when we try to open the doors and merge with the elements.

I pour warm *Liebfraumilch* into paper cups. I had hoped to cool it in the sea, but the enraged breakers won't let me. If I venture down there I will be blown away, with my slim green bottle. I roasted a chicken last night and we sit with linen napkins on our knees; it is not what I visualized but we are enjoying it. I had forgotten the strength of the elements up here, in the North Country.

I see the Ranelagh up on the cliff. I point it out to Simon. He trains his binoculars on to the building and tells me it has a sign outside, banging in the gale. 'Self-Catering Apartments, Vacancies', it says.

'An odd place to have lived,' he says.

'Blackpool or the Ranelagh?'

'Both. But I like the town – it isn't at all what I had expected. It has more charm. All that 'thirties lettering, street names and so on, it can't have changed much since you were here. It has a certain battered grandness.'

'Like me.' We laugh. I catch sight of my face in the driving mirror and wipe a scrap of chicken from my mouth. It hasn't changed, my old town, it is virtually untouched, from redevelopment or traffic. Thank God for trams, I think, recalling the mess of Oxford, and practically everywhere else.

'Innocence, that's what it has, and vulgarity, but honest with

241

it. It's a bit like you – and the book.'

'Oh, thanks.' It is a compliment, a bit of a back-handed one, but that is how I like them.

'I hope you don't have masses of trusty relations to visit?'

Now how can he say that, just after the other remark? He can't have understood the book, then. Or me. How can he have known me so well, and still think I have anyone to visit?

'I haven't – and wouldn't.'

'Ah, one never knows with you provincial types. You always discover your roots, sooner or later.' *Provincial types?*

'You know I never belonged. You've read the book.' (And you are directing the film for television.) 'I'm just slumming, like you.' I sound sharper than I intended. And we are having, were having, such a good picnic. I shiver.

'Cold?'

'Someone just walked across my grave. Let's go. You must see the town.'

We drive away from the rain-lashed promenade, and along through deserted streets.

'It is going to be great, terrific,' shouts Simon, peering at the Winter Gardens, the Tower, all the hackneyed old landmarks.

'We'll use the real places, my places, won't we?' I know the answer to that one, really.

'Well, the Ranelagh isn't quite right, is it, love? I mean, we need something a bit more like you describe – grander, perhaps?'

I huddle into my raincoat. He asks if it matters to me.

'No, not really. You can't repeat the past.'

'Can't repeat the past? Why of course you can!' He smiles at me. Dear, quick, literate Simon.

'Thank you, Jay Gatsby,' I say.

'Think nothing of it.'

I find it odd that the place means so little to me. I don't feel nostalgia or hurt, or anything very much. Catharsis, I suppose. What did I expect, the old Proust-madeleine recollections, with the Guermantes way and the Méséglise way (or their Blackpool Sarah equivalents, the Ranelagh way and the Encino way)? No. Only the Tower retains any kind of potency, and that is because it is still an unfulfilled challenge. The place hasn't as much resonance for me as, say, Aldeburgh, or Oxford, or Nice. *Nice?* What would young Sarah say to that?

The wind has dropped, the sun is trying to make an appearance.

'I'd like to go and stand on the steps, going down to the sea.'

'But the tide is in,' says logical Simon.

'It always was. I used to will it to go out.'

'All right, Canute, let's do it.'

We stand on the steps with the sea whirling beneath our feet.

'This is idiotic,' he says, enjoying it. But he has his needing-to-telephone look. He can never last long without telephoning and organizing something.

'Let's find a hotel and you can do your telephoning,' I say.

'Is it so obvious? How well you know me.' Not said nastily, but not too happily, either. I must watch that. I have done it often before. A mother of adolescents learns not to know too well. Nothing annoys more. The eighth deadly sin. Let be; I tell myself, let be.

We find a small two-star hotel, with Egon Ronay and motoring association recommendations studding its front, like medals on a general. We book a twin-bedded room with TV, bidet and all the other modern conveniences far removed from the boarding houses of my youth.

'Ye gods,' I say, the old schoolgirl slang coming out, 'a bidet, yet. When I was young people used to sleep in the bath.'

'You want me to sleep in the bath?' He climbs in and mimes snoring. It offends me, I don't quite know why. Perhaps because we, in our fashionably faded jeans and sloganized T-shirts and our Slick Willie clumpy shoes, are treading over the past when people had to holiday like that or not at all. There is no reason why he should know. He climbs out, crestfallen, as one of my sons used to be when a joke misfired.

We stare at our reflection in the narrow looking-glass.

'We look like unisex Viking twins,' I say, removing my sheepskin coat. Simon fumbles in his pocket for a joint.

'You want to watch out. They are all Northern puritans up here, you know.'

'Including you?' He has cottoned on to my down mood.

243

'I'm going to have a bath. You are free to do your telephoning.'

'I'm ringing Abigail. Any message?' He grins round the bathroom door. I throw a cake of hotel soap at him. I miss.

I run the bath and soak. I look at my body. Strange to think it was transported around this same place by the young Kate, or *Sarah*. Circling endlessly with Ellie (Eva). Is it the same body, or have the renewed cells left the child? – it is like the old puzzle about the Zen monk, going up and down the mountain. At what point does he pass *himself*? There is a point. Or so one is supposed to believe. The answer is to extend the time to infinity. I look for young Sarah's body under the soapy water. It isn't there. Do I notice the squaring-off of the figure I notice in other women of my age? Not yet, I am in fact thinner than during the maternal years. Perhaps I am in for a phoney adolescence. Let's hope so.

Young Sarah wanted to be Ginger Rogers. I'm older now than Ginger was then. I no longer wish to be Ginger Rogers – but I'd like the lust Sarah felt back again. Oh for the lusts of childhood, when one would feel like dying for whatever it was one wanted. A bar of chocolate, a bright comic, a new toy everyone else seemed to have.

Those impossible hopes, to be world-champion ice skater or a great ballerina. They are all there within one's grasp when the dreams are potent. Better than anything one has later. You learn quickly not to have them – until you can't raise them again, no matter how hard you try. It is known as growing up – and should be called scaling down.

I lie on the bed and watch Simon perform on the telephone. He is alive, vital. Who is the recipient of all this charm? Abigail, of course. He winks at me as he says, 'Of course you can, don't be silly – I have complete faith in your ability', etc., So it is not just me who gets all that.

I think about it. I did it for Jenni, Miles and Peter. And Dom. All the time. The great little encourager. I sometimes think I smothered them with my attentions, my hopes and my *knowing*.

He hangs up at last. Flops down on the narrow twin bed beside me.

'She is a little gloomy. The television thing went basically wrong, at least she thinks it did.' Abigail had been doing Nina, in *The Seagull*.

'Did you ever lust after anything, when you were a child?' I ask him.

'Only the girl next door. No, I lie. I lusted after one of those Hamley's airplanes, the ones that actually flew.'

'And did you get one?'

'Of course I did.' *Of course.*

'Did you like it when you got it?'

He scratches his head.

'I liked it, but, you see – it never flew. I had agitated a whole year for it and then it never flew. My brother, the mechanical genius, my dad and I would go to Primrose Hill every weekend and try and get the damn thing in the air. The propeller whizzed around, it looked as if it would take off, but it never did. We gave up. I lasted longer than the others, hoping it would fly, but even I gave up in the end.'

'What happened to it?'

'I don't remember, isn't that strange?'

'When was that?'

'Oh, a long time ago. 1960.'

1960. Peter was one. We might have passed each other on the slopes of Primrose Hill, me with pram and infant, he a lanky schoolboy with his model plane.

'Have you lusted after anything lately?'

'Only Abigail.' I hit him.

'I want to know,' I say.

'No. It goes, doesn't it? I thought I would faint that morning when I saw they had bought the airplane model. It was so beautiful I had to keep shutting my eyes, then opening them quickly, to see that it was still there. I was testing the reality of it.'

I know what he means. I did that with my first lover.

'About Abigail,' I say.

'Not Abigail again?' He leans over me, propped on his elbow. 'What is it that worries you about her? I'm not opening and shutting my eyes to see if she is there.'

No, and you are not opening and shutting them for me, I

think. You know I am here.

'Will she be a good Sarah?'

'Bloody marvellous. She probably was a marvellous Nina. She just needs support. Of course, she'll have to suppress her natural charm a bit, to play a lumpen Northerner.' He is trying to make me laugh. Now he thinks I am annoyed, because I haven't laughed. I wish I could get angry again but I don't. It is known as maturity, I think. All that has passed, just as I passed young Sarah on the beach, and didn't notice her.

'I didn't mean that – about the lumpen Northerner,' he says.

'Oh – I was miles away.'

'Then come back to me, Laura.' Laura? He hums Rachmaninov's Second Piano Concerto. I'm good at this game.

'Brief Encounter.' We both sigh.

'They don't make them like that any more.'

'You could,' I say. Would he want to?

'Never. We haven't got the – whatever it was...'

'Innocence. Your favourite word these days.'

'That's it – we are too self-conscious; they just did it and that is why it is still touching. Now we think, "can't do that, it is too David Lean or too Fellini".'

'Which is mine to be?'

'What would you like?'

'A touch of the Fellinis would be very nice, thank you.'

'Why don't we go up the Tower now?' he says, suddenly.

'Why?' I freeze. I can't, even with him.

'I'd like to get a feel of the stretch of the town. Then I have to meet the others at the station.'

'I can't go up the Tower.'

'Why not? You've never been up, even though you lived here?'

'I never could. My strongest weakness is cowardice.'

'You can't have a strongest weakness, it's an oxymoron.'

'I have, though.'

'Nonsense. You are a very strong lady. I mean that.'

'Come and see me on the Golden Mile. Strong Lady booth.'

He laughs and hugs me but it isn't going to develop into making love, because he has the Tower and Abigail to go to, and I, for once, have to telephone.

I get off the bed.

'Where are you going?'

'I have to telephone the hospital.'

'I thought Eva was better?'

'She is, but I still have to telephone. And I must ring home, to see if everything is all right.'

I light a cigarette and dial. The hospital say Eva is comfortable, a remark that amuses me; Eva has never been 'comfortable' in her life. She can come out at the weekend, they say. Pauline, the girl I hired to look after Macheath and keep an eye on the pot plants tells me that Jenni has been telephoning. That is unusual. I tell Pauline the name of the hotel and the number, in case she should telephone again.

I slip on to the twin bed again. Simon is reading my Mishima paperback, which I resent. I don't like people to poach my reading matter.

I go and lie on the other, pristine bed.

'What's all this? What did I do?'

'Oh just read your book. I want to take a nap.' I fall into a half-sleep, comforted by his reading presence in the room, as a child would be.

As I drift, images emerge; of the old Ranelagh, high on the cliff, like an Austrian *Schloss*, without the hanging sign saying 'Self-Catering Apartments, Vacancies' – the sea pounds and roars and a stray Alsatian barks. The black iron Tower shadows the yellow sands.

I sleep longer than I intended, and wake to read Simon's note.

Gone to pick up the others. I was too late for the
Tower – I fell asleep too! I will take them out for
dinner. See you in the bar at about eleven. Love, S.

Bless him; he knows I would like time to wander about alone. I go out, with headscarf and raincoat, into the bleak seascape. A fisherman, garbed in black oilskin so that he resembles a London garbage bag, shouts at me: 'Hello, lass. Rotten evening.' I nod at him, he has made me feel at home.

To warm me, I buy a cup of tea in a garish snack bar on the front.

A sullen lad, with a bad case of acne, serves me. He gives me a full cup with milk substitute floating in fatty globules like the pimples on his skin. He seems to wonder why I am there at all. I am the only customer. I would like, in a sudden excess of feeling, to embrace him, and tell him that this, terrible as it might seem to him, is what it is all about, and that he must not be conned into thinking there is anything else. What a dreadful thing that would be to do to him. It would be an indignity, a cheek, and what is more, probably not true. He is lit in the neon like an illuminated picture in an Italian church. It has taken me a long time to see him that way, and quite a journey. An epiphany, I believe you called it, Mr Joyce? I go over to pay him. He thinks me a mad old woman and he is right. I will be if I get the chance. The whole secret is in the choosing. I might make my way back.

At the hotel the owner's wife is chatting to someone in the foyer. I slip past them. It is about ten o'clock; I have time to collect my thoughts before meeting Simon and the others.

'Mrs Wainwright—' I turn. The owner's wife is looking particularly professional. 'Someone to see you.'

The visitor walks up to me. It is Jenni. I am so surprised; I haven't seen Jenni for a year or so.

We go up.

She is apologetic, which is unusual. We embrace, but not fondly.

'Sorry to come and disturb you. Pauline told me where you would be. It is important.'

I think about her posture of fear. Surely I haven't encouraged it? It must be something to do with her message – because however much she might mouth the dismay at disturbing me, she and the boys never worried about it over much when they were growing up – hence my final belligerence. She asks me if Simon is here – and looks around the room, sensing his spoor.

'He's gone to meet the actors. I didn't know you were back in London. Have you seen Eva?'

She ignores that, picking at her cuticle, as she always does when worried.

'I came to London to see Miss Blair – your gyno lady. I'm

whatever they call it these days, up the spout, in the pudding club. Pregnant.'

I have to smile and she catches it.

'My God – you are the last person I would think might be pleased. I mean, you made such a fuss about the whole deal wrecking your life.'

'Maybe I wasn't smiling because of that. I smiled involuntarily, I suppose, because I never thought you would do anything so – messy.'

'Oh, I know. Ridiculous, isn't it, these days, when we are all supposed to be so *au fait.*' She sounds just like Dominic. I have to smile again.

'I wish you wouldn't do that. It isn't funny, however old hat it might seem to you.'

'I'm really smiling because I'm glad to see you; it just breaks out.' Can it be she has come for advice? I don't believe it. She never liked my opinions, all the way along.

'You put me off motherhood. All that grumbling – the wasted years, you used to say.'

'It's hard when you are in the middle of it – you say anything. It needn't affect you. My generation is different from yours. You don't have to go through with it if you don't want to.'

'I'm not sure I am going to,' she says. 'Oh, I know the abortion laws are being tightened, but that doesn't make much difference if one can pay, does it?'

'No, it never did,' I say. I look at the tight little face of my daughter. We never had the closeness the boys and I had, she was definitely Dom's child. Good old Freud.

'Have you asked Dom – Daddy?'

'Good heavens no. Lois is pregnant again, did you know?'

'No.' The poor old sod.

'What are your feelings about it, then?' I ask, reaching for a cigarette. She grabs the pack from me and lights up. I never even knew she smoked.

'About the abortion thing? I've marched, you know I have – and I have shouted about a woman's right to control her own body, but now I am beginning to wonder if the foetus hasn't got rights too.'

249

'Well, I suppose it has.' She is so different from me. She is rocked by this in a way I wasn't – I suppose I didn't have time to be; I was too worried about where to find the money for my back-street abortion. Twenty-five pounds. It was more money than I had ever owned in my life. I had to pay it back to the middle-class cow I borrowed it from, one pound a week for twenty-five weeks. Abortion on HP. The moral question may be the same for Jenni, but she is making rather a meal of it.

'I don't like asking your advice. I wouldn't if I wasn't desperate.'

'I know. I don't like giving it.' I flash her a look of recognition. We are, in spite of everything, alike. Mother and daughter, female.

'You are going to go through with it. Otherwise you wouldn't have come up. How did you get here?'

'Drove up. It was fast, the motorway was clear. I shall go back tonight. I have to work tomorrow.'

I ring down to the owner's wife and get her to bring coffee and whisky.

'So you think,' she says, 'that I wouldn't have come if I had not made up my mind?'

'I think so. You'd have just gone ahead, had the abortion. It can't be so unusual, in your group, can it?'

She laughs.

'You know, it's funny, but none of us seem to conceive. I mean, I'm the first.'

'Then you must go on with it. Perhaps the human race is dying out.'

'It's not funny. A lot of my friends find that when they finally decide, well – they can't. But that isn't a reason for going on with it. I came up for support, really. The fact is, you always hated motherhood so much – I fear I might too.'

'What gave you that idea? I was bloody compulsive. My later reactions, which are the most recent for you, were just me trying to push you all out of the nest.'

'Mm.' She doesn't believe me. Had I been so dreadful, all those years? I look at her objectively. She is a neat package, she has good clothes and figure, Dom's cheerful earnest expression, she is good at her job, very good in fact – in public relations – and she earns enough to keep herself and however many children she would like to have. She has, as far as I know (and of course I do not know), never been in love, not even to the extent of the hand-holding corny romanticism of Dom and me in our early days together. As for the all-consuming passion that some girls (including me) wreck themselves for, I have never seen signs of that in her – or in any of her generation. So how will she cope with the dreariness if she never knows the magic? It is all too planned but then she was ever a planner. I decide to try two or three things.

'You can convert part of the house if you want. I was thinking of selling – but there isn't any reason why I should. You can have most of it. I'm happy living in a sort of bed-sit situation and anyway I want to drift about a bit.'

Her expression lifts.

'Oh, that sounds wonderful. Are you sure? I could keep on working, in that case – get someone to look after the – *it*.'

I hope she doesn't think I am the someone. Much as I love babies, with a physical besottedness I hope for her sake she never feels, I don't want to end up that way.

'Feel free about that aspect. The moral thing is your own.' I hope she isn't going to go on about the sanctity of life after settling the material details.

She begins to cry, silently, the tears just running down into her untouched whisky.

'I can't tell you how much it means, to have your support – I really do want this child. I wanted you to convince me.' How did I convince her? All I did was offer shelter. Perhaps that is enough. I watch her misery of the past few weeks leak out.

'You can't drive back in that state. I'll get you a room here,' I say. She blows her nose vigorously.

'No, I've disturbed you enough. We both have work to do.' She gets up from Simon's bed, and puts on her coat. We embrace, in a way we have never done before.

She leaves, turning at the door, holding up her arm in a kind of triumphant gesture – half-wave, half victory salute, like a ballet dancer's exit. Then she closes the door.

She forgot to tell me if she visited Eva.

I polish off the whisky in her glass, as well as my own. I look in the mirror. In six months I could be a grandmother. Ye gods, as young Sarah would say.

I go down to meet the performers.